Whispers in the Rigging

Blue Moon Investigations

Book 9

Steve Higgs

Text Copyright © 2018 Steven J Higgs

Publisher: Steve Higgs

The right of Steve Higgs to be identified as author of the Work has been asserted by him in accordance with the Copyright, Designs and Patents Act 1988

All rights reserved.

The book is copyright material and must not be copied, reproduced, transferred, distributed, leased, licensed or publicly performed or used in any way except as specifically permitted in writing by the publishers, as allowed under the terms and conditions under which it was purchased or as strictly permitted by applicable copyright law. Any unauthorised distribution or use of this text may be a direct infringement of the author's and publisher's rights and those responsible may be liable in law accordingly.

'Whispers in the Rigging' is a work of fiction. Names, characters, businesses, organisations, places, events and incidents either are the product of the author's imagination or are used fictitiously. Any resemblance to actual persons, living, dead or undead, events or locations is entirely coincidental.

Dedication

To the men and women of the Armed Forces. Now, then, and always.

Table of Contents

Trapped. Friday, November 25th 1222hrs

My Office. Monday, November 21st 0847hrs

Chatham Dockyard. Monday, November 21st 1018hrs

Big Ben. Monday, November 21st 1115hrs

The Office. Monday, November 21st 1157hrs

Lunch. Monday, November 21st 1237hrs

Medway Hospital. Monday, November 21st 1401hrs

Bluffing an Entire Business. Monday, November 21st 1447hrs

The Dockyard. Monday November 21st 1511hrs

Cleaning Crew. Monday, November 21st 2000hrs

Whispers in the Rigging Room. Monday, November 21st 2031hrs

Ghosts. Monday, November 21st 2105hrs

A Late Start. Tuesday, November 22nd 0912hrs

Upnor. Tuesday, November 22nd 1103hrs

Family. Tuesday, November 22nd 1222hrs

Lunchtime Flirtations. Tuesday, November 22nd 1249hrs

The Office. Tuesday 22nd November 1316hrs

Chatham Royal Dockyard. Tuesday, November 22nd 1412hrs

Chief Inspector Quinn. Tuesday, November 22nd 1530hrs

Tea and a Book. Tuesday, November 22nd 1640hrs

What about the Strippers? Tuesday, November 22nd 1830hrs

Cleaning Duties. Tuesday, November 22nd 2030hrs

The underground. Wednesday, November 23rd 0037hrs

Murder. Wednesday, November 23rd 0715hrs

Round Two with the Chief Inspector. Wednesday, November 23rd 0900hrs

The Invitation. Wednesday, November 23rd 1042hrs

Alex Jordan. Wednesday, November 23rd 1101hrs

Baby. Wednesday, November 23rd 1143hrs

Man stuff. Wednesday, November 23rd 1600hrs

Stag Night. Wednesday, November 23rd 2051hrs

Rude Awakening. Thursday, November 24th 0800hrs

Alex Jordan's Office. Thursday, November 24th 1128hrs

Dirty Truth. November 24th 1142hrs

Captive. Thursday, November 24th 1201hrs

Not Trapped. Thursday, November 24th Roughly 1220hrs

Tunnel Fire Fight. Thursday, November 24th No Idea What Time it is. Don't Really Care.

Henchman are Hard to Beat. Thursday, November 24th (still no idea what time it is)

Mopping Up. Thursday, November 24th 1504hrs

Going Home. Thursday, November 24th 1522hrs

Coomer Castle. Friday, November 25th 1000hrs

The Wedding of Jagjit Singh and Alice Windecote. Friday, November 25th 1630hrs

Postscript: Call from Hilary. Tuesday, 29th November 1809hrs

More Books by Steve Higgs

More Books by Steve Higgs

Free Books and More

Trapped. Friday, November 25th 1222hrs

I rubbed my wrists as if I could rub away the pain in them. The bindings had been tight enough to cause some numbness in my fingers and the process of freeing myself from them had caused them to cut into my skin. Pins and needles now as the blood returned to my digits.

How long before they came back to check on me? I had worried they were going to be diligent enough to leave a guard on me. It would not have been possible to free myself with someone watching and very difficult to subdue them with my hands behind my back.

The room I was in had only one door, so there was only one route for my escape. I had no idea who or what might be outside. The bag over my head on the way in ensured I was disorientated and hadn't seen what lay beyond the four walls I could see.

I stepped carefully to the door. There was a keyhole, an old mortice lock but I hadn't heard them lock it as they left. I pressed my ear close to the small gap between the frame and the door, listening for any sign of a person outside. I stilled my breathing, making myself as quiet as possible. After a few seconds, I decided there was no sound to hear.

Okay. Now what?

I still didn't know what was outside the door, but I was going to have to go through it anyway. I was inside their base of operations, below ground and cut off from everyone. My only chance of escape, before they came back to kill me, was through that door. If I was lucky, I would find myself near to where I wanted to go, even though I would not know which direction was which until I found a point of orientation. Also in my list of most desired outcomes, was for there to be no one wandering the tunnels as I snuck about in them. To get to the next part of the plan I had to escape and possibly fight my way out. Just me against as many of them as I came up against.

A weapon would be good.

I looked around the room, a quick search that turned up a picture frame – no use, a plastic bucket – might be a distraction if I threw it at someone, a small table – too unwieldy to carry around. Largely drawing a blank on the weapon front, there was a rag in the corner which I had ignored, but having looked everywhere else I figured I might as well look under it (just in case someone had hidden a bazooka). No such luck, but the oily rag did have a pipe wrench beneath it.

I permitted myself a lopsided grin as I hefted it. It wasn't much, it was all I was going to get though, so rather than acknowledge that I was stalling, I turned the door handle and slipped silently out of the room.

Beyond was a tunnel. I could go left or right, but since I didn't know where I was, either direction held the same probability of success. I had a rough map of the underground tunnels and rooms in my head. I knew where I needed to get to in order to escape, I just needed to work out where I was.

I picked left but only got three paces before I heard voices coming from that direction. I froze, it was instantly clear they were coming toward me from around the corner ahead. Behind me, the tunnel stretched on for a hundred feet before the next corner. The safest option was to slip back into the room I had been in. But what if that was where they were going?

I ran. Strong, hard strides that quickly became a sprint. Finding out where I was in relation to where I wanted to be was suddenly a secondary concern. Avoiding capture was more important.

I had planned for the worst as I always did but bringing weapons with me would have tipped them off and would have been confiscated anyway. The one thing I did have was my phone because I forgot to remove it. They had taken that soon enough. It was just me and my wits now.

Was I making too much noise? Convinced the voices coming toward me must have been able to hear my shoes slapping against the stone floor, I denied myself the desire to look over my shoulder. Could I hear them running? Had they heard me already and given chase?

The corner was coming up. If I could get there I would be out of sight and just maybe I would recognise something and be able to orientate myself. I wasn't having that kind of luck though. With a pace left before I swung around the corner, I heard their shouts.

In the next breath, I made the turn and glanced back down the dingy corridor I had just fled. Three of them were after me, two of whom were guards I had seen previously. Their shouts were going to attract a lot of attention really quickly.

Rounding the next corner with adrenalin sending my heart rate through the roof, I was rewarded with a sight that changed the game.

I knew where I was.

The underground system had three entry points. One I was yet to find, one was in a secret stairwell that connected to a door in the back of the Admiral's office (the one I had been led down) and one that sat right at the edge of the river, hidden from view but accessible by water. All three ran into a set of linked chambers. One could hide an army in here and no one above ground would know. On the map, two of the tunnels that led to the chambers were curved, the other was straight and had intersecting paths. The straight one was the one that led from, or in my case, to the water and it was right in front of me.

I could see at least two hundred yards. Light was provided by overhead lamps, but like elsewhere they were too dim and too few to hold back the dark as the tunnel stretched into the distance. I stopped running and did the only thing I could in the circumstances.

There were three men chasing me. I was injured and tired and badly outnumbered. So, I attacked them.

I figured they would be sprinting after me, running full tilt with their pulses drumming in their ears like mine was and they wouldn't think twice about throwing themselves around the corner after me.

I had two or three seconds before they would reach me, so I relaxed, took a couple of deep breaths and as they hit the corner, I hit them.

As planned, it caught them all by surprise. The tool in my right hand scythed upwards to connect under the chin of the second man, not the first, as I sidestepped and tripped him. I could hear him stumble and sprawl on the floor behind me. It bought me a few seconds.

With one man down but unharmed and one man falling backward from the blow to his jaw, I was able to continue my forward motion into the third man. The half second of warning had been enough for his brain to get a message to his muscles so he was abating his own forward momentum to avoid running directly into me.

It was all too late though. As they had rounded the corner, I had already thrown myself at them. Even if the slowest of them had been able to come to a complete halt in the space of a few feet, I would still have closed the distance before he could get his arms up to defend himself. As it was, all the third man had time to do was look surprised before I hammered my left hand into his throat with a stiff arm.

He was still moving forward, the sudden blow to his neck caused his head to stop moving while his body pivoted about my arm.

He wouldn't be badly hurt but he was out of the fight for now. Behind me, the man on the floor was scrambling to his feet. It was the one that had held me for the beating on Tuesday night.

Time to even the score.

He was up and setting himself into a fighting stance, but found time to reach behind his back to produce a knife. Thankful that it wasn't a gun, I too positioned myself. Arms loose, feet spread for even balance and knees flexed and ready to move.

He grinned at me. Whether it was forced false confidence designed to make me feel uneasy or he genuinely believed he was the superior fighter was something I would find out very soon.

Then I heard the footfall of a small crowd coming down the tunnel we had all just run along. The three that had spotted me had either raised the alarm or had made enough noise to be heard and now all their friends were coming for me.

Bugger.

He grinned at me once more as shouts started to echo along the tunnel. They had spotted me.

'Feeling lucky?' He asked.

Time was not my ally and he was blocking my escape route. I either went through him or I was going to die. I had about five seconds.

He didn't bother to come at me. Why would he? All he had to do was keep me in place long enough for his friends to arrive.

So, I went to him. I swung the wrench like I was going to throw it at his head, he flinched, and I threw it at his feet instead. It struck home on his left foot, causing him to howl in pain and denying him the focus he would need if he wanted to stick me with the knife.

I punched his face as I ran by, landing a hard blow to his left temple that shocked my hand and might have broken a couple of knuckles. He was behind me now though and I was running for all I was worth.

I had one chance of escape: I had to get to the river entrance.

In my head, I counted as I ran. The horde was behind me and there was going to be guys in it that were faster runners than me. I had a small head start but no way to know if I could outrun them.

I got to three Mississippi before the sound changed and I could tell they had just rounded the corner behind me. I was once again visible to them which would spur them on to close the distance. It took rigid discipline to not look back and focus only on getting to my destination.

There was nothing in the brick-built tunnels I could use to slow them down, no convenient trolley of cleaning products one always found in a movie chase to throw in a pursuer's way. I just had to keep going.

I was sure they were gaining, and my breath was coming in ragged lumps now. I had already run more than two hundred yards as fast as I could when the floor of the tunnel started to slope downward. I pushed myself on, buoyed with hope as I was certain the river entrance was not far ahead of me now.

In the dim light of the tunnel ahead, I thought for a moment that the lights had been turned off. However, worry that I might have to run virtually blind was replaced by elation as I realised it wasn't a lack of light ahead of me, but the door that would lead out to the river.

Beyond it was going to be a dock. A dock that was underground and could only be accessed from the river. Behind the door was salvation.

I risked a glance over my shoulder.

My pursuers were falling behind. They were slowing down.

And they were laughing.

I reached the door and stopped.

'It was a good try, Mr. Michaels.' A familiar voice echoed in the confined space. 'Unfortunately, that door only opens from the other side.'

I glanced at the door. He was right. There was no handle this side.

My Office. Monday, November 21st 0847hrs

Four days before the race through the tunnels and oblivious to the trouble I was about to get in, I was making coffee in the high-end machine I had decided to buy for the office. Amanda and I had both closed cases and billed clients with a confident regularity and both she and I and James/Jane had a real love for coffee. So, I splurged on a machine that would take fresh beans and make glorious, glorious, strong, dark brew.

My father was in the hospital in a coma that was the result of a blow to his skull. It had rattled his brain, but the doctors assured me he was not in danger. His brain activity was normal, their expectation that he would come around naturally in a few days. Until then he would be cared for and monitored for any changes.

There was nothing I could do other than visit and try to comfort my mother. Visiting hours were not until after lunch but thoughts of checking on his condition were entirely secondary to my plan to find whoever had injured him.

Almost two weeks ago, he had been telling me that there was something odd happening at the Royal Dockyard, a local tourist attraction that used to be the Royal Navy's largest shipbuilding port. It was hundreds of years old but had closed in the eighties as either technology had moved on or spending on defence had cut back. I didn't know which it was, and it might have been a simple case that there were no more large warships to build. That, in itself, was something to celebrate.

Dad had retired after a long career in the Navy but had found himself in need of something to keep him occupied occasionally and I think he also missed the camaraderie and banter, so when a part-time job as a tour guide on the retired vessels in the yard came up, he took it.

Now he was in the hospital and I was going to find out why.

The aroma of coffee brewing under my nose was making me salivate. In the final stage of its process, the machine made me wait while I watched dark liquid pour down the twin shoots and into the tiny espresso cup sitting beneath them.

I took the cup out, reset it to make another and took the steaming brew across the room to my assistant Jane. I had hired Jane a couple of months ago when the number of enquiries was getting too much for me and when I took on another detective to assist me with the mounting workload. I had worried what the overhead would do to my profit and loss figures as the assistant would not be billing any hours and was, therefore, pure cost.

It turned out that it didn't matter because she was so darned efficient that I was solving twice the number of cases. She was fantastic with all the IT equipment, somehow automatically knowing how everything worked best and she was a demon at research. One might want to call her a geek, but the term didn't fit the profile as she was also a petite blonde with trim legs and a toned bottom and a pretty face.

I didn't think of her in those terms, of course. Not because I am her boss and wouldn't entertain stray lecherous thoughts about an employee in my head. No. I didn't have those thoughts about Jane because she also has a penis.

Jane was actually a man when I employed him but was one of the new-wave of gender-neutral persons that now seemed to be everywhere. It had no impact on me, so I made no comment either way. I will admit that I was curious about what underwear was worn when the Jane personality was dominant. No matter what might be happening on the outside there was still meat and two veg to put somewhere underneath and I doubted I would be comfortable balancing mine in a tiny thong.

Jane thanked me as I handed her the miniature porcelain cup and saucer, but barely looked up from the array of screens in front of her. Like me, she liked to get in early and she was genuinely excited to do her job it seemed.

I scurried back to the coffee maker as it was now spitting out my cup-full of excellence.

I heard the back door of the office open as my colleague Amanda walked in. I refer to her as my colleague for two reasons. The first is that I have found myself mostly uncomfortable with the concept of employees.

I want to work with people, not have them work for me. It made me feel too much like an overlord. That probably said something negative about my personality but so be it. The second reason was one I had been trying to avoid or deny ever since I met her: I was pretty much in love with her.

She was dating a multi-millionaire and I was certain she had no interest in me or I would have found a way to express my feelings by now. For my part, I was dating someone too, but I had already half admitted to myself that the relationship had no future and had made no move to advance our relationship beyond a few dinners and kissing. For the last few days, I had been resisting seeing her at all, convinced she was going to drag me through her front door and take off her clothes.

Natasha, the lady I have been dating, is a very attractive woman. A stunner most would say, but it was my inability to see beyond Amanda that drove me to believe it was love I was experiencing. So my wasted heart kept beating on despite the belief that she would never be mine.

'Hi, Guys.' She waved as she swung into her office to drop her bag and coat. 'Wow! Smell that coffee. Is one of those for me?'

The machine finished the second cup as she crossed the room toward me, smiling and gorgeous and everything I wanted. I handed it to her reluctantly. My adoration had limits.

'Thank you, Tempest.' She had her eyes closed and the cup raised to just under her nose to breathe in the scent.

I had all but forgotten the coffee because I had just got a whiff of her perfume. It is my understanding that a given perfume smells different on everyone that wears it. The scent interacts with the person's own biology to subtly change the way it smells. Whatever was in Amanda's skin made perfume on her smell like heaven. It was a magnet to my libido. Or maybe I was just horny and she was the most beautiful and perfect woman on the planet.

She had her eyes closed still, so didn't notice my guilty glance at her body. Seeing her naked a while back didn't help my ability to resist picturing her reclining on my bed.

As I placed yet another cup under the twin spouts, Amanda opened her eyes and moved away to see what Jane was up to.

The machine beeped to let me know it was out of hot water. Irritated, I stomped through the office to get more from the tap.

Fifteen minutes later, I was buzzing from the two cups I had drunk and wondering if I should impose a personal limit of one. Amanda had spoken with Jane as she was doing some research for her and let me know she was going out. Her client was a lady that believed she had a cult of devil worshippers living next door. It was one of those odd cases where we could investigate but had limited options on what to do about it if we could show the lady that she was right.

I was sitting at my desk scrolling through information on the Dockyard and making notes as I taught myself more about the place. There was no client for this case unless you wanted to say it was my parents, but the point was that I couldn't bill anyone for my time. Regardless of that fact, I was going into full investigation mode to find out who had hurt my father. The police had been informed and had conducted a cursory inspection of the scene. It wasn't a serious enough crime though and would not attract hard effort to track down the miscreant responsible. I was going to have to do this myself.

Besides, one of dad's colleagues at the Dockyard, Alan Page, had backed dad's story that there was something going on. Whispers in the rigging room he had said. He regaled me with tales of ghosts in naval costume being reported by the night crew of cleaners and security. I didn't know how much was hyperbole or embellishment and how much was true but had vowed to find out for myself.

I wanted a map of the yard to pin on my wall and I wanted the names of persons in key positions at the yard. My initial plan was to gain the attention of the chap that ran the place. If he would endorse my investigation, I might be able to move more freely or get a pass that would allow me access to places tourists couldn't go.

The CEO of the dockyard was easy enough to find. It was a man in his late thirties if the photograph on the website was current. His name was

Alex Jordan. He had an MBA from a London business school and was a Royal Navy Reserves Officer. The Dockyard business website was separate from the tourist website. It, no doubt, existed for affiliate firms that did business with the Dockyard, but there I was able to find Alex and other personalities such as Julia Jones. Julia was head of facilities management so, in all likelihood, she ran the night crew of cleaners that came in after the tourists left for the day. The head of security was a man named Danylo Vakhno. He looked like a strongman competitor with his head like a bowling ball and crew-cut hair. The photograph of him only showed his head and shoulders, but even from that limited shot, I could tell he had some serious muscle.

I dialled the number for Alex Jordan. A man answered.

'Alex Jordan's office.' His voice was short but not terse, proficient and well-practiced like someone who answered the phone hundreds of times a day and had arrived at a response that did everything it needed to without any fluff. It was also heavily accented with an Eastern European twang that I could not pinpoint.

'Good morning. My name is Tempest Michaels. I'm the son of Michael Michaels, the employee that was injured yesterday.'

'Oh, goodness, yes. I heard about that. How is he? Mr. Jordan insisted we send a care package to him today.' He sounded genuinely concerned and upset.

'He is still unconscious, but they believe he will make a full recovery.'

'Oh good, good. How can I help you, Mr. Michaels?'

'I am a private investigator by trade and I want Mr. Jordan's permission to look into the circumstances that led to my father's attack.'

'Oh. Um.' My request had caught him off guard. 'I'll, ah... I'll put you on hold for a moment please.'

He was gone, leaving me to listen to nothing as they had no hold music. The wait was less than twenty seconds though.

'Can you visit here this morning, Mr. Michaels? Mr. Jordan will make time for you.'

Perfect.

I thanked him for his time, advised that I would be along within the hour and disconnected.

Chatham Dockyard. Monday, November 21st 1018hrs

I got to the Dockyard in twelve minutes. It was a straight shot through Rochester High Street to Chatham and the river bordered the route most of the way there. Now that it was a big tourist attraction there was plenty of parking and access to the Dockyard itself was easy – I just had to buy a ticket.

I had been to the Dockyard a couple of times to collect my father when he had been working a shift and we had made plans to catch a movie or something, so I was familiar with the layout of the place. I realised though, as I looked around, that most of the real estate was buildings that were not part of the tourist attraction. Staring at one building now, I acknowledged that I didn't know what it was or what it had once been or even whether it even had a purpose now. There were lots of buildings around it, beside it and behind it that I could classify in the same bracket.

I was facing away from the river, so behind me in the dry docks were the submarine, Ocelot, a destroyer called Cavalier and a 19th-century wooden sloop named Gannet. In front of me were the buildings I could not identify and to my right, quite some distance away was the rigging room.

To my left, was the entrance with its cafeteria and shop. I walked back to the entrance to see if there were maps of the grounds that labelled all the buildings. Perhaps a historic pictographic version that would show their original use.

I scanned around until I found a flip-display of posters. What I wanted was the second to last poster I looked at – an aerial photograph of the dockyard taken several decades ago by the look of it. Running down the right-hand edge was a numbered list that corresponded to numbers on the poster. I had the name/purpose of each building.

Satisfied, I walked to the cashier and paid the £9.99 asking price. As the lady there bagged my item, a book next to the till caught my eye: The Hidden Mysteries of Chatham Royal Dockyard. I picked it up, quickly leafed through it, and read the blurb on the back of the jacket. I became aware that the cashier was waiting for me to take my bag and leave and that the next person in line was becoming impatient.

I handed the book over. 'I'll take this as well, please.' It was rung up, my card tapped against the reader once more and pocketed after it beeped to confirm it had taken my money.

The book might be a wasted expense but might also prove useful. I would only find out later.

Inspecting the Dockyard was a task I could perform after I had met with the man that ran the place. He was expecting me at some point soon, so I asked the cashier where I could find him, a question which drew a deliberately audible sigh from the lady impatiently waiting to be served. The cashier's directions were easy to follow as she needed only to point to a desk on the other side of the room. Above the desk, hanging from the ceiling, the word *information* was written in large letters.

I thanked her once more, smiled at the women in the queue behind me and took my book and poster.

The lady at the information desk was a carbon copy of the cashier. She was polite and efficient though, so in under a minute, I left the shop and ticket area with a day map of the Dockyard that had a wobbly line drawn on it to get me from where I was to the Admiral's office where I would find Alex Jordan.

Getting into the building that housed his office was less simple though. The building had a number on it, high on the right-hand side of the front façade as one looked at it. There were no other identifying marks, but it corresponded with the map and clearly had people moving about inside in what looked to be an office setting.

A large oak door, the original entrance, was set into ornate masonry where it dominated the front of the building. An electronic pass reader had been installed for staff to gain access, but my repeated knocking failed to attract anyone's attention. After a minute that felt longer, I gave up on the door and found a window to knock on instead. The windows were above my head though, the ground floor of the building raised, probably as a flood defence so I could see the people inside moving behind the windows, but they could not see me unless they came to the window and looked down.

Fortunately, a lady in designer glasses was curious enough about the knocking noise to investigate.

'Can I help you?' She enquired politely.

'Good morning. I have a meeting with Alex Jordan. I believe he works in this building but cannot seem to find a way in.'

She smiled with a half chuckle that told me I wasn't the first person to encounter this issue. 'There is a side door at the end of the building.' She pointed to my right. 'That is where reception is. We have said they need to erect a sign, but they don't want to spoil the front of the building and they won't let us come in the door because we are not grand enough. We have to sneak in around the side.'

'On this side of the building?' I confirmed by pointing as I set off and nodded my thanks.

The building was long enough that I walked for a minute from its centre point to get to the far end. Once there though it was clear I was at the right place from a small sign asking visitors to report to reception and an arrow pointing through the door.

Inside, an older man in a cheap suit checked by making a phone call to confirm that I was expected before directing me through the inside of the building and upstairs to where I would find the Admiral's office.

The lady that had spoken to me through the window spotted me on my way through and gave me a small wave of triumph.

I smiled at her but kept going.

I reached a grand wooden staircase that led to a wide landing that wrapped around the stairs on the first floor. It met a series of large windows at the front of the building where it faced the river to provide an unrivalled and uninterrupted view over the panorama outside. The windows continued along the entire front face where it formed a corridor to give access to the many offices the upper floor housed.

The landing was so vast it also housed a small open plan office where three ladies were working at separate desks. They all looked up as I broached the top of the stairs.

'Mr. Michaels.' One said as I approached them. 'Mr. Jordan's office is located at the far end of the hall.' She indicated that I needed to turn through one-hundred and eighty degrees and go the other way. 'His personal assistant will be expecting you.'

I thanked her, turned around and walked for another minute to reach the far end of the building. It was eerily quiet, the only sound, other than muffled voices from the three ladies behind me, my own footsteps.

I arrived at an office door, which in contrast to all the ones I had just walked by, was facing me. The office at the end of the building dominated the entire end of the building. The door itself was of an ancient carved wood that might have been hewn from a derelict warship but looked able to keep out a horde if closed and locked. It was ajar but was opened fully by a man roughly twice my size before I reached it.

'Mr. Michaels, yes?' Said the man as he extended a hand that was roughly the size of a trash can lid.

'Indeed. Good morning.'

'Mr. Jordan is expecting you.' A fact that had been made clear by everyone so far. 'I'm Andriy Janiv. I am Mr. Jordan's personal assistant.' We were crossing the room toward yet another imposing door. The end office was in fact split in two so that the Admiral had a man on hand, presumably another senior Royal Navy Officer, that acted as his personal assistant even back then. Andriy's accent was thick with Eastern European tones. I could not place it, but it sounded Russian to my untrained ear. Perhaps he originated in one of the former Russian states.

He knocked on the final door with thick knuckles, received an instruction to "Come" from inside and pushed the door open for me.

'Mr. Michaels.' He announced as I stepped inside. The door closed behind me as Andriy shut himself back in his portion of the office.

I had to admit it was an impressive place. The ceiling was high and ornately decorated. The walls were adorned with wood panels and the furniture, which might have been centuries old, looked priceless. Dotted about the walls were oil paintings in wide frames, each of them a different seascape and each probably more than one hundred years old. I wondered whether he got a private bathroom since the building and indeed the room preceded indoor toilets. Then I spotted a door on the wall to my right. It blended with the wood panels so well I had missed it at first. No doubt it had been fitted out with a bathroom sometime in the twentieth century.

Alex Jordan was getting up from his desk to greet me. He looked just like his photograph and young to be commanding such a large facility. He was short and slight with fair hair parted to one side on the left.

I closed the distance to him as I extended my hand. 'Mr. Jordan, thank you for seeing me at such short notice.'

'Not at all. Terrible business with your father. You said he is recovering?'

Alex had a good handshake with a solid grip and he met my eyes when we shook. I liked him instantly.

'The doctors believe he is. I will reserve my judgement until he is awake and talking.'

'Of course.' Alex had moved back to take his seat behind his desk. 'Sit, please.' He requested before taking his own chair. As I put down my bag and relaxed into the ornate chair with its arms of gold brocade, he asked me, 'What is it that I can do for you, Mr. Michaels? I am given to understand that you are a private investigator of the paranormal. Is that right?' He touched his right ear.

'I run an agency that specialises in cases with a paranormal or unexplained element, yes.'

'Hmm.' Alex spun in his chair to face away from me, deep in thought. 'You are aware we have ghosts here?' He turned the chair back to face me as he asked the question. As he did so he touched his right ear again. What I had taken to be an action brought about by an itch now looked deliberate as if he was signalling something to me that he could not say.

'I am. It seems likely they are part of a ruse to conceal what is really happening and will be in some way connected with my father's attack.'

'What is really happening? You think there is something untoward occurring at the Dockyard?' His eyes were boring into me as he made the odd movement to touch his ear again. This time looking at the phone on his desk. I had no idea what he was trying to convey, but then it hit me that he might have Tourette's and the motion I has seen him repeat was involuntary. I chose to look away, conscious that I was now staring at him. As I did, I noticed a Ukrainian – English Dictionary on his desk. The accent I heard earlier today must be Ukrainian though I wondered how many Ukrainians he had employed that he felt a need to learn their language. Surely, they would all be fighting hard to learn English but perhaps it was a clever tactic to learn at least a little so he could greet them in a tongue they recognised. More good-boss points right there.

'I will confess I have not the slightest notion what might be happening here. Whether the ghosts have even been seen by anyone or are just a daft, wild rumour. I do plan to find out though. I am offering my services free of charge. This will all be at my own expense. All I ask is that I am granted free passage to go where I may.'

'I'm afraid I cannot allow that.' He spun away from me to face the wall again, his fingers steepled in front of his face and his lips pressed to them. 'The head of security would never allow it, quite rightly I am sure, but more importantly, I don't want you to catch the ghosts. They are a massive tourist attraction and we don't even need to do anything.'

I cocked my head slightly and waited for him to continue. 'Attendance is up twenty-four percent since rumours of ghosts here started. It has only been a few weeks and we are suffering slightly because almost half the night shift cleaning staff and many of the security detail have quit in fright, but the entrance fee has never generated more revenue.' He spun back to face me again. 'No, I'm afraid the investigation will have to be left to the police, Mr. Michaels. I have no doubt you mean well, you may even be a capable detective, but I cannot have an amateur running about the Dockyard, going where he pleases and interrupting our business.'

I fixed him with a serious look. 'Mr. Jordan, the police will perform a cursory investigation but will be distracted by bigger crimes. The likelihood of my father's attacker being identified is slim unless you have a person dedicated to discovering the truth. Don't you want to know what motivated the attack?'

'Perhaps it was random.' He replied.

I cocked my head. 'My father was found in a bin.'

'Maybe the attacker panicked. Maybe he wasn't attacked at all and it was an accident. The point, Mr. Michaels, is that I cannot permit you to poke around while you try to uncover what you deem to be the truth.'

I nodded. Regretfully, I had to acknowledge that I had been expecting his response. My ideal scenario was for the Dockyard to hire me to investigate their ghosts, for in so doing I would uncover what had happened to my father. It was not to be though, and I believed any further argument to be futile.

I stood up and gathered my bag. 'Mr. Jordan, thank you for your time.'

We shook hands once more, he bid me a good day and wished my father a speedy recovery. Then, as if by magic, Andriy opened the door behind me to let me out. I had to wonder if he listened at the door. As I left the room, I saw a clock on the wall opposite Alex's desk. It had been behind me the whole time, placed as it was so that Alex need only look up from his desk to see the time. It stood out in the office because in striking contrast to every other item in the room, it was modern. A glass and chrome thing. Then I was out of the door and going through Andriy's outer office.

Walking back down the long corridor that would get me out of the building and out of the Dockyard, I was forming a plan in my head. My first shot had not achieved the result I wanted, but my course was not to be swayed.

I had a case to solve and Mr. Jordan was going to know nothing about my actions until I presented him with the solution.

Big Ben. Monday, November 21st 1115hrs

I knocked on Big Ben's door. He lives in a penthouse suite in a private gated complex that borders the river Medway as it runs through the centre of Maidstone. His place looks out over the river itself, but the view wasn't anything to get excited about. On the other side of the river was more apartments and beyond that yet more apartments. It passed as high-end for Maidstone though.

The security guy managing traffic in and out of the complex knew me well enough to wave me through, plus my bright red Porsche was easy to spot and remember.

There was noise inside, voices that were clearly not Big Ben's and I wondered what kind of debauched orgy might be going on behind the closed door. Wondering was all I did. I certainly didn't want to find out. I had already rung the bell though and could hear someone approaching from the other side of the door.

I heard the lock slide back moments before Big Ben's big beaming head appeared around the door.

'Hey, buddy.' He said as he opened the door. 'Was I supposed to be expecting you?'

I followed him in and closed the door behind me. 'Not at all. This is an unplanned visit. I need your help, mate.' Big Ben was naked from the waist up and wore a pair of loose-fitting track pants on his legs with no socks or shoes. He had underfloor heating though and the apartment was warm.

He led me through from the lobby to the main living area where there were four scantily-clad but still technically clothed ladies watching daytime TV.

One of them turned to see who it was and smiled. I said, 'Good morning.' But her response was to turn back to watching whatever mundane program they were engrossed in.

Big Ben picked up a mug of coffee as he folded himself into one of his sumptuous white leather chairs. 'Coffee?' He asked.

'Sure.'

He turned his head slightly to one side to call across the room. 'Brunilda. Be a love and make some coffee.'

'Ja, sweetie.' A brunette with long flowing locks and nothing on but sports underwear from Pink said as she stood up. 'Darf Ich fur sie etwas anderes tun?' She asked as she went by. My knowledge of German was sufficient to know that all she had asked was if she could do anything else for him, but the voice she used to ask it would have given an erection to a corpse.

'Nein, danke.' He replied and kissed her arm where she had draped it around him. She skipped off into the kitchen to make me a beverage.

'What's it like being Hugh Hefner's better-looking prodigy?' I asked enviously.

He grinned at me and stretched in place. 'Friggin' brilliant.'

Stupid question really.

'So, what do you need me for? Are we storming a castle?'

I considered the question; he wasn't far off the mark. 'We need to infiltrate a military base posing as staff and perform a clandestine operation under the noses of the criminal gang that operate there to expose the truth and save a princess.'

Not used to me exaggerating ever, he took a second to realise that I had been. He blew out his breath as he laughed. 'You had me for a moment there. What are we actually doing?'

'All of it except for the princess bit.' He stared at me, wanting more information than I had given him. 'My father got attacked yesterday at the Royal Historic Dockyard where he works sometimes. He spoke to me last week about strange events, but I didn't react and now he is in a coma. They whacked him on the head and dumped him in a wheelie bin.'

Big Ben's eyes flared. 'So, we are off to find out who did it and teach them some manners?' Big Ben was good at teaching people manners.

Brunilda reappeared with my coffee. It was strong and dark and unctuous, just the way I like it. She winked at me as she leaned in to hand it over, an act that sent a zip of electricity straight to my groin.

I was already starting to get hot in my clothes as Big Ben's heating was set to a temperature designed to sustain girls in their underwear. I peeled off a layer, paused and peeled off another which left me in just a shirt and jeans.

I answered Big Ben's question. 'Basically, yes. I just visited the chap that runs the place, but he was disinclined to give me free rein to investigate. They have rumours of ghosts spotted by the night cleaning crew and security guards. That is where I plan to start.'

'You know I am in, man. Whatever you need.' Big Ben had a serious expression for once. We didn't need to exchange words, we had been through enough together to be confident each of us would be there to support the other when the occasion called for it. This was such an occasion.

I nodded. Nothing further needed to be said. 'I want to infiltrate the night crew. Ideally, we would join the security detail, but I already know the cleaning crew is short staffed. They lost numbers when the ghost rumour took hold. Are you up for that?'

'Join the cleaning crew? Doesn't sound too taxing. I guess we do a bit then sneak off to explore, right?'

'Pretty much.'

'Any idea what is going on there?' He asked.

'Not yet. But I'm going to find out. When I leave here, I am going to the office to have Jane manufacture some fake CVs for us. I will call the lady that runs the facilities management side of the operation as the manager of a bogus outsourcing cleaning firm and offer the two of us as cheap labour. I'll let you know how it goes but I expect to start there tonight. Can you make that work?'

He held up his index finger, imploring me to give him a moment. 'Girls! Playtime is over. Time to go. Big Ben needs his space.'

From the sofa, a chorus of disapproving sighs and complaints came in response, but they collected their things and left, still in their underwear for the most part.

When they were gone, he asked, 'How is your dad? Better yet, how's your Mum?'

'Dad's still unconscious. The doctors have said he is fine and will come around in time. Mum seems to be holding up well enough. I'll be taking her to the hospital to see him later rather than letting her take herself.'

He nodded. 'Since we are probably going to be there tonight, I'm going to need some sleep. I didn't get much last night.' He didn't elaborate.

'I'll send you a message later, once I have arranged something.'

As I went to the door, he called after me, 'Tempest.'

'Yeah?'

'We'll get them.' I nodded grimly. It was very much my intention to *get them*. You don't get to mess with my dad and laugh about it afterward. Not for long anyway.

The Office. Monday, November 21st 1157hrs

My belly was starting to grumble as I parked my car behind the office. I would find Jane inside, working away at something for Amanda most likely. I hadn't given her anything to do recently as my cases had been too simple to require much research.

I had tasks for her now though and it all needed to be done quickly. Not because I was hungry and needed to get home to feed myself and walk the dogs, but because I had to infiltrate the Dockyard and I could feel the clock ticking inside my head.

'Hi, Jane.' I called as I pushed the door open. The smell of coffee hit me instantly.

'Hi, boss.' She called back in her normal deep voice. To compliment her female persona, she had been practising speaking with a voice that sounded less manly. She could hide the adam's apple with a scarf but losing the baritone was a tougher challenge. Today, she wasn't trying.

I went straight to the coffee machine. Earlier I had left the office jittery from all the caffeine, but it was long gone from my system now and I wanted a fresh shot.

'Want some?' I held a cup up to show Jane. She lifted a cup from her desk to show she had just made one for herself. 'Are you able to switch tasks?' I asked as I busied myself filling the machine.

'Sure. I'm looking into 17th century French demons for Amanda but I think it can wait.' It was something to note that her research topic, which sound ridiculous anywhere else, was just par for the course in our office.

Coffee in hand, I went to her desk and outlined the task I needed her to perform. It involved creating a website, falsifying a staff list, creating CVs and then emailing Julia Jones with a speculative email offering her contract cleaners at a reduced rate. Alex Jordan had admitted they needed them. I was going to present a solution.

To be fair, it was quite a list of things to achieve in a short space of time. Jane acknowledged the challenge presented, cleared her desktop and got started.

I went to my office to craft the email we would send to Julia Jones. It was all a complete blag and would come apart fast if she looked for the fake firm on Companies House because we didn't exist and there was no way to create and register a firm that quickly. After twenty minutes of drafts I was happy with the letter and the official-looking letterhead I had created. It was convincing enough so I forwarded it to Jane.

'Don't forget to take a lunch break.' I called as I got up to take my own.

'No time if you want this done.' She called back. 'Bring me a sandwich. I'll take the hours later.' She probably wouldn't, she seemed to love her work enough to be in early and stay late every day. I took her on for part-time hours originally but shifted her to full time because she kept working the hours anyway. She was invaluable. Having that thought, I made a mental note to ensure her value was reflected in her Christmas bonus.

I reminded Jane that I was taking my mother to the hospital after lunch, but I went to the sandwich shop a couple of doors along from the office and paid them to make and deliver lunch to her. With that done, I slid into my sleek, red Porsche and gunned it for home.

Lunch. Monday, November 21st 1237hrs

My house sits in the corner of a street at the north end of a small village called Finchampstead which in turn is located on a hill overlooking the much larger town of Maidstone in the South East corner of England. The village was a pretty little place surrounded by vineyards and orchards and countryside with one road in and one road out. My four-bedroom detached house was larger than I needed but I liked having the space and had bought it at a time when the housing market was depressed following a global mortgage scandal.

I pulled onto my driveway at 1237hrs according to the clock on my dashboard. I was hungry now, already fighting the voices that wanted a dirty, fat sandwich with the sensible part of me which knew I had just lost nine pounds through hard effort and monitored eating and really didn't want to put it back on.

As I opened my front door, the two furry beasts inside tumbled out to greet me. I live with two Dachshunds, both black and tan with short hair, and brothers even though they were not litter mates. Bull and Dozer were excellent companions, but they could be relied upon to be deliberately problematic if I made them go too many days without something tasty from the treat cupboard.

Once I had ruffled their fur and petted them, they ran to the backdoor. This was usual routine: I came home, they greeted me, they went out and barked at wood pigeons on the lawn.

Through my kitchen window, I watched them tear across the lawn after a blackbird that had dared to touch down on the grass. They barked the whole way, stealth not a tactic they had ever learned. I filled the kettle and flicked it on. As it began to get agitated, I pulled prawns from the freezer and couscous from the cupboard. The hot water went on the couscous, the prawns into my wok along with cashew nuts, scallions, peppers and spinach leaves.

Five minutes later the dogs were in the living room crunching on cold pieces of carrot I kept in the fridge for them and I was tucking into my lunch. I had added some hot sauce for flavour and served it with cold milk to drink.

After lunch, with dogs clipped to leads, I set off for a stroll around the village. They probably didn't need it, it was hard to gauge what they did need, but prudence dictated I give them exercise when I could, plus it was dry today and despite the cool air, it was nice out.

Mrs Comerforth, my next-door neighbour was just coming through her garden gate as I went out of mine.

'Hello, Margaret. Been shopping?' I asked rhetorically as I observed her bags.

'Yes, dear. Just stocking up on provisions.' Her provisions appeared to be gin and some chocolate biscuits. I was a little envious. 'Will you be needing me to have your doggies any time soon? I do like their company.'

Mrs Comerforth and I had an almost symbiotic relationship. We both had what the other one needed in that I had dogs and she felt she was too old to have one of her own and I had to go on stakeouts or night time investigations or sometimes (gasp!) a date. The latter was the least common, but whatever the occasion, if I was going to be out for any length of time, I could rely on my neighbour to keep the dogs safe and warm and with company at her house. Better yet, if I was going to get home late, she would put them back in my house before she went to bed.

'Actually, Margaret, I will be out tonight.' I gave her a basic run down on my planned nocturnal activities without explaining the boring detail about my father. She was excited to have them for company and would pick them up herself if I didn't drop them off. I wasn't sure what time a shift at the dockyard might start, since I hadn't even applied for the job there yet, so I could offer no advice on what time I might go out or be back.

It didn't matter to her. The dogs were pulling at their leads to get going. She saw them and said I should get going. It was too cool for her to stay out anyway.

She was right about the temperature, but it was concern for my little dogs rather than my own needs that curtailed our walk. Ten minutes after setting off, we returned home, the two dogs pulling excitedly to get in the house and the warm.

I settled them back on the sofa with a blanket, gave them a pat and left them behind again as I set off to fetch my mother.

Medway Hospital. Monday, November 21st 1401hrs

'Hello, Mother.' I took her hand as she stepped out of her house and down to the street.

'Hello, Tempest.' She was dressed nicely, as one might for church, because she felt there was a need to look respectable when speaking to doctors. I opened the passenger door of my car for her to get in then closed it gently behind her. 'Goodness, Tempest. Why can't you get a sensible car?' She asked as she made a big show of getting down to the seat.

Mum was sixty-four and had no trouble whatsoever with her mobility but liked to have something to moan about. Right now, it was the proximity of my German Sports car to the ground. I did not engage with her comment.

'Have you heard anything from the hospital today?' I asked to change the subject.

She shook her head. 'Not a word.'

'Then his condition will be unchanged.' This was neither good nor bad. The doctors had told us he might take several days to come around. He was in no danger, but the blow has caused a minor brain bleed and some swelling. He had simply powered down until it could fix itself.

Mum jabbered about having to make dinner for herself and how she kept turning around to ask Dad something only to find herself remembering that he wasn't there. I made sure I listened and said yes and no at appropriate points. Letting her talk would most likely help her deal with whatever emotions she was feeling.

It was the middle of the day, so traffic was light which allowed me to zip through the towns to the hospital where for once I found a parking space easily.

Dad was in the special care ward where most of the patients were not able to care for themselves. 'Hello, dear.' Mum called out as she went into his room. She leaned in to kiss his cheek. 'He looks so peaceful.' She commented. Then she took his hand and started talking to him, one of the things the doctors said we needed to do. 'You missed the snooker last night. Mark Bingham was putting up such a fight against Ronnie O'Sullivan. The final is this weekend so you need to get home in time for that.'

I moved in to check his colour. He did indeed look peaceful, though I refrained from saying it because it sounded too much like what one said about a dead relative. Looking at him in the hospital bed made me angry, my rage rising despite the company. He had a dressing on his head still and a tube going into his nose to feed him. He was breathing by himself but the nurses were having to wash and clean him and deal with waste.

Mum had more to say, 'I miss you in the house. It's quite lonely without you there. Especially at night. The bed is awfully big for just me.' Just then the sound of gas escaping from beneath the covers stopped whatever she was about to say next. 'Well I don't miss that.' She stated grumpily as she sat down grabbed her knitting bag.

A noxious scent of bum-filtered methane began seeping from the sheets. I backed away wondering what they were feeding him.

From the knitting bag came a part-finished jumper, a ball of wool and two knitting needles. Seconds later the familiar click, click, clickety sound started up as she added another line of wool to the garment. Her blurring fingers seemingly working by themselves as she never once looked down.

I had no intention of staying. Other than bringing mum so she didn't have to come alone, my visit was to see how he was doing for myself. His colour looked good, his breathing was even. He just looked like he was asleep.

I fetched mum a vending machine coffee from around the corner and was about to leave when three of dad's retired Navy buddies from the dockyard arrived. Leading them was Alan Page, the chap I had met here last night.

'Hello, chaps.' I shook their hands as I introduced myself. The men accompanying Alan were Stuart Cobb and Fred Radford. They both looked to be in their late sixties but were sprightly still.

'We can't stay long. We snuck out on our lunch break.' Alan told me. 'How's he doing?'

I shrugged. 'The same.'

Alan inclined with his head. He wanted to talk outside in the corridor. Once outside he said, 'The boys and me want to help. I told them what you do for a living and that you were planning to look into what happened. Well, we want to lend a hand.'

'Okay.' I said as I nodded my head. 'I haven't got very far yet. But I'll let you know if I come up with something I think you can help with.'

Stuart had something to say. 'We have certain skills that might be of use.' His voice all but a whisper. 'Skills honed over decades.' He was piercing me with his gaze. He was pretty intense.

They all were for that matter. It made me wonder what branch of the Navy they had served in. The comment about taking decades to hone their skills hadn't been missed though. To me it meant they were getting on a bit. I would never call them old, but if I was asked if I wanted to have my dad getting into trouble with me, the answer would be a hard no. These chaps were the same age or older.

'I'll keep that in mind.' I replied. 'I met with the CEO, Alex Jordan this morning. He was disinclined to help me. He thinks the ghost rumours are helping business. However, I plan to join the night cleaning crew today so will be able to get into the Dockyard at night to look around.'

'Join the cleaning crew?' Remarked Alan. 'Good luck with that. They only employ Eastern Europeans there now.'

'Not just the cleaning crew.' Added Fred. 'They are replacing everyone with Eastern Europeans now.'

I thought about the Ukrainian personal assistant the CEO had and the dictionary on his desk.

'You know there's only two English guys left on the security detail?' Alan asked the other two. 'All the others have been replaced already.' He turned back to me. 'You should speak with them about the ghosts.'

I pulled out my notepad. 'Their names?'

'Dave Saunders and Dave McKinnon.' He supplied. 'They have both seen them. The ghosts that is. They work the night shift, but I don't know for how much longer. I do know they are both worried about their jobs and how long it is until they are pushed out as well. I think management would get rid of us if they could.'

'Don't be too sure they won't.' Said Fred. 'You think they will keep us on as tour guides because we were in the Navy, but would the public really care if it was a foreign chap answering their questions and guiding them around?'

'Cheap labour.' Commented Stuart.

I noted the two names. I would track them down tonight. Then I thanked the chaps for their time and promised to call them if I thought of a way they could help me.

'We'll just go and pay our respects to your mum.' Alan said, and the three men filed into dad's room.

I left them and the hospital behind as I went back to my office. I would return at 1700hrs to collect mum.

Bluffing an Entire Business. Monday, November 21st 1447hrs

Jane had not moved from the position I had left her in more than two hours ago and I wondered how much she had managed to get done.

'All of it.' She boasted when I asked her. 'It was much easier than I thought.' She pulled out a cardboard folder, the type with a flap at the front which opened to reveal a pocket beneath. In it were several sheets of paper which she began to fan on her desk. 'Here are CV's for you both. I just copied these from templates on the internet and adjusted them to make you look like cleaners. Here is the letter you wrote earlier. I changed the font and the logo but otherwise it is unchanged.' She had also found time to create a website which displayed the fake firm, listed its achievements, company history and mundane rubbish like health and safety policy.

'How did you do all this so quickly?' I asked.

'Like I said, most of it was easy, almost cut and paste. Even the website was a simple task. All I had to do was find one similar to what I wanted and use a clone program to rip off the html code, embed it in a new webpage and populate it with some images.'

Easy for Jane maybe. It would take me a year to do the same thing. I picked up the documents. They looked convincing to me. My next task would be to call Julia Jones, the lady responsible for hiring the cleaning staff and convince her to employ me and Big Ben.

Should be easy, I told myself.

She answered on the third ring. 'Julia Jones. Good afternoon.'

'Good afternoon.' I launched into the patter I had been practising in my head. 'This is Jeremy Carter of Kleaneeze. We supply outsourced cleaning staff and I understand you are in the market to hire some.'

'Actually, I am. But I have strict instructions on who I can hire. I am being provided with additional cleaning staff soon.'

I grimaced at the news. 'Are you saying that you cannot hire anyone, no matter their qualifications and experience?'

'I'm sorry.' Was all she said in return. Whatever the reason was, she wasn't going to let me get into the Dockyard the way I had hoped to. Maybe it had been a long shot, I hadn't thought so at the time.

I thanked her for her time and disconnected.

Nuts.

I called Big Ben. He answered with, 'Whaddup?'

'We have a minor setback. The plan to go in as cleaners is a bust. We are going to have to go full ops mode and break in.'

'Roger. What happened?'

'I'm not entirely sure. The lady that needs to hire new staff isn't allowed to hire new staff. She was a little cryptic about it.'

'She? What's her name?'

'Julia Jones.'

'So, what's the new plan?'

'Tactical gear. I'll come to you at 2000hrs. We go over the concept of the operations, infiltrate the Dockyard and spend a few hours trying to find out what is going on. It'll be harder this way. We will have to put more effort into dodging the guards and there will be consequences if we get caught.' I was thinking as I talked. If we were caught it was likely there would be a criminal prosecution as a result. Under different circumstances I wouldn't consider this course of action, if it were for a client for instance. But someone had hurt my dad and I was going to find out who.

I wanted to tell Big Ben that I didn't need him, but he wouldn't believe me. There was a distinct possibility that he could get into deep trouble by coming with me, but he and I had the kind of brotherhood that meant that even though we would never talk about how we felt we would also never let the other face things alone.

'I'll be ready.' He said. 'See you at eight.'

Sitting at my desk after the call, I ran through some scenarios in my head. Where was the best place to enter the Dockyard unseen? I had to get us in and out without triggering any alarms, using any of the actual entry routes and without encountering the guards. Then I remembered the two Daves that Alan had told me about.

If I could find them, maybe they would help. Suddenly I had an option. What did I do with it? If they worked the night shift, I wouldn't be able to find them at work now. I hadn't taken a phone number for Alan or anyone else, so I had no way to contact them. I was going to have to go back to the Dockyard if I wanted to talk to anyone.

Rummaging through my pockets and then my wallet, I found the entry ticket I bought this morning. Having to pay to enter again was insignificant but I was still happy that I had a day pass and could just waltz back in.

I had planned to get some sleep before spending a good portion of the night snooping around, but I would have to go without. I grabbed my keys, told Jane I was going out and headed back to the Dockyard.

The Dockyard. Monday November 21st 1511hrs

I had some very specific tasks for my second visit. One of which was to see if I could pick up a contact number for the two Daves. Their assistance, if I could obtain it, might prove pivotal in my ability to investigate this case. I would speak with Alan and the other tour guides on the various ships and attractions certain that someone would be able to furnish me with a number for them.

I also planned to have a good look around the Dockyard itself. It was a big place with lots of buildings. I would be here at night and trying to evade the security, so a good knowledge of the layout would be my ally. I wanted to see the security for that matter. I spotted a pair of them ahead of me, moving away from me toward buildings at the far end of the facility. I followed.

They were both big men, taller than me and had an ex-forces look about them. They were walking ahead of me which denied me the chance to see their features. I wondered if they would also be Eastern European.

There were crowds of people for a Monday afternoon in November. I had no idea the Royal Historic Dockyard was so popular. I moved through them, trying to memorise the position of the buildings relative to each other and the river and making note of little alleyways that ran between some of the buildings, but which were not visible until one walked right in front of them. I hoped it would not come to pass, but there existed a very real chance that I would be spotted by the security at some point and have to evade them. Knowing which turn led where might prove invaluable and I like to be prepared for the worst.

The pair of security guards I was following met with two more that rounded a corner just ahead of them. The two new men were facing toward me and both possessed the blockish features I associated with Eastern European men. They too looked well-trained as if all four were part of a military unit.

After a few exchanged words they separated, the two I had been following continuing on the way they had been going.

Using the mental map in my head, they were heading straight for the rigging room. A guess that proved to be correct as a sign declaring rigging room became legible as I neared it. They went inside with me following no more than a few yards behind. I approached the door they had gone through intending to peek inside and catch them doing something incriminating. Would careful observation reveal something?

The answer to that question was no as the rigging room turned out to be full of tourists. A tour was in fact in full flow, the gentleman giving it gesticulating wildly as he explained what the piece of equipment behind him did. I joined the back of the small crowd for a while.

The rigging room was long. Like really long. Its original purpose to craft the long ropes that would control Royal Navy warships back in the day when they had sails. Running down the length of it was a contraption weaving and winding the rope together. It wasn't making a lot of noise, but there was certainly enough to drown out any whispers that might be there to hear. That was why they could only be heard at night when the machine was off. Another task for me tonight then.

While I was listening, I lost sight of the two security guards I had followed in. They were no longer in the room so far as I could tell although it was possible they were behind one of the pieces of equipment further down the room.

I moved on, looking for them. 'Please stay with the tour group, sir.' Called the guide.

I stopped, caught in indecision. If I ignored him, he would likely call after me again and I did not wish to draw attention to myself. Instead, I went back outside, leaving the rigging room behind. I would be back soon enough.

I wandered around some more, orientating myself and trying to remember the buildings and the surface beneath my feet. A lot of the streets between the buildings were paved with old, worn cobble stones, their dull grey blockish tops looking very much at home as the entire vista appeared to have been frozen in time. In several places though, the cobbles had been replaced by tarmac. The look, sound and feel of it was not only different but seemed wrong. Like fitting an amplifier to a flute, to me one thing did not go with the other. I could only assume the cobbles had to be taken up at some point during the 20th century and budget at the time dictated a cheap solution be employed to repair the hole. It would have been before the Dockyard was recognised as a national treasure so might have occurred just before it closed and had been considered a huge drain on the economy.

Whatever the case, there were only three places that I found the tarmac, so if I did end up running away from the guards at any point it was something I could use to work out where I was.

I walked back to the ships that were sitting in dry dock by the river's edge. They were the main tourist attraction, at least that was my understanding from talking to my father. He took tours around the submarine mostly, a cold war artefact he had once lived in for months at a time.

I spotted Alan. He had clearly spotted me first as he was heading toward me with Fred, Stuart and a new man I had not met yet.

'Young Mr Michaels.' Alan said in greeting. 'This is Boy George.' He introduced the new man. 'We call him that on account of he is the young one on the crew and because he is so pretty that he must be a wooftah.'

'You can suck my plums you miserable, ugly old git.' Replied Boy George. George, assuming that was his actual name, couldn't have been a day younger than sixty, but if that was his age, he probably was the youngest one of them by a good margin. He was my height at around six feet tall and it was obvious he would have been aftershave model material a couple of decades ago with a chiselled jawline, piercing blue eyes and a mop of blonde hair. The hair was mostly grey now, but the looks had not left him. I had no intention of asking about his sexual orientation.

Instead, I shook his hand. 'Tempest Michaels. Good to meet you.'

'You're going to help us find out what is going on here?' He asked.

'Something like that.' I answered. 'I will be investigating. My only real purpose is to find out what happened to my father, but I understand there are ghosts here and that usually means someone is doing something they ought not be doing. If I stumble across one thing while investigating the other, then so be it.'

Alan spoke up. 'Don't forget to enlist our help when the time is right, young Mr. Michaels. I know you was Army, but we can forgive you for that and work with you this once.'

'He was Army?' Echoed Boy George. 'Goodness, you'd never know to look at him, would you?'

Banter between the various arms of the services was normal. Stepping into a Navy environment I had expected some nonsense to surface and here it was. Oddly enough it was almost always the Royal Navy boys that started it, spouting off about being the senior service as if there hadn't been armies first. The individual Regiments all had names like The Duke of York's Regiment or the Duke of Wellington's Regiment as they were raised and paid for by Lords as fealty to their king. It was a proud mark of stature to have a Regiment of soldiers at the nation's disposal. Who could afford a Navy though? The Royal Navy was created through taxing the nation, so as a singular service the Navy did indeed come into existence first. It was just several hundred years after the armies were formed but the Navy boys tended to brush over that inconvenient bit of information. By comparison, the Royal Airforce were so new the paint was still drying on the planes they flew, and they tended to stay quiet.

I wouldn't normally rise to the bait, but I recognised that they wanted the banter. 'Really? You old knackered turds want to trade insults just because I didn't feel like hiding two hundred miles offshore and went to wherever the action was instead of working on my tan? Tell me, what was the second world war like for you?'

They all grinned. 'You're going to fit right in.' Said Alan.

'I need a number for the two Daves. Or at least one number for one of them. I might need to enlist their assistance.' I didn't say that I might be sneaking around the Dockyard at night. The fewer people that knew my plan the better.

Boy George whipped out his phone and gave me a contact number for Dave Saunders. I would try it shortly and see if I could meet with him before he started work tonight.

I thanked the chaps and turned to move away. Alan caught my right arm in a vice-like grip. 'Don't forget. We can help.' His eyes were boring into mine. The three other men came to stand beside him. 'We have… what was it the chap on the film said? Oh yes, a particular set of skills.' Once again, I noted just how intense Alan was and wondered again just what he had done in the Navy.

I assured them I was just going to quietly conduct an investigation and was unlikely to need any help unless I needed some questions answered. As I shook each of them by the hand, they drifted back to their stations and were immediately gobbled up by tourists with questions.

Off to one side, away from the stream of human traffic, I dialled the number Boy George had given me.

'Dave Saunders.' A man's voice answered.

I launched into a quick explanation, 'Mr Saunders. My name is Tempest Michaels. I am the son of Michael Michaels, one of the tour guides at the Dockyard. Are you aware that he was attacked and injured recently at the dockyard?'

'Here, are you that ghost detective bloke?'

'Yup. That's me.'

'I heard about you. What can I do for you?'

This was off to a helpful start. 'I may need your help. Can we meet tonight before you start your shift?'

'I'm free now if that is convenient.' He replied straight away. I took his address in Gillingham, thanked him and promised to arrive in the next thirty minutes. I checked my watch when I disconnected: 1612hrs.

It was dark. The sun had been starting to get low when I arrived. Now floodlights high above the street were illuminating the main tourist areas and more lights set into the ground were highlighting the old buildings. The Dockyard took on a romantic tone in the dark, but I hoped the lighting would be switched off once the tourists left to preserve electricity. There was far too much light for me to sneak about. I would be visible from one end of the Dockyard to the other like a dancer on a stage being tracked by a spotlight.

I would find out soon enough. It was time to go, but as I headed back to the carpark, wishing I had been able to secure a job on the cleaning crew and thus not need to sneak about tonight, a familiar voice called out to get my attention.

I turned to see Big Ben approaching. What the hell was he doing here?

Cleaning Crew. Monday, November 21st 2000hrs

Several hours later, I nodded to Dave Saunders as we filed out of the briefing room. Big Ben and I were new, so we had been assigned to work with two of the longer serving cleaners, two Ukrainian ladies named Anyanka and Anna.

If you are wondering how it is that we came to find ourselves on the cleaning crew after I had failed to secure employment, well… I guess you don't know much about Big Ben. He had asked me the name of the lady that did the hiring and firing and once he was off the phone he had driven to the Dockyard, asked for her in an insistent way and then seduced her in about ten seconds flat. He had finished the deed and was leaving when he had spotted me.

I still didn't know quite why his smile and a few words were enough to make ladies throw their knickers in the air, but it worked ninety-nine percent of the time and he was at it again now because the cleaning crew were almost entirely female. The three men out of the forty cleaners, if one didn't count Big Ben and me, were almost pensionable age, so my tall, handsome colleague, and to a lesser extent even I, were getting eyed up a lot by the ladies around us as the supervisor, also female, handed out the assignments.

The supervisor was something different though. Standing roughly five feet nine inches in flat shoes, she was almost as broad as she was tall, but it was all muscle. Like the head of security, she looked like a bodybuilder combined with a strong man competitor. Even her jaw muscles appeared to be developed. I was impressed because of the effort, determination, focus and sacrifice that went into transforming one's body like that, but I was equally horrified at the same time. To me it was not an attractive look. I could barely tell she was a she. From behind I would have assumed it was a man with a lady's hairstyle.

Pasha had eyed Big Ben and me suspiciously but had made no comment about our employment yet. She had made it clear we were not being trusted with even a simple task though, which was why we had chaperones. However, I had seen the faces of the two ladies we had been paired with when Pasha made her announcement. They were over the moon at the prospect. Next to me, Big Ben had winked at them, eliciting a giggle and some nudging between the pair. It was already clear that Big Ben's plans and theirs were about to align.

Our first task was to empty out the many bins located around the open areas of the dockyard. Anna had a map which showed where all the bins were located. The task seemed simple enough but there was a list of things to do after that.

I wondered how fast we could get the work done and how we would lose the two girls so we could snoop about by ourselves. Big Ben had a plan for that as well. As we left the room, he delivered a playful nudge to Anyanka's hip with his own, then whispered in her ear.

She giggled at him and danced away as he tried to grab her. Anyanka was a thickset woman with wide hips and a roll of fat hanging over her belt. In her later thirties or perhaps a little older, she was no kind of catch and way below the batting average for Big Ben.

So how was it that we came to meet Dave Saunders? I need to backtrack a little to explain that. When we left the dockyard at 1617hrs, I had been on my way to visit Dave Saunders at his place in Gillingham. We found his house easily enough from the address he had given. It was not far from the Priestfields football stadium where terrace houses were packed in like sardines. Parking was difficult, but we found a spot around the corner that would take both our cars, locked them up and walked back to the address he had given me.

He had seen me coming and was unlocking the door as we mounted the steps that led to it. Welcomed inside, we could see how he had observed our approach - the front door opened directly into the small living room where his couch was located adjacent to the only window in the room.

'Come in, come in.' He beckoned.

There was not much space in the room for furniture, a single arm chair, a battered looking corner table and the sofa he had been sitting on. The wall opposite the sofa was dominated by a huge wide-screen tv which we found ourselves facing as we wedged ourselves side by side onto the surprisingly uncomfortable seat.

'Thank you for seeing us, Dave.' I started. 'This is my associate, Ben Winters.'

'You know Alan Page, don't you? He called just before you to say I should expect to hear from Michael Michaels's son. I guess that's you.'

I nodded.

'Alan said you were going to be looking into what is happening at the Dockyard, is that right?'

'It is. I want to find out what happened to my father. I don't trust the police to get the job done.'

'Neither would I, mate.' He agreed. 'So, how can I help you.'

'I have a few questions for starters.' I had my notebook out and a pen ready, so I pressed straight on. 'Have you seen the ghosts?'

He nodded as he spoke. 'Several times. Dave and me, that's Dave McKinnon, we have heard the screams from the cleaners and gone running to find out what was going on. Sounded like people were being murdered sometimes, but when we found the source of the noise it was always someone that had been scared by the ghost. Sometimes it was cleaners, sometimes it was other security guards and once or twice it was other people working late, like folks that work in the offices. A few times we arrived quickly enough to see the ghosts vanishing in the distance.'

'What did they look like?'

'Like sailors from the 18th century. All white wigs and fancy white tights with one of those long coats that has all the gold brocading on it. Only... Only you could sort of see through them. They looked misty.'

I made a note. 'Anyone ever hurt before my dad.'

'Yeah, several people. Mysterious falls down stairs, a few accidents where the person appeared to have hit their head but would then swear blind that something had hit them. A couple of occasions where the ghosts have chased people and they have fallen in the dark and hurt themselves.'

'What was said about that? By management, I mean. What did they do?'

'Hushed it up mostly. There was never any proof. The victims, if I can call them that, were accused of being clumsy or of making it up to cover up their own accident. Lots of them have left. Some through indignation that they were not believed but most of them through fright that it might happen again.'

'I see. There seem to be a lot of Eastern Europeans taking jobs at the Dockyard. What do you think about that?' I had a vague theory forming.

'Not Eastern Europeans, Mr. Michaels. No, it's far more specific than that. They are Ukrainian. Every last one of them.'

'Really?' That didn't sound like a coincidence. 'Are you saying that as the old staff are being scared away, they are being replaced by Ukrainian nationals exclusively?'

'That's what I am saying. You can check I am sure.'

Julia Jones had claimed she was under instruction on who she could hire. 'How come you and Dave are still there?'

'I doubt I could get another job. Not one as convenient as this one. I can walk to work from here, the pay is okay and up until all these problems started, I never had to do anything much. Dave and I would find a quiet corner and watch movies on his iPad.'

I remembered nights performing pointless guard duties during the early part of my army career. A nook out of the wind where you could while away a bit of time was a blessing on many a cold night. Next to me Big Ben was nodding his understanding.

So, I had a Ukrainian chap as the CEO's personal assistant, a Ukrainian head of security and the entire facility was now being flooded with Ukrainian staff as the old staff were being scared away. It was very specific, and it seemed the ghosts were being used to perform the scare tactics.

'You're not scared that you might meet with an accident?'

'I am actually.' He admitted. 'Dave and I never leave each other's sight these days. We are the only two left on the security detail that are not Ukrainian, and they are making it more and more uncomfortable for us to stay there.'

'In what way?' Big Ben asked, speaking for the first time.

Dave turned his attention to Big Ben. 'Small stuff really. Our packed meals would go missing, our mugs got broken, we would always get the crappiest duty and if it was raining, we would have to be outside all night. I think Dave would have left if I hadn't begged him to stay a bit longer. If he goes, I don't know how much longer I'll be able to continue.'

I thought for a moment. I would have more questions, but I didn't have any more at the moment. Dave was clearly prepared to aid us in our investigation, so I outlined what Big Ben and I would be doing and when and where. He had no questions for us, so it was time to go. We were starting the cleaning shift at 2000hrs so were getting short on time to change and eat and get back to the Dockyard.

'Anything else you want to know?' He asked.

I shook my head, but Big Ben said, 'Yeah. Are there many fit girls working there at night?'

I slapped him on the arm with my notebook.

That had ended the chat with Dave, who had then promised to look out for us at work and would give us whatever help he could. Big Ben and I had met back at the Dockyard fifteen minutes before we were due to start our shift. I used the time to feed myself and to feed and walk my dogs before dropping them off with Mrs Comerforth.

Now, as Anna led us to the wheelie bin we would be pushing around to empty the bins into, I wondered how we would slip away. The answer, at least initially, was that we wouldn't. The cleaning still had to get done, otherwise Big Ben and I would last no time at all no matter who he shagged next.

Our presence had been spotted by several of the Ukrainian security guards. They were eyeing us warily while they discussed us in their native tongue. We were not followed though, so soon enough, with Anna directing our actions, we were emptying bins into the big wheelie bin and then pushing it to the next destination on the map. It was easy work, but monotonous. As Big Ben and I emptied each bin by yanking out the bag inside and tossing it into the larger receptacle, Anna put a fresh bag into each bin and placed it back where it came from. The simple task would be unpleasant in the rain, but tonight it was still and dry and really not that cold. It could have been much worse.

The girls were chatting constantly in Ukrainian while Big Ben and I were mostly silent, but after ten minutes of the slow, boring task Big Ben sidled up to me and whispered, 'We need to lose the girls.'

'Yup.' I nodded.

'How about we shag them and offer to leave them tackling one of the easier indoor tasks while we race around and get this done so we can sneak off.'

I glanced at Anna. She was smiling at me.

'I reckon you're well in there, mate.' Big Ben observed.

It didn't sound like a thing to be happy about to me. Anna was no more attractive than her friend Anyanka. Not that I was being judgemental, I just didn't wish to put my penis anywhere near her. Besides that, I really couldn't see how I converted pushing a wheelie bin around into us all taking our clothes off for sex.

'How about an abridged version of that plan where I don't have sex with anyone?' I suggested.

'Really?' Big Ben looked confused. 'I thought you were still suffering a dry spell. You said you hadn't shagged Natasha yet. Haven't you been on like seven dates now?'

'Six actually.'

'Six dates? With a girl as hot as Natasha? A girl that you were lusting after for months. Yes, you were!' He snapped when I opened my mouth to disagree. 'You do realise that life will be simpler for you if you just come out of the closet.'

'Suck it, douchebag.'

'There you go. Telling other men to suck it. What more proof do you need? Just get yourself a tee-shirt that says, "I love cock" and wear it proudly.'

'You are not helping, and I am still not going to have sex with Anna in order to distract them.'

'Okay, length-lover. I'll just have to do them both while you empty the bins.'

He peeled off and fell back a couple of paces to where the girls were chatting as they followed us. I couldn't hear what he was saying, however, the result of his words was that Anyanka took his hand and began tugging him toward the nearest building. Anna didn't go with them though.

As Anyanka was fiddling with a large bunch of keys on her belt, a bunch that I had not spotted until now but most definitely wanted to get my hands on, Big Ben was gesticulating to me urgently. Quite exactly what message I was supposed to perceive was lost but it was probably something along the lines of, "Sorry, I tried, but you are going to have to shag her yourself."

Not happening, I told myself as Anna came toward me, smiling in what I assumed was supposed to be a demure way.

It could be worse, I told myself. I could do this. It might even be nice. I was trying to gee myself up for the task, but no matter how I phrased it in my head, I still couldn't get Mr Wriggly to engage. It was like turning the ignition key, but the starter motor was broken. Bottom line: Anna was short and ugly and she smelled a bit odd. She also had missing teeth, a misshapen nose and a large hairy brown mole on her right cheek. Nature had not been kind to Anna, but my sympathy couldn't extend far enough to give her an orgasm.

'Hello, Tempest.' She smouldered at me while lounging herself against the wheelie bin. They didn't give us a uniform to wear, I guess that cost them more, so all the staff wore whatever crappy clothes they had at home. Anna had chosen a torn and dirty coat to ward off the cool night air and partnered it with ripped jeans, that were skin tight on her bulging thighs, and a pair of ratty trainers for her feet. Not that putting her in a fresh outfit from Victoria's Secret would have made a difference, but the bag-lady look wasn't doing her any favours.

She gave up on the indirect approach, pushed herself off the wheelie bin and advanced on me. Mr Wriggly hid beneath my right testicle.

'I think our friends are getting warm and comfortable inside. Wouldn't you like to do that too?'

I really wanted to blurt out that I would rather take a cheese grater to my balls and then douse them in vinegar before setting them on fire, but I kept the less-pleasant thoughts locked inside my head.

Instead, I said, 'I, um. I like cock?' It came out more as a question than anything else as if I was asking if she would believe my lie.

Her face was sceptical. 'Your friend said you were shy and that you have a small penis, but I should be sympathetic and let you try your best.'

I was going to kick him in the nuts.

'Sorry, no. I'm just gay. Gay, gay, gay, gay, gay.' I said, trying to get myself into the role.

'Oh. Oh, well. I guess I misunderstood.' We sort of looked at each other for a few seconds, waiting for the other to speak.

'Shall we continue with the bins?' I asked as I grabbed the wheelie bin again and started pushing it toward the station of bins I could see in the distance.

'I should, ah. I should wait for Anyanka.' Said Anna, then thought better of it. 'Maybe I should check on her actually. Make sure she is alright.' Clearly, she had struck out with me and fancied her chances elsewhere.

Fine by me. As she hurried in the direction Anyanka and Big Ben had gone, I revelled in finally being alone. I checked my watch: 2022hrs. It was dark near the water, but the floodlights I had seen during my earlier visit were still on, bathing the Dockyard in pools of bright light. I figured I could bluff that I was looking for a toilet if anyone wanted to know why I had wandered off, so I abandoned the wheelie bin, orientated myself against the map in my head and started jogging toward the rigging room.

Whispers in the Rigging Room. Monday, November 21st 2031hrs

I was being careful not to make any noise as my feet hit the cobbles, a task made easier by wearing an old, soft pair of trainers. I didn't want to draw attention to myself and knew that if I was a security guard at night, I would react to the sound of a person running.

My stealthy movements would also allow me to hear others who were not trying to mask their progress. I could hear women chatting and laughing around the corner ahead of me as I approached it. I paused, checked around the corner and crossed between buildings while they were not looking my way. I had covered more than half the distance to the rigging room but had not yet seen any security guards. Perhaps they considered the site to be safe and were more relaxed than I expected. It could be that they were all hiding in the warm somewhere.

I reached the rigging room and slipped inside. The lights were off inside the long, thin room suiting my intentions perfectly. Light pouring through the windows from the flood lights outside provided enough illumination to see by and plenty of shadows for me sneak through.

No doubt it was set to be cleaned at some point this evening, the crew assigned to it on other tasks first. Alan had said there were whispers in the rigging room, which was cryptic and non-specific, but I had to acknowledge that those two things were my wheelhouse – an area where I generally operated.

Creeping through the room, dodging around ancient wooden equipment and stacks of rope positioned to give the visitors the look and feel of the room when it was in use a few hundred years ago, I could detect no noise. It was a long room though, so if I was listening for whispers, I should expect them to be hard to hear.

Every few yards I stopped to listen, stilling my breathing to prevent it interfering. Several minutes had elapsed when I judged I was over half way and then I heard it.

I froze on the spot, straining my senses. Nothing. Then it came again, a murmur of human speech too faint to understand. I turned slowly in place trying to pinpoint the direction it was coming from. Down the centre of the room ran what was essentially a raised table on which the rope was worked, the vast lengths required to rig a boat needing to be completely laid out in order that connections could be made at appropriate points along it. I climbed over it now to the other side in search of the noise.

The voices were intermittent which made them far harder to find and my paranoia was telling me I had already taken too long on this task and was going to be missed soon. I was committed though, the noise I could hear was part of this mystery.

It sounded like an echo. The realisation that the garbled sound I could hear had a certain quality I associated with being underground put me on all fours on the floorboards. I began crawling around the floor, moving a few feet and pausing to listen, then repeating the motion, each time waiting for the noise before moving again.

It was coming from more than one place. It had to be and that was why I couldn't pinpoint it, then as I moved forward, I caught the whispered voice right by my ear. It was coming from a pipe.

I turned to face it and sat on the floorboards to inspect what I had found. There was a pipe coming out of the floor. To the touch it felt like it was made of lead, which made sense given the age of everything here. It rose to a height of about three feet and was tucked between wooden boxes that might have been built as tool chests or part stores but were fixed to the floorboards. They did a great job of concealing the pipe which was probably easy to see if the lights were on and all but impossible without.

I placed my ear over the hole to listen and was rewarded moments later by more voices drifting out of it. Even with the sound going directly into my ear I still couldn't make out what I was hearing.

I sat back to consider what this told me. The first answer was that there was something beneath the Dockyard. Was there a cellar underneath the rigging room and all I could hear was a couple of guards playing cards where they thought they would never get caught? Or was it more than that?

I checked my watch again. Too much time had gone by for me to hang around any longer or to begin searching now for a way into whatever was beneath me. Maybe I would be able to slip away again later.

At a slow jog, I made my way back along the room to the door I had come in through and made my way back to the wheelie bin.

Ghosts. Monday, November 21st 2105hrs

I found Big Ben and the girls not far from where I had left them. Anyanka's hair had a dishevelled look to it that I made no comment about.

'Ah, there he is.' Said Big Ben as I came into view. 'I had to tell the girls about your weak sphincter muscle from too much getting it hard from hairy men and how it means you have to go the toilet more often because things just won't stay inside.'

He was trying not to grin because he knew I couldn't disagree without exposing the lie but was failing as he smirked at his own humour. All three of them were looking at me, waiting for me to say something.

'Yes. Sorry about that. I had a... call of nature.' Anna patted my arm.

Big Ben gave the wheelie bin a shove and we set off again, my toilet troubles put to one side thankfully. I moved to help Big Ben push the bin and so I could quietly speak with him.

'I thought the plan was to leave them doing something indoors, so we had more freedom of movement?' I whispered.

'It is. On our list of places to clean is a gallery down by the water beyond the ships. We are heading there now. Anyanka said it would take them half an hour to hoover and dust by which time she expected you and I to have finished emptying all the bins. She is a bit bossy actually.'

I looked at him, waiting for him to expand on the last sentence.

'Yeah, she was shouting instructions at me the whole time. Harder. Faster. Grab my hips. I think she likes that she is in charge of us here and gets to tell me what to do.'

'Okay.' I didn't really need to hear how she liked it. 'Did you find time to quiz her about anything more pertinent to our current investigation?'

'Of course.'

'And?'

'I asked her about the ghosts and whether she had seen them. Her response was that she hadn't but that lots of others had and that she had seen a lot of new faces in the last few weeks because the cleaners were getting scared and leaving. She also remarked that she was surprised Julia Jones had hired us. Everyone else employed in the recent weeks has been Ukrainian.'

'Yes, there is a distinct Ukrainian theme here. I want to believe there is something to that.'

We stopped at another set of bins. They were full of the day's detritus. Empty cans and plastic bottles and a broken umbrella. It all went into the wheelie bin as the girls reloaded the bins with fresh plastic bag liners.

After just one more stop to empty bins we arrived at the gallery. Anyanka pulled out her bunch of keys, sorted her way through them and, finding the right one, opened the door.

As the lights came on and Anna went inside, Anyanka gave Big Ben and me instructions and a thirty-minute deadline for getting the rest of the bins empty. She sure was bossy. It suited me though, we needed to sneak off and look around untethered to our Ukrainian chaperones, and now we could.

'What do we do about the bins?' Big Ben asked as we wheeled the heavy bin away at speed. I had the map in one hand and no intention of wasting much time doing what we were expected to do.

'Grab a few as we pass them, lose the map and if anyone even notices that some weren't emptied, we claim we couldn't find all the bins. I am not concerned about keeping this job beyond the next couple of days.'

'So where are we heading?'

We were jogging with the wheelie bin between us, pushing it along the cobbled street at the best speed we could manage and being rewarded with vibrations juddering all the way up our arms to our skulls as it skipped across the uneven surface.

'I found voices coming through a pipe in the rigging room. I think there is a room beneath it, so that is where we are going. Something is going on here. Under normal circumstances I would have no interest, but…'

'Someone hurt Mr Michaels senior and we have a judicious slap or two to hand out.' Big Ben completed my sentence.

'Something like that.'

I felt the bin drag suddenly, it's resistance to forward motion markedly increased as Big Ben deliberately slowed it. He had spotted or heard someone. With a nod of my head we aimed our trajectory at a bin station just to our left and were pulling the full bags out of them as a pair of guards rounded the corner ahead of us.

'I saw their shadows.' Big Ben said quietly as he threw them a wave.

Neither man returned the gesture as they eyed us. They were both large men, all the Ukrainian guards were as if they had kidnapped a bodybuilding team. The two Daves contrasted this by having skinny arms and tubby bellies.

The one on the right spoke into a lapel microphone without taking his eyes off us. Then the pair backed away, disappearing around the corner without breaking eye contact.

Big Ben said, 'That was odd.'

I nodded. 'Let's move.'

The bin got abandoned. We could come back for it later. It had seemed as if the guard were looking for us and had then reported our location to someone else. Not staying where we were was the only prudent course of action. We stayed stealthy though, keeping to the shadows and making as little noise as possible.

Our dash to the rigging room took two minutes as we tried to make sure we were not seen. When we got there though we began a search of the building's exterior. It would have been safer to stick together, but the two-hundred-yard-long building would take too long to inspect that way, so we split at the first corner. I instantly regretted not bringing radios with me, I had them in the office sitting idle. It was too late now though.

Big Ben had gone right as I went left, which placed me on the lee side of the building away from the river and in the dark as this portion of the yard wasn't floodlit. I was looking for a door, a ramp leading down, an obvious manhole cover, anything that might indicate a way into the room I believed was beneath my feet somewhere. Halfway down my side of the building, I had still not found anything that wasn't solid cobblestones and judged that I had gone further than the point where I found the pipes inside.

Another minute later I reached the end of the building and turned the corner at the far end. As I stepped back into the floodlit area, Big Ben rounded the corner opposite me.

'Anything?' I asked.

He shook his head. Okay, nothing so far. I quelled my annoyance and checked my watch: 2117hrs. Anyanka's deadline was fast approaching, and we had emptied only two bins. It was not something I cared about but I would need her to believe we were trustworthy, so we could ditch them again later or tomorrow or the night after that.

I clapped Big Ben on the shoulder. 'Let's get back.'

Silently we fell into pace, side by side as we began jogging back to collect the wheelie bin. We didn't get far though. About halfway back to where we had abandoned our cleaning duties, what I could only describe as an apparition appeared in front of us.

It was there one moment and then it was gone. It was a hundred yards ahead of us but we both saw it, and both knew what it represented. It hadn't been visible for long, though it was long enough for us to see the horrifying death mask of a face beneath the ornate navy-blue bicorne hat. It looked right at us, its lips drawn back in rigor to reveal its teeth. It also had the misty quality that Dave Saunders had described. It was grey where it should have colour, but I couldn't see through it.

We paused, both momentarily frozen by what we had seen but before we could react it appeared again. This time closer and began coming toward us. From between its lips a rasping moan escaped.

It was quite terrifying.

Big Ben laughed. 'That thing actually looks real.' He said.

I nodded my agreement. 'Yeah. Let's get it.'

It was right ahead of us on our way back to the river front and the gallery where we had left Anyanka and Anna, so we started running toward it. As I expected, the pace of the advancing apparition faltered, then slowed to a gradual halt. Then it vanished.

My brain didn't like that it had just vanished and was questioning why I was still running toward the dead sailor. Neither one of us slowed our pace though, reaching the spot we had last seen it only a few seconds later to discover that it hadn't vanished, it had stepped into a shadow and then ducked down another alley way. Lord knows the Dockyard is littered with narrow alleyways that run between the buildings. They had been designed with foot traffic in mind at a time when even a bicycle would have been a feat of engineering genius.

'Hey!'

Big Ben and I had been about to explore the alley to see how far the ghost had gone or if there were an open door it could have slipped through to escape when Pasha's voice rang out. It carried in the dark where this close to the water there were very few sounds to compete with it.

'Where the hell have you been?'

Big Ben turned to speak with her as she approached across the cobbles looking angry. 'There was a ghost, angel.' He said.

'Was it emptying the bins?' She snapped back at him. 'They won't empty themselves, you know?'

'Where are the two stupid women I left you with?'

Big Ben looked confused. Girls don't usually have questions for him to answer. Unless perhaps the question is: How do you want to do me? Instead, especially after he has given them the best shag of their life – his opinion not mine, they remain eternally grateful.

As his lips moved and no noise came out, I answered instead. 'Hi, Pasha. We saw a ghost, or what was supposed to be a ghost. It went down here so we were following it.'

'Why?' She asked. It seemed to be a reasonable question. Pasha came to a stop in front of us with her hands on her hips in clear frustration. 'You have work to do. Chasing ghosts is not what you are being paid for.'

'Haven't ghosts scared away most of the staff? Are they not a problem that needs to be resolved?'

She eyed me suspiciously for a moment. 'Wait. You're telling me that you really saw a ghost?' Her eyes widened slightly, then her brow knitted again. She didn't believe us. 'If you saw a ghost, what did it look like?'

'Like an 18th century Royal Navy 1st Lieutenant. Gold brocade to the epaulettes, bicorne hat, white stockings. It looked very dead.'

Now her eyes widened again. I guess it matched with the description she had heard from other people. 'Why on earth would you chase it? Everyone else has run away terrified.'

'We don't scare that easily.' Big Ben answered. Then he stepped forward and took her right hand in both of his. He gave her his best smouldering look as he gently said, 'Kitten, you didn't really come looking for me to ask me about the bins, now did you? Wouldn't you rather help me have this place renamed the Dickyard?' He was turning the charm on. For him it was a tactic that rarely missed.

Pasha was immune though. 'I have a boyfriend and he is super badass and would beat the crap out of you so don't go getting any ideas.'

Big Ben replied, 'Babe, I never have any ideas.'

Stunned silence. Her mouth twitched in a smile and I couldn't tell if Big Ben had made himself sound stupid by accident or on purpose. She considered his reply for a moment then turned on her heel to start walking away. 'Come on, morons, you still have work to do. I will escort you back to Anyanka and Anna. I want a word with them about their diligence. You can stay late to finish emptying the bins.'

I wanted to see where the ghost could have gone but couldn't see a way of ditching the girls again immediately without raising suspicion or directly disobeying Pasha who seemed likely to fire us both if we gave her the slightest reason to. I only needed the job for a few days. I could suck it up that long. Tomorrow in the daylight I could explore again. It would be easier to look around then.

As we followed Pasha back to the gallery, Big Ben had a question for me. 'Did you see its teeth?' He asked meaning the ghost.

It wasn't just me then. He had seen it too. 'Yeah. Bright, pearly whites and it had a very convincing shadow too.'

A Late Start. Tuesday, November 22nd 0912hrs

It had been just before 0300hrs when I got home. The dogs were already in the house as was the normal practice for Mrs Comerforth. She had a key and would let them back into my place as she went to bed. I had been too tired to stay up to fuss and pet them, and they had not seemed all that interested in being awake. Instead, I had lifted them onto the bed and had them curl into me for comfort – theirs and mine.

They were still there when I awoke, two gently snoring warm lumps in the duvet that showed no sign of wanting to rise even though I had given myself a late start.

The lazy hour was more to do with the knowledge that I was going to be back at the dockyard until late again tonight than it was to do with being tired. I had applied the soldier's rule of sleep when you can because you never know when you might next get some.

Sitting on the edge of my bed and scratching myself idly, I ran through what I had learned the previous evening. It was a short list which had at the top of it that Pasha was so engaged in managing the cleaning crew that she could not be distracted by Big Ben's attentions. I had to admit that most women were putty in his hands once he turned on the charm. She, however, was not, but while it was unusual, there was nothing in it that I considered to be suspicious.

Beyond my thoughts on Pasha, all I had was voices coming through pipes in the rigging room and the belief that there was a room of some kind beneath it. It was close to where my dad had been found and perhaps formed the epicentre of the mystery so far.

Then there was the scary ghost that had not been scary at all if one assumed it was a buffoon in a costume. We had both spotted the ghost's perfect rows of teeth as they shone in the light. Three hundred years ago no one had teeth and those that did had terrible ones that were falling out of their heads. Of course, had I been asked what I thought the ghost was before I had seen it, I would still have said it was a person in an outfit, but then, unlike everyone else that might come across it, I did this for a living.

I had a rough plan for my day and it was all about getting to the bottom of what had happened to my father. More normally, I would be off to the gym or going out for a run, but I felt an enhanced pressure to focus all my effort on this case to the point that I was dismissing everything else.

As I got up to make my way to the shower, I remembered that Natasha had sent me a text last night. In it she had politely pointed out that she hadn't heard from me and was hoping we could see each other soon. I hadn't replied, which was mostly because Anyanka had heard the incoming text and had raised a warning eyebrow at me so I would know she felt I didn't have time to answer it. I had to acknowledge though that I also hadn't answered since then because I wasn't sure what to say.

I doubt my situation is unique, but I find myself rather enamoured with a woman I am not dating; my colleague and employee Amanda Harper. I cannot even explain what it is about her that transfixes me, other than my belief that she is womanhood perfection personified. Natasha is gorgeous. Utterly beautiful, engaging to speak with, intelligent and delightful to have in one's company. Yet when we kiss nothing happens. In my head that is. Plenty is going on about three feet south where an angry beast is screaming to be set free. In my head and probably in my heart, I know that I have no future with Natasha. I always hated breaking up with women though, cowardly in my preference that they would ditch me.

Rinsing shampoo from my hair, I forced myself to promise I would text her back and explain what had happened to my dad and where I had been for the last couple of days. That would buy me some time, but I was supposed to be taking her to Jagjit's wedding on Friday. She was my date and we had a room booked at the wedding venue that night. It was inevitable that we would have sex and I knew she was getting impatient.

Mr Wriggly thought it was about goddam time and was mocking me, *oh no, you'll have to have sex with the single, available, large-breasted, gorgeous woman. However will you cope?*

He had a point and was beginning to stir at the thought of her abundant chest and what it might be like to get my hands on it. I didn't have time for him though, there were things to do.

'Come on, lazy dogs.' I called as I went back into the bedroom, drying my skin and hair as I went. My outfit for the day was business casual as usual. I found myself wanting to wear heavy boots instead of stylish men's shoes so as I slipped on the supple, brown-leather oxfords, I yet again found myself questioning whether I would have to fight someone in them. It was my ability to deliver a kick without hurting myself that was driving the desire to don something sturdier. All too often, my innocent investigative work led to confrontation and the need to defend myself. Shoes had a habit of coming off in a fight. You don't see soldiers wearing loafers, do you?

The dogs plopped off the bed to the carpet where they each performed a complex series of stretches – a sight to behold on a miniature Dachshund I can assure you. I scooped one under each arm to carry them downstairs, then fought to hold onto them as they struggled to break free and get to the back door.

With maniacally excited barking, they cleared the lawn of wood pigeons as I filled my kettle and thought breakfast thoughts.

My phone rang. I had a mug in one hand and the tea caddy in the other. It was my cross-dressing assistant at the other end though. The tea caddy was discarded so I could thumb the phone to speaker.

'Good morning.' I hallooed, deliberately not addressing my assistant by name as I could not tell which one would be in use today.

'Hi, boss, It's Jane.' She helpfully supplied. 'Are you coming to the office today? I have some interesting details on the Dockyard.'

I had tasked her yesterday with researching recent newsworthy events. She was a whizz at digging up information and had a nose for what might be pertinent. Much like Amanda, the other detective I had taken on to share the workload, she was worth her weight in gold.

'I'm just getting some breakfast, but I'll be there in half an hour.' I replied. Jane was used to me coming and going as I pleased. Not because I owned the business and I wasn't to be questioned, but due to my semi-regular stakeout activities and nocturnal ghost hunts. It was the nature of the job that some of it had to be done at night.

The dogs barked to be let back in. They wanted their breakfast, as did I, so I disconnected the call with a promise to see her soon and went to let them in.

Twenty-eight minutes later I pulled into the parking space behind my office. Amanda's car was absent, not that I had a specific need to see her, I just liked to touch base to see how she was getting on and whether she wanted my help with anything. I had only seen her in passing yesterday which meant the last worthwhile conversation had been Friday and then it was via a phone call.

We operated independent of each other, tackling our own cases and billing hours. I had taken her on only a few weeks ago with little plan as to how it would work. There were so many enquiries I could probably take on a third detective if I wanted to. But it was confusing enough for me with just the two of us for now and hiring a third would mean we had to office share somehow as the building only had two rooms at the back which gave Amanda and I an office each.

I made a mental note to call her once I had checked in with Jane and let myself in through the back door. The two dogs scampered ahead of me to reach the next door as fast as they could, then waited impatiently once more for me to open that, their little tails whipping back and forth in excitement. That they could find such pleasure in the most basic events was a marvel.

They were both butting the base of the door with their tiny heads as I turned the handle to open it, then moving their feet so fast they could scarcely keep their grip on the short office carpet tiles. They bumped each other continually as they rushed in, turned left and hurtled toward Jane at her desk.

I found it quite notable that where some people found Jane's choice to wear ladies' clothing odd or distasteful or some other negative emotion, the dogs couldn't give a monkey's. They wanted to be petted and fussed and given treats. The person supplying said treats could be a serial killer in a tutu and biker boots for all they cared. They judged people by a different set of rules.

'Hi, Jane.' I called as I hung up my coat. The coffee machine was next on my list of things to do. I called out, 'Want one?' As I made my way to it.

'Yes, please.' She answered in return. When the last office burned to the ground, I lost mundane items such as the kettle I had there, so when I went to the electrical retailer to replace it, they had a stand inside the front doors displaying funky hi-tech coffee machines.

Let's just say the salesman didn't have to work hard for his commission. The only drawback was that the coffee in my office was better than the stuff at home now and I sometimes found myself wondering if I should take the machine home with me at night for safekeeping.

As I took Jane her delicate porcelain cup, I asked, 'What did you find?'

'Well, firstly, they have an odd employment policy going on somewhere because everyone taken on in the last few months is Ukrainian. That can't be an accident.'

I nodded. 'I met some of them. Almost the entire night-shift cleaning crew is Ukrainian. Big Ben and I stood out.'

Jane looked at me.

'Well, more than normal I mean.' People say I look dominating and surly when I am not smiling. I don't see quite how I can manage to look intimidating when I usually have two miniature Dachshunds at my feet, especially since both of them can be relied upon to either fall asleep or roll on their backs for a tickle whenever I stop moving. Big Ben though, he does tend to stand out. He would anyway, just because at six feet seven inches tall he is always the tallest person in the room, but he is also the most strikingly handsome man most people have ever seen either in the flesh or on the big screen. When you add to that, that he carries a surprising amount of muscle for a person that is not a professional bodybuilder, well, he stands out, that's all.

'There are a few people left in key positions that are British, most notably the CEO and the Facilities Manager, and the tour guides themselves appear to still be British Nationals, but anyone new is not.'

While she was speaking a series of dots were joining in my head. 'Big Ben and I saw the ghost last night.'

'I thought it was ghosts?'

'A valid point. We only saw one, but of course there can be as many as they want since it is just some tit in an outfit. I am thinking that the ghost thing, which started a few weeks ago now, could be aimed at the local persons that worked there. Get rid of the locals, or more generally the British, and replace them with Ukrainians. The ghosts are used to scare away the people they want rid of. Almost all the guards are now Ukrainian. There are only two of the original guard left.'

'To what end?' Jane asked.

I nodded again. 'That's the question. If it is deliberate, and it certainly feels like it is, then what are they trying to achieve?'

'Who stands to gain?' Jane echoed the thought in my head. It was a standard question I asked myself with most cases.

I parked the thought until I had more pieces of the puzzle. 'What else have you got?'

Jane tapped a few keys. 'I was looking at staff employment as a general background check when I stumbled onto the Ukrainian thing. All the staff that left have done so voluntarily, no sign of people being sacked. Except for this chap.'

Jane swivelled one of her screens toward me, so I could see the face of the man it showed. He was in his sixties and bookish, which is to say I would guess librarian if someone asked me to name his profession. His hair was mostly gone, a few wisps clinging to the sides of his scalp above his ears. His nose was a little red and veins riddled his face. The picture was a head shot, the sort taken for a staff photograph that is then used for your ID badge.

I asked, 'What's his story?'

'He was sacked on November 3rd. Summarily dismissed according to the HR database.' My instant thought was to ask Jane how she was reading from the HR database of the Dockyard, but I already knew the answer would be that she had hacked it. Getting caught wasn't something I was worried about, not for a private firm where we were not using the data against them.

Instead I asked, 'Does it say why?'

'No, however, I thought you might be interested to know his address is in Upnor.'

I looked away from the screen. Upnor was no distance from the office at all. Maybe fifteen minutes if I got caught in some traffic. The tiny village bordered the river and only existed at all because it had a castle right at the water's edge. I forget the purpose or reason the castle was built now but remembered a school trip there when I was much younger.

The dogs could have a good walk along the beach if the tide was out and I might learn something from the man.

I was going out.

Upnor. Tuesday, November 22nd 1103hrs

The man's name was Cedric Tilsley. Jane hadn't been able to find a number for him, so I was going to have to knock on his door and hope he was in, but Upnor is a small place, even compared with my home village of Finchampstead. The road through the countryside swept downhill to the river coastline where it hugged the water with houses bordering the inland side until it terminated little more than two hundred yards after the village started. Despite its tiny size, it had two pubs which I knew maintained a steady trade through the warmer months when tourists were drawn to the castle grounds and the yacht club regattas.

Though I hadn't been to Upnor in some years, the public carpark I remembered was still there. Whether it ever got busy I couldn't guess, but on this dingy, damp Tuesday morning in November, mine was the only car in it.

The dogs had sensed that we were arriving somewhere, their reaction as always to climb up the door so they could peer out the window. As I pulled to a stop, they ran across the seat and leaped the transmission tunnel to arrive on my lap. They wanted to explore, and for once, given that Upnor was basically a dead end, I opened the door and let them go.

They shot off toward the water, crossing the path and jumping down to the pebbles below where there were undoubtedly many, many smells to draw their attention. I stopped to open the boot where I kept an old pair of army-issue boots. I had learned early on in my career as an investigator that all too often the footwear would prove to be inappropriate for the environment I was drawn into. With the boots securely tied to my feet, I ambled after them, taking my time and enjoying the view across the river. I took in the vista, which stretched to the left to show me Chatham and Rochester, plus a glimpse of Gillingham in the distance and to the right where the newly developed St. Mary's Isle was jutting out into the water. The sky was grey, but it did not cause California Dreaming, rather it felt right for the time of year. As the land swept upward on the opposite side, the wide expanse of open land known as the Great Lines could be seen beyond the few tall office blocks in Chatham city centre. On the other side of that was Medway hospital and my father.

Snapping back to the present and thinking about the case, I remembered my intention to call Amanda, fished out my phone and wandered after the dogs as they scurried along the beach together.

It rang for a few seconds before it connected. 'Hi, Tempest.' Her wonderful voice pulled at my heart and my libido simultaneously. To me it always sounded like angels laughing.

'Good morning, Amanda.' I replied. 'I'm just calling to check in. To make sure you have all you need and have not been kidnapped by a voodoo priest or anything.'

She laughed at me though it was hardly a joke. I wouldn't say she needed regular rescuing, no more than I did at any rate. However, it was a genuine concern whenever I hadn't heard from her for a while.

'Thank you for checking on me. I am not currently kidnapped.' She assured me with amusement in her voice. 'How is your dad?'

'He is still unconscious, so no change there, but the doctors seem convinced he will wake soon and make a full recovery. Thank you for asking. Are you on a case?'

'I have three cases currently. Actually, I am lurking in a doorway in Canterbury, waiting for my target to appear on one of them.'

'Anything interesting?'

'That would depend on how one defines interesting, but what I have is a client whose family have been losing sleep for many months because of moaning noises in the night. When I started investigating, I discovered that it wasn't just them, there were fifteen families in the same street affected by the nightly event. I think I have traced it to a single person, an old man that lives on the same street. I am calling him the sandman for now, but I cannot work out how he is doing it, or why, or even if it is deliberate. So, I am following him around and building a picture of his activities.'

'The sandman, huh? Good name.'

'It seemed to fit. Ooh, here he is. Gotta go. I'll message later.'

The line went dead in my ear. I had wanted to touch base with her and I had. She was completely capable of managing her time and workload and was billing three times what I was paying her, which was twice what she earned as a police officer. The surplus money was going directly into the firm's bank account and was therefore mine. Something about that made me uncomfortable though. Acknowledging that I was a terrible businessman because I didn't like profiting from my employees, I already knew I was going to make Amanda a partner at some point. I would be more comfortable once I had although there was a voice at the back of my head telling me that she would then no longer be my employee so any romantic pursuit I might engage in would be less creepy.

I put the phone back in my pocket while berating myself for yet again daydreaming about my perfect employee with her perfect smile, perfect figure and…

FFS.

I shook my head to rid myself of her image. By the water the dogs had found something. They were always finding something to sniff but it was usually a dead fish or something equally smelly. Their latest find was a brown cardboard package.

When I got closer, I could see it was a box. It had been in the water and lost its square shape although the glue sealing the flaps on the lid had not yet lost its bond. It was roughly square and about fifteen inches along each side by about six inches high.

I said, 'Move along, chaps.' To keep the dogs going, but as I dismissed the box, I noticed writing on the top. It was not English. Now, I couldn't tell what language it was, but it looked Eastern European to me. It wasn't German or French or Spanish but had the gibberish jumble of letters I would associate with Welsh only with lots of accents added. Was it Ukrainian?

As I crouched for a closer look, Bull and Dozer moved in to see what I was doing, both sticking their noses where I was trying to place my hands.

I had seen Ukrainian written on the wall in the room the cleaners congregated in for their briefing last night. This looked the same. It was two lines of typed text on the upper lid which looked to be a manufacturer's mark.

It might be nothing, but I was going to check it out anyway. Resolving to pick it up and take it to the car must have been a thought I was projecting though because Bull instantly lifted his back leg and widdled on the nearest corner of the box. He even locked eyes with me when he did it before trotting off content in a job well done.

I muttered to myself, but grasped the box anyway, taking care to avoid the freshly damp bit where he had peed. As I lifted though, I discovered that the glue on top might have retained its integrity but the glue on the bottom had not. The box lifted to a height of about six inches before the flaps beneath yielded and the contents spilled all over the beach.

I allowed myself a pointless display of angry, ironic defeat until the paper the box had contained began blowing across the beach. Then the dogs and I played a great game where I tried to grab the paper to stop it littering the area while they ran around excited by my jerky movements trying to bite my hands and trip me. Some of the paper went into the water and was lost but I was able to retrieve/rescue ninety-nine percent of it. Over half had stayed where it was because it was damp and stuck together. The half that was not told me that the box hadn't been in the water long.

With an armful of paper, I snagged the now deflated box with one hand to go back to the car. I stopped though, looking down at my hand in horror. The part of the box I had grabbed was the exact spot Bull had relieved himself on. It was still warm.

Perfect.

On my way to Cedric Tilsley's house, I dropped the box and paper into the boot of my car and put the dogs on their leads. We were walking through a village which meant there would be cats and the dogs would not only cause havoc if they saw one but would attempt to chase it and get lost.

Cedric lived at number two Pearson's Lane. I knew the lane itself lay perpendicular to the main street that bordered the river and it was easy to find using the map in my head. It was a short, stubby street that terminated less than fifty yards after it started when the land began to slope sharply upwards. There were three houses on each side of the lane, all good-sized Victorian detached places. His was on the right in the middle, a bright white, double-fronted place with sash windows and a chimney gently emitting smoke in the middle of the roof.

As I knocked on the door, I hoped the smoke meant he was in. A dog barked somewhere deep inside the house, the sound getting closer as it bounded toward the door. In return Bull and Dozer began barking their response. I couldn't tell what the three dogs were trying to communicate but it sounded angry and aggressive.

The dog on the other side sounded larger than my two, but it would be fair to say the odds of that were high. I had eaten cheese sandwiches that were bigger than my dogs.

I retreated a pace to stand behind the gate as a shadow moving toward the door preceded it opening. A playful, excited Dalmatian attempted to bound out, barely held in check by its owner Cedric. Cedric looked just like his photograph. He might even have been wearing the same clothes. His face was open and friendly, almost smiling and might well have been were he not struggling to control his exuberant dog.

I had to hush my own dogs, so I could speak. 'Good morning. My name is Tempest Michaels.' I offered him my card. 'I am looking into some events at the Royal Dockyard and hoped you might be willing to answer a few questions for me.'

He eyed me suspiciously. 'What sort of questions?'

'My father worked there as one of the guides. He was attacked recently while looking into strange noises coming from the rigging room. Lots of the staff have been scared away by the ghosts that have been reported there.' He looked at my card again, understanding the connection now. 'You are the only person whose departure in recent months wasn't voluntary. Do you mind if I pick your brains a little?'

He nodded his understanding. 'Who is your father?'

'Michael Michaels. I'm...'

'Tempest Michaels.' He supplied. 'You gave me your name already.' He smiled pleasantly. 'Please come in.' He remembered his exuberant dog as it leaped about again, trying to break free of his grip on its collar. 'I'll, err. Just give me a moment, won't you?'

He retreated into the house, dragging/coaxing the bouncing Dalmatian as he went. The house had a long corridor splitting it in two down the middle. He went all the way along it before turning to the right, returning just a few seconds later without the dog.

He grinned in a congenial way and beckoned me to join him. As I opened the gate, Bull and Dozer shoved their way through and strained at the leads to get into the house. I was going into another person's home, a person that was generous enough to let me bring the dogs in, so they were staying on their leads and under control until he suggested I do otherwise.

Ahead of me, Cedric was holding open a door that led into a study. It was an impressive room, filled floor to ceiling with books, models in glass cases, artefacts that appeared to be antiques taken from ancient warships and even some aged looking oil paintings. All of it was naval themed.

He had a desk with a wheeled office chair against one wall and two very old, but very solid looking three-legged stools in a corner.

'You said you had questions for me Mr Michaels. What is it that you would like to know?' He was sitting at the desk but had turned the chair to face into the room. He indicated I should take a seat on one of the stools.

The dogs pulled against their leads but recognised that I was not going to let them explore so curled into balls and lay down to sleep as I sat. Placing my bag on the carpet next to the stool and trapping the dogs leads under my foot, I removed my trusty notebook and pen. 'Can I start with some basics? How long have you worked at the Dockyard, what your role there was?'

'I was a curator, Mr. Michaels. I studied history at Bristol in the seventies which led me to a job in the library at Eton. It was then that I developed a passion for British Naval history. When it was announced that the Dockyard in Chatham was to be converted into an historic tourist attraction I applied for a position. I was promoted to curator three years later and have held that position ever since.'

'I believe you were recently dismissed. Can you tell me how that came about, please?' His face clouded as I asked the question. Unsurprisingly, it was a sensitive subject.

'Dismissed.' He repeated the word as if trying it out in his mouth to see how it felt. 'Dismissed. I was fired for doing my job.' He closed his eyes and sighed. When he reopened them, he had stilled the rage inside himself and was ready to talk. 'As curator, I am responsible for all of the museum artefacts. I am sure you will understand that there is far more in storage than there ever is on display. I was performing a relatively routine inspection and discovered that there were items of uniform missing. I called my staff to confirm they had not been requested for use in a new display I was somehow unaware of and that they had not been *borrowed*,' He made little quote marks with his fingers. 'for use as a Hallowe'en costume.'

'When was this?'

'When I found they were missing? That was November 4th. I had visions of one of the younger chaps we employ borrowing two uniforms for a party and wrecking them. They all swore that wasn't the case though.'

'So, then what happened?' I asked.

'I reported the loss to the CEO, Alex Jordan. He is my immediate superior. I expected him to approve my wish to involve the police. The uniforms are priceless artefacts, hundreds of years old and irreplaceable. Instead, he blamed me for their loss, berated me for thinking it was a good idea to have the police scaring away the visitors and fired me on the spot. I was escorted to my car and ejected from the premises.' He was still angry about the dismissal two weeks on, which given the nature of the event was not surprising. He slumped back into his chair when he finished speaking and sat on his hands to keep them still. He had been gesticulating wildly until that point.

I had questions queuing inside my head regarding what he planned to do about his dismissal, but they were not pertinent to the case so remained unasked. Instead my next question was about the buildings.

'Cedric, do you know anything about basements or rooms beneath the buildings at the Dockyard?'

He gave me a mystified look. 'Rooms beneath the Dockyard? Why do you ask?'

'I was there yesterday. There were voices coming through pipes in the floor of the rigging room. I couldn't find any trace of an entrance leading down though. There are no skylights outside to let light in and no steps leading down. Also, I spoke with some of my father's colleagues, the other tour guides and they have also heard the voices but knew nothing about rooms beneath the buildings. Could it just be a cellar?'

Cedric thought about what I had said, his fingers now steepled in front of his face. 'This I not something I am familiar with, the geography of the Dockyard, that is. I can reel off endless facts about the ships built there and where each one sailed and served and fought and even who the captain and crew were at the time. I believe though that tunnels exist beneath the Dockyard. They were dug in the early 18th Century I believe, but long since abandoned. I have worked there for more than two decades and never heard anyone talk of them. I'm not sure they are even accessible, or where the original access point might have been. I do recall seeing a map that shows their layout though.'

Tunnels.

Now he had my interest. 'Where is the map?'

'In the archive of course.' He replied. 'A place I can no longer get to.'

'Would you be able to guide someone to it?' I was leaning forward, anticipation making me agitated. The existence of tunnels beneath the Dockyard would provide an explanation for the voices I had heard.

'You mean, do I know exactly where it is?' He steepled his fingers again to think for a moment. 'It must be ten years or more since I saw that map, but it will be in the chart section of the archive. There are many, many charts in there, all catalogued and labelled. It will be with them.' He paused. 'You do know the difference between a map and a chart, yes?'

I nodded. 'I have sailed.' Charts were maps of the sea, there being nothing to draw on the map if all one was looking at was a huge expanse of water. So, a chart was a sea map, if you like.

'Jolly good. The map will be in there, but to pinpoint its location any better than that...' He realised something and met my eyes. 'You're planning to break in and get it, aren't you?'

I briefly considered lying. It was not a habit I endorsed though. I replied with, 'Yup. Someone hurt my father and left him for dead. I am beginning to think there is something nefarious going on at the Dockyard. I intend to find out what it is.'

His face took on an impressed expression as he nodded his approval. 'I think then that I had better start being a bit more helpful. Fancy a tot of rum?'

He was already getting up from his chair to retrieve an old-looking telescope from a shelf laden with books. Settling back into his chair with it, he slid the cap from the far end. Two shot glasses plopped neatly into his hand with a clink. Then, from the narrow end, he unscrewed a cap and poured two neat glasses of rum.

Passing one to me he said, 'Let's get the buggers, eh?'

Family. Tuesday, November 22nd 1222hrs

When I left Cedric's house, I had a better understanding of where I could find the map. Not its exact location but I knew which building it was in, where I needed to enter that building and where the map room was in relation to the building's layout. I wouldn't be able to get to it until tonight and to achieve that I would have to slip away from our chaperones again. I worried that task might be harder tonight as Anyanka had watched us like a hawk after our run in with the ghost last night.

It was down to me to work something out and important that I did because I had a big advantage now in the form of a small bunch of keys that Cedric had given me. Naughty Cedric had copied some keys many years ago when constantly signing them in and out from the guardroom had grown boring. Six keys in total opened a side door to the museum, the library, the archive which then led to the map room, the museum store rooms (two keys) and the final key opened the front door to the Admiral's main building.

How many of them I might get to use I could only guess.

On my way back to my house in Finchampstead, my phone rang. The caller ID on my dashboard claimed it was my sister calling.

'Hey, sis. What are you up to?'

'Why didn't you tell me about Dad?' She demanded.

'Good to hear from you. How is the weather there?'

'Don't evade my questions. I only found out when Mum called to ask how I was doing.'

'How are you doing?'

'I am four days overdue and ready to burst. My feet are swollen, my back is killing me, my nipples won't stop dribbling and if Chris ever comes near me again, I am likely to cut it off.'

'So, enjoying pregnancy then?'

'You are being annoying, Tempest.' I hadn't called my sister because I knew she would only start worrying and would most likely attempt to get to Kent to see him in hospital and give mum a hug. My plan had been to call her once dad was awake. Too late for that now. I explained my thoughts though.

'I am coming anyway. I have had two babies, it's no big deal anymore.' My sister was just as determined as I could be when I had decided on a course of action. I recognised the futility in trying to sway her.

'When will you arrive?' I asked.

'I'm already here. Or at least, I am just coming off the M26, so I will be at Mum's in ten minutes or so.'

'You're driving?' I asked, incredulous that she could even get behind the wheel.'

She made an exasperated sound. 'Yes, Tempest. I'm pregnant, not crippled. Plenty of women drive themselves to the hospital to have their babies.' I wasn't sure that was true. 'In some countries the women don't even stop work. They are out in a field picking crops and have the baby right there on the dirt, not in a nice hospital like we get here.'

'Okay, Rachael. You can stop beating me up now.' I interrupted before she got into full lecture mode. 'Will you be taking Mum to the hospital this afternoon?'

'That is my plan.'

I gave that some thought. 'Did Mum tell you I am looking into what happened?'

'She did. Is it safe?'

I shrugged to myself before I spoke. 'That would depend on one's concept of safe or what we were comparing it with.'

'That sounded like a no.'

'It is what I do every day.'

'And you keep ending up in hospital.' She pointed out.

It was a fair point. 'Nevertheless, someone hurt dad, and no one is doing anything about it.'

'The police won't catch them?'

'Stretched too thin to spend much time looking into an injury that could be an accident. There are no witnesses, so unless dad comes around and says he was attacked, they don't even have a crime to investigate.'

We both fell silent for a few seconds. It was me that spoke first. 'I could do with some time to focus on my investigation. Can you handle Mum by yourself this afternoon?'

'Will we see you later?'

'I have taken a job on the Dockyard night cleaning crew, so will start at 2000hrs. I can call to check in by phone before I start but will not get home until well after you have all gone to bed. I can call in at Mum's house tomorrow morning though.'

'Okay. Chris has the kids for the next couple of days. I doubt Mum will give me too much trouble. Please try and stay out of trouble yourself. I don't want to have to visit you *and* Dad in hospital.'

We said goodbye and disconnected. My afternoon was suddenly free for research and investigation. How could I best employ my time?

There were a few things I needed to do that had nothing to do with the case, among which was final admin tasks for Jagjit's stag party on Thursday night and to finish writing my Best Man speech. I had expected to have to do these things in my evenings, but my evenings were now spent at the Dockyard. Even if I solved this case in the next couple of days, I was fast running out of time to make arrangements.

I pointed the car toward home. I needed to visit the Dockyard again this afternoon because I would be able to see better in the daylight. The dogs were going home because I would move more freely without them and they had enjoyed plenty of exercise already. Thinking about their exercise on the beach reminded me that I needed to boil my right hand when I got in. The use of a wipe thingy to perform an initial clean hadn't satisfied my need to expunge the dog wee from my skin.

Lunchtime Flirtations. Tuesday, November 22nd 1249hrs

My stomach was rumbling by the time I stopped the car and got out. I had remembered the box of paper in my car and diverted my route to arrive at the office instead. I had research for Jane to do and I could grab a boxed salad from the coffee shop across the street.

Hunger dictated I deal with food needs first. Despite their walk along the beach, Bull and Dozer had a determined gait again. I guess the sleep at Cedric's house plus a twenty-minute power-nap on the ride back to the office had recharged their batteries.

They were pulling me toward the High Street from the car park with all the effort their tiny legs could muster. Before we reached the point where the alleyway between the buildings exited into the main thoroughfare, I saw what was propelling them forward. There was an abandoned kebab on the concrete. No doubt if my nose was as close to the ground as theirs, I would be able to smell it also.

I had to reel them in like fish to shorten the lead as they struggled against it and then chastise them for considering the discarded meal as a viable snack opportunity. My explanation regarding the poor nutritional content of their choice fell on deaf ears though. In the end, wrestling them in the tight confines of the narrow passage while trying to sidestep the offending article became too great a battle. I picked them up and carried them over it.

They both made grumpy noises as they strained to peer around my arms for a final glance at their elusive prize.

In the coffee shop, I promised them a gravy bone. I had some in a pot behind my desk. They looked at me, their expression hard to read but they did not seem to be placated by my offer.

'Next please.' Called the lady at the counter. It was a woman I had not seen before. Her badge read Kateryna and she had a thick Eastern European accent.

'Tall Americano, extra shot of expresso, skim milk, no foam and a twist of hazelnut please. And a Waldorf salad, dressing on the side please. Both to go.'

Through the gap behind her that led to the kitchen, I saw Hayley go by. She was preparing food instead of serving at the counter. Three feet below my eyes, someone twitched as he remembered Hayley's impressive chest and supplied an image to my brain of her sitting astride me, her hands on my chest as she rocked back and forth.

'Hello?' Kateryna, said for the third time as the lady behind me gently touched my arm. I had been staring into space while I reminisced, the sound of her asking me to pay for my lunch completely missed.

'Sorry. I was distracted.' I smiled at my odd behaviour. 'Can I ask if you are Ukrainian?'

Kateryna looked up as she waited for me to tap my card on the reader. 'Yes. How can you tell?'

'I have a couple of Ukrainian friends. I am trying to learn the differences between accents.' It was sort of true. Anyanka and Anna were not friends, but they were ladies that I knew, so I wasn't exactly lying.

'You have a good ear.' Kateryna threw me a nice smile as she held up my cup. 'This is where you have to give me your name.'

'Tempest.' She looked at me confused. I laughed lightly and spelled it for her.

'I need your phone number too.' She said, pen still poised over the cup. She was still smiling, although her cheeks had now coloured slightly in embarrassment over her forwardness. She risked a glance at me. 'New company policy.' She explained. 'All hot guys have to give up their phone numbers.'

'Can you two hurry up?' Asked the woman behind me, getting impatient. She tutted and sighed.

Caught out by the unexpected flirtation, I provided my digits, got a wink in response and moved to the end of the counter.

Waiting for my coffee and food, I gave Kateryna a closer examination. She was tall and slender, her figure athletic with narrow hips and chest. She seemed perfectly pleasant, but I was not attracted to her. Mr. Wriggly questioned my sanity. She was pretty enough, her short, pixie cut hair suited her and she had lovely blue eyes that a chap could swim around in. As I looked without lingering long enough to be caught staring, Hayley came out of the kitchen bearing food. She walked behind Kateryna with a plate in each hand and a third balanced on her right forearm, saw me and winked.

'Hi, Tempest.' She murmured in a sultry tone on her way around me.

It was enough to curtail any notion of agreeing to a date if Kateryna called me. I assumed she was going to record my number and maybe add hers to my cup so that I could call her. I seriously doubted I could sleep with a second woman from the small pool of them working in the coffee shop and not have it blow up in my face. Besides, I already felt guilty about giving her my number when I was supposed to be dating Natasha.

My coffee was placed next to my salad on the counter. I grabbed them, ushered the dogs into motion and escaped to the sanctuary of my office.

The Office. Tuesday 22nd November 1316hrs

'Hey, boss.' Called Jane as I came in through the office front door. She was sitting on the comfy chairs by the coffee machine reading a magazine and eating a sandwich that looked home-made. 'How did you get on?'

'With the curator? He was very helpful.' I let the dogs off their leads and took a seat opposite Jane. The dogs, now free of their leads went nowhere. I had food, which to them meant there was a chance I might drop something, or perhaps, if they concentrated hard enough on their stares, I might receive their unvoiced message and just place my lunch on the carpet tile for them to eat.

While Jane and I were sitting, I did my best to ignore the dogs' eyes boring into me and told her about the tunnels under the Dockyard. Then I explained my need to find a way into them and about the map Cedric had provided rough directions for.

'When will you go after that?' She asked.

I finished my mouthful, sucking bits of walnuts from my teeth before I spoke. 'Tonight. Big Ben and I need to slip our guards and find it the first chance we get.'

'They put guards on you?' Jane was mystified by the concept.

'Not exactly. We were paired with two ladies that have worked there for some time. One is in charge of us and quite bossy. I think Big Ben likes it.'

'Oh.' She said, now understanding what I meant. 'How will you get to where the map is? Won't it be locked away?'

I fished the keys from my pocket and jingled them in the air.

As I finished my salad and acknowledged that it was nutritious and balanced and sensible and therefore boring and unsatisfying, I said, 'I found something on the beach in Upnor. I need you to see if you can identify what it is or what it is used for.'

'Okay.'

'I won't be a moment. Come along, dogs.' They trundled after me as I went to the back of the office. Before I went back out to my car to retrieve the paper, I gave them each a gravy bone from my office supply.

Returning sixty seconds later, with the soggy, pee covered box and the paper I had carefully placed back inside it held gingerly in my hands, I met Jane at her desk.

Looking around I said, 'We need something to put this on.'

'Oh, ah. Is it very wet? The carpet tile is only short.'

'And the dog peed on it.'

'Eww.' Said Jane in a very girly manner before fishing her abandoned magazine from the trash. Opened to the centre spread, it made a mat for the box to rest on. She peered at it, not wanting to get too close. 'What is it?'

'That is the question. I think the writing on the outside is Ukrainian. Something fishy is happening at the Dockyard involving Ukrainians. I have no idea what yet and this box might be nothing or might be something. There's a maker's mark on the outside. Do what you can to find out what the contents might be used for please.'

Jane simply nodded, opened her handbag to retrieve a pair of eyebrow tweezers from a small manicure kit and used them to touch the box. I thought she was being overly delicate, but I kept my mouth shut.

'It smells a bit.' She complained.

'Be quick then?' I offered. I was going back to the Dockyard. 'When you are done with it, please move it to the back room. Don't throw it away as it might be evidence.'

As I went to the back door with the dogs trotting behind me, Jane settled at her desk to see what she could find.

Chatham Royal Dockyard. Tuesday, November 22nd 1412hrs

There was a very light drizzle coming down on my drive back to the Dockyard. It was only just enough to demand I swish the wipers once a minute, yet I knew the dogs would not approve. I could leave them in the car, I liked them with me though, so they could have damp fur for once. My intention to leave them at home this afternoon had been overruled both by a desire to get on with the investigation and not lose most of an hour on the round trip, but also by the knowledge that I would be out half the night and not with them.

I parked in almost the exact same spot as the previous day. Then, I had fortuitously spotted a gap near the entrance, today, the grey sky and threat of rain had reduced the number of visitors, so the car park had far more spaces available to pick from.

The lady at the ticket stall recognised me from yesterday. She was cooing at the dogs more than paying attention to me though. An experience I was used to.

'Aren't they lovely?' She commented to her colleague. The pair of them had abandoned their station to get a proper look.

The dogs replied by flipping onto their backs for tummy tickles.

'We don't get many here two days in a row.' The first lady said looking up at me.

She was questioning what could have brought me back so soon and had left her observation hanging in the air like a question for me to answer. 'I am writing a research paper.' I supplied. It was enough of an answer to quell any further interest.

Once the two ladies had clambered back up with an accompaniment of groans and complaints, I handed over my payment card, bought another day pass and went into the Dockyard.

The wind was picking up. This close to the water it was able to whip along the exposed area of the river, channelled as it was in the valley the river formed. In between the buildings, the air tumbled and spun, the last of the summer's leaves creating patterns as they danced to show how the wind was moving.

I pulled my coat tight as I set off for the rigging room once more. The dogs would most likely get cold after a while so I revised my plan for looking around to make my visit brief instead. The map I bought yesterday had gone on the wall in my office, held in place by some handy drawing pins. Looking at the photograph of it on my phone now, I had to zoom in to find the key and then out again to locate the building I wanted. Once I had inspected the cobbled streets around the rigging room in the daylight, I was going to locate the museum so I would not have to waste precious time searching for the entrance I had a key for in the dark tonight.

Looking up to orientate myself after squinting at the small screen on my phone, I discovered I was standing beneath a sign post. One of the arrows pointed to the museum.

Tutting at myself, I changed direction. The museum was close by, allowing a circuitous route to the rigging room to include a visit there first.

The original use of the building that now housed the museum might have been anything. It looked like accommodation to me, where perhaps the Petty Officers were barracked when ashore. Long and thin like most of the buildings in the Dockyard, it was two stories high and symmetrical about a central entrance door. Sash windows dominated the front fascia.

A sign mounted above the front door told visitors that this was the museum. Cedric's key was for a side entrance he had said. No other door was visible on the side of the building I was looking at, but I found one around the next corner.

The bunch of keys he had given me had only two types of key on it. This was a modern Yale lock which gave me two options. As I put the first key in the lock, I said a silent prayer that there would be no one on the other side of the door. With the dogs around my feet, hugging into them to avoid the cool breeze, I slid the key in. It was a fit. I gave a quick experimental turn and satisfied I could get in tonight when no one was here, I left it at that.

I would find out what was on the other side of the door later.

My search around the rigging room was as fruitless in daylight as it had been at night. Wherever the space below the rigging room was accessed from, it was not where I was looking. The wind had not abated, so in acknowledging that I was beginning to feel the coolness in my hands and feet and face, I also acknowledged that it was time to get the dogs back into the warm.

'Let's get home, shall we, chaps?' I asked them needlessly as I started back toward the carpark. They pulled ahead of me, whether sensing they had turned toward home or understood my words, I could not tell.

I pulled them to a stop though as we passed the Admiral's building. In a parking space designated for the CEO, was a Humvee bearing Ukrainian plates. It had not been there on my previous trips. Alex Jordan drove an Audi A7 or at least that had been the car in this spot on my last visit.

Telling myself that it might just be the car of a visitor to the CEO or perhaps that of another senior employee who, perhaps knowing the CEO was away, had elected to park there. I took a picture anyway.

The dogs were trying to move on, making me worry they were, in fact, cold. I hurried my pace back to the car. Once inside, with the engine running and the heated seat on to warm their paws, I sent a message to Jane with the picture attached to it.

Can you find the owner for this car? It might be important.

Seconds later a reply pinged back.

Give me thirty seconds.

A rap on the window startled me. The car was just beginning to warm, so it was with reluctance that I powered the window down to speak with Alan. Boy George, Fred and Stuart were behind him.

'Mr. Michaels.' He acknowledged. 'I'm glad I caught you. How is the detective work going?'

'It is going. That's about all I can claim after twenty-four hours. It would be better if I keep the details of my activities secret though.'

'Oh, I think you can trust us with secrets, Mr. Michaels. Besides, the two Daves already told us you had infiltrated the night crew of cleaners. Rumour has it you got chased by a ghost last night.'

I stared at them, waiting for the follow up remark.

It was Fred that volunteered, 'We was a bit surprised, truth be told. We thought you Army boys would be less easy to scare.'

I rolled my eyes. I wanted to reply that we had chased it, not the other way around, but defending myself would be ridiculous.

Boy George stuck his head between his colleagues. 'Here, are you alright, Mr. Michaels? You look awful cold.'

'I'm fine thank you.' I replied with a forced smile.

'Leave him be, Georgie.' Chastised Alan. 'Army boys don't get hardened to the cold like we do.'

It was another jibe. Their banter was good-natured, but unwelcome. I was sure they were trying to get a rise from me, poking me to see if I would get annoyed. Showing my irritation would only encourage them to poke more fun and it would embarrass my father if I didn't give as good as I got.

'Chaps, it saddens me that you couldn't make the grade to get into the Army, but please retain some dignity and keep your envy in check.'

Four pairs of eyes widened at my insult. 'Couldn't make the grade.' Echoed Alan.

Fred said, 'We're the senior service, lad.'

I eyed the four of them. 'You most certainly are the seniors service. I would add your ages up, but I don't have the time to count that high. How many of you have your letter from the Queen already?'

'Cor. That was a low blow.' Laughed Alan. 'Don't forget we are here to help when the time comes.' He said, suddenly serious again. Then he pulled his coat, jumper and shirt to one side to reveal a tattoo on his right deltoid. The tattoo looked to be a hundred years old. The piece of wrinkly leather it was inked on no longer retained the tension it once had, and the ink had lost the sharp edges it might once have had.

As I watched, the other three men reached up to tap their shoulder in the same place. I nodded my understanding, and as they stood up and began to move away, I closed my window. It was time to go home. I wanted to get ready for tonight, I needed to eat and settle the dogs and I had some research to do.

Just as I began to pull away, my phone pinged. It was Jane.

The car is registered to a firm called Global Import Services. They operate out of the Ukraine, but I cannot find any trace of a trading history in the UK.

I texted back my thanks. What did that mean? I had Ukrainians involved in whatever was going on here. My gut said it was something criminal though I had no clue what it might be, and the Import Services firm sounded like a front for something else.

Was there a Ukrainian gang operating in the area? The question had swum into my consciousness and deserved an answer.

I knew just the man to ask.

Chief Inspector Quinn. Tuesday, November 22nd 1530hrs

Chief Inspector Quinn and I had a tenuous relationship. I wasn't sure what had started it, but he didn't like me and his decision to voice that made me not like him either. That and he had me arrested several times.

I recognised that he was a well-connected, resourceful and knowledgeable police officer though and believed that because we didn't like each other, he was more likely to listen to me. I might be wrong about that.

I paid for parking in the secure car park next to the police station in Maidstone. I had dropped the dogs off at home as I had to drive by the village to get to Maidstone. They wouldn't be welcome in the police station and were far happier at home asleep on the sofa.

The desk officer today was a young woman I had seen before. She recognised me and waved a hello. She undoubtedly knew Amanda and thus saw me as a person she knew. Her wave drew the attention of the sergeant sitting behind her. I knew him too. His name was Butterworth and he was a bit of an arse. At least when it came to me, he was.

'Good afternoon. I wish to speak with Chief Inspector Quinn.'

The young lady in front of me opened her mouth but was silenced by her sergeant speaking over the top of her. 'Solved another crime have you, Mulder?'

'Can you let him know, please?' I asked her, never swaying my eyes from her to acknowledge he had spoken.

Sergeant Butterworth wasn't done though. 'You'll do no such thing, Andrews.' His gruff manner was beginning to bother me.

Any further attempt to have the young lady fetch Quinn would just cause her grief. I turned my attention to her superior. 'I have a question for Chief Inspector Quinn. Is there a good reason why you are preventing me from asking it?'

'A good reason? A good reason like I already know your question will be some ridiculous nonsense about a ghoul or a wizard? Then, yes, I have a good reason.' He folded his arms across his chest. He was trying to look immovable. 'Is your enquiry not about a ghoul or a wizard?' He asked, his tone mocking.

The sergeant hadn't noticed that while he was staring at me and filling the space at the front of the counter, his subordinate had slipped out the door at the back of the reception while miming that she was off to fetch the person I wanted.

She stepped back through the door behind him, gave me a cheeky wink and set her face to innocent when sergeant Butterworth turned to see what I was looking at.

Before he could annoy me any further, CI Quinn appeared through a different door in the wall to the right of the reception counter.

'Mr. Michaels. I understand you want to see me. I do hope you are not going to waste my time.'

I offered him a hopeful expression. 'I need no more than a few moments.' He indicated back through the door and held it open for me to follow him. 'Thank you.' I called out loud enough for the desk officer to hear me.

The Chief Inspector was leading me to an office, but I started asking my question as the door to reception closed. 'What do you know about Ukrainian gangs operating in the area?'

Rather than answering, he asked, 'Why do you want to know about Ukrainian gangs?'

Quinn wasn't going to give me anything without a reason. I gave him the full story. 'My father works at the Royal Historic Dockyard. He was attacked and injured there recently.' He nodded and murmured words of sympathy as one automatically does. I gave him a brief chance to do so before continuing. 'He will be fine, but I am investigating what happened to him and have stumbled across something. I don't know what yet, but there is something going on at the Dockyard. Something criminal.'

'What makes you think that?'

I gave him a level stare. 'Chief Inspector, in the short time you have known me, and bearing in mind that you loathe everything about me and seem determined to catch me out, when have I ever been wrong?'

He didn't reply for a few seconds. He just held my gaze. 'When have you ever been wrong.' He repeated. 'That's all you have to go on? I should base the application of my resources on your ego?'

'Quinn.' I started, then paused while I decided whether I should keep going, give up and walk out, or go with my gut instinct and punch him in the ear. I sighed. 'Quinn, yet again I am going to solve a case that you refuse to acknowledge until it is too late for you to be involved. I am not trying to do you a favour. I just want the people behind my father's injury to be caught. If I am right about the gang thing, I may need your help.'

'If you are right about the gang thing, you won't live out the week.' He assured me. 'I wish you luck with your endeavours, pointless and foolish though they are. If you find any actual evidence, please let me know.'

'I already have evidence, Quinn.'

He cocked his head quizzically. 'Why not lead with that?'

'I wanted to see if you would persist with your standard game of being an annoying tit.' I gathered my bag from the floor and began to rise.

'What evidence do you have?' He asked to delay my exit.

I leaned across the table to get into his face. 'One day, Quinn, you will work out that we are on the same side.' I opened the door to let myself out.

'The evidence?'

'Missed your chance, Quinn.' Having failed to get what I wanted from him, which was some information and perhaps a little assistance, I instead took the upper hand and left him feeling small. All that was left was to magnanimously waltz myself out of the police station, which I would have done a great job of if I hadn't instantly taken a wrong turning and found myself in the toilets.

'This way, Mr. Michaels.' Called Chief Inspector Quinn while crooking a finger at me.

Silently seething, I let him show me the way out. Going down the steps that led back to the carpark, I checked my watch: 1612hrs. It was already dark out and it felt like a long day. I yawned. Heading back to the Dockyard later for several hours of detective work while I pretended to clean didn't exactly appeal, but in addition to my desire to find dad's attacker, I now needed to show Quinn that he was wrong.

I headed for home.

Tea and a Book. Tuesday, November 22nd 1640hrs

Ninety-nine percent of the preparation for Jagjit's stag night had been arranged more than a week ago. Since he had given us a scant month between the engagement announcement and the wedding, there had been options we might have pursued that were simply not possible, however, I was content with the program of events in place. This afternoon I had gathered the attendees, less a couple of apologies, to go over final minutiae.

It had been agreed that we would meet at the pub in the village since a good portion of us lived here, but I had been forced to change the time of the event to allow for my investigation at the Dockyard. I had to leave at 1930hrs to ensure I would get there on time but moving the meeting forward to 1800hrs had meant that a couple of the chaps working in London were not going to make it until we were about finished.

There was nothing to be done about it and everyone had assured me that they had taken time off tomorrow to accommodate the driving experience I knew Jagjit would love.

I checked my watch: 1640hrs. I had enough time to get myself some food and grab a shower before heading out. The dogs were well walked today, their trip to the Dockyard more than sufficient to exhaust their tiny legs. They would go to Mrs Comerforth next door before I went to the pub and would be quite happy to do so.

I had some pre-prepared meals in my freezer that I made in batches, days or even weeks in advance because it was generally easier to make a big pot. This evening's meal of meatballs with a stack of veg was reheating in the oven while some wholemeal pasta boiled on the hob. I was sipping a mug of tea at the kitchen breakfast bar and reading through the book I had bought at the Dockyard yesterday morning. It was not a thick book and it had a lot of photographs in it, but the author claimed there were secret chambers beneath the dockyard that were dug after the Dutch invaded in 1667. They were then extended as the dockyard was extended.

While the author knew they were there, he had not seen them, was not able to describe them in any useful detail and, most unhelpfully, did not know where they connected with the surface. I was just going to have to get the map. It was a mission for tonight. I put the book down, disappointed that it didn't provide me with the giant shortcut to the end of the case that I had childishly hoped for.

The dogs had taken themselves for a snooze on the sofa while I sat at the breakfast bar, only appearing in the kitchen when they heard me serve food to my plate. I shooed them away as they had already had their dinner and tucked into mine.

I continued reading the book, but it revealed nothing further of interest to the case. Learning about who had designed which building and what ships had been made in the Dockyard had no bearing on the appearance of ghosts now nor the motivation behind the attack on my father.

I set the book to one side as I cleared my plate, tidied up and went upstairs to get clean and change my clothing. While steam started to billow from the shower to fog the mirror, I inspected my body. I found that I constantly struggled with my weight. I could gain pounds just by thinking about eating a cheeseburger and had done exactly that through actually eating one (or two) on a break in Cornwall a month ago. My usual diet of vegetables and lean meat, pulses, wholegrains and lots of water kept me on the right path, but it had been a fight to lose the excess I had quickly gained when I decided to take a break and eat what I fancied.

I slapped my stomach and twisted in front of the mirror. It was far from perfect, but I could just about see my abs again through the thin layer of fat over the top of them and the love handles had gone. With a mental slap for my vanity I climbed into the shower.

Getting dressed in the bedroom, my phone beeped the arrival of a text. I leaned in to press a button. The text appeared on the screen. It was from Hilary, confirming the time we were meeting. I hadn't seen him since the incident with the witch at my house two weeks ago. He had messaged twice to say he was not able to meet for a drink as we usually would on a Friday. Big Ben had commented that his wife had put him under house arrest, labelled him as pussy-whipped and suggested we might never see him again. I wondered if Big Ben had it right. He was coming tonight though and was attending the stag party tomorrow, so I would find time to ask him how things were going after the near break up with his wife.

I texted him a reply, finished getting dressed and headed downstairs. It was 1737hrs, time to drop the dogs off. For my own amusement, I jangled their collars and called them to the front door. As always, nothing happened. A causal guest might not even know I had dogs. I took two paces which brought me into the kitchen where I grabbed the handle of the fridge and yanked it open. I called them again but could already hear them moving as they tried desperately to untangle themselves and get off the sofa. I had watched them do this on many occasions. They would happily sleep next to, on top of or intertwined with each other, the shared body heat adding comfort to the reassurance that the other was nearby. When they then heard someone at the door, or, as in this instance, heard the fridge open, they exploded into motion but generally they each hindered the other in their struggle to get upright and moving.

Two seconds elapsed, and they arrived by my feet, skidding to a stop across the slate tile. 'Hello, chaps.' I said, grinning as I shut the fridge door again.

They knew they had been tricked and were less than pleased about it. I snagged them both before they could slink back to the sanctuary of the lounge though. With collars on we headed out the door, around the fence and up the path to Mrs Comerforth's house. Once they saw where they were going their pace increased. They were predicting an evening of snoozing on her sofa instead of their own and couldn't wait to get started.

The dogs strained to be released when they saw her shadow approach the frosted glass of her door, but I kept them in check until she had the door open.

'Good evening, boys.' She said in greeting, her eyes on them not me. 'Are you ready for some Coronation Street?' I doubted they cared whether she watched soap operas, documentaries or action films, their tails beat even harder now that she was addressing them.

'Ready?' I asked her.

'Yes.' She chuckled and mimed getting into a wrestler's stance to deal with the threat of excited Dachshunds. They were gone a nanosecond after I unclipped their leads, accelerating from a standing start to maximum velocity before they reached her doorstep less than a yard ahead. Bull went to the right of her left leg, whipping between it and the doorframe, Dozer ran blindly through her skirt making the hem whoosh with his passage.

Mrs Comerforth was already turning to go, 'I'll pop them back in your house before I turn in, love.'

'Thank you.' I called after her. I got a final wave and the door was closed against the cold.

'Pub o'clock then.' I said to myself as I set off.

What about the Strippers? Tuesday, November 22nd 1830hrs

Basic, Big Ben and two of Jagjit's four brothers were already in the pub when I arrived. Jagjit was the youngest of five boys and the only one yet to produce grandchildren for his parents. They had plenty from the older four boys and he said the pressure on him to meet this requirement seemed to have diminished in the recent couple of years. He was marrying a white girl, but I didn't know, and wouldn't ask, what that would mean in terms of his parent's expectations.

All four brothers were coming to the stag do, however Rajesh and Vihann both worked in London and could not get back in time to meet this evening. I hadn't enquired what they did although I believed they were both in banking or possibly real estate management. Jagjit had told me about them at some point but the information hadn't stuck.

Big Ben saw me coming through the door, 'Alright, maggot muncher?' He asked in greeting. Always the charmer.

Arjun and Aditya waved from the bar where they were just being served. Arjun gesticulated that he would grab me a drink while he was at the bar.

'Just a sparkling water, please. I have to drive later.' He nodded and spoke to the Landlord.

'Good evening, Ben, Basic.' I approached the table they were sitting at. There were two other chaps there that I didn't know. Jagjit had provided a list of persons to invite and indicated where he knew them from. Thus far all contact had been by email or phone as some of them had to travel and were staying overnight, hence the meeting this evening.

I introduced myself, but the chaps knew me already. As I wondered how, they introduced themselves as Kit Granger-Smith and Ross Jarrett. 'We were in the office when you burst in and busted Mrs Barker.' Ross said. They were friends of Jagjit from his job in Canary Wharf.

'That was quite the show.' Kit agreed. 'Everyone still talks about it now.'

'Is that good or bad?' I asked.

'Definitely good.' Kit assured me. 'You saved the firm a lot of trouble that day. It would have come out sooner or later that she was defrauding us.'

I wondered about that. Mrs Barker had done a pretty good job of framing her stepson for his grandfather's murder. I had got lucky on that case. Had I missed a vital clue, she might have got away with it and never been caught. I thanked them anyway, both for their comments and for coming.

Arjun and Aditya took their seats. 'Thanks.' I said as Arjun handed me my water. 'We are just waiting on Hilary.' At that moment, the pub door opened behind us. Hilary came in grinning from ear to ear.

He said, 'Evening, all.' As he closed the door. 'Sorry I'm late. I was… busy. I'll just get a drink if that's okay. I've worked up quite the thirst.'

Hilary was different. Big Ben saw it too. He was more confident, more buoyant, more everything perhaps.

At this time on a Wednesday evening we were the only people in the pub, the jukebox was silent, and Hilary would hear me from the bar eight feet away, so I started talking.

'Chaps, thank you all for coming. Some of you have travelled farther than others of course, but we are all here to celebrate Jagjit passing from bachelorhood to the sanctity of marriage thus we have a duty to see him off in a suitable style.'

'Strippers!' Said Big Ben with some cheer and volume. The landlord looked up but didn't comment.

I pressed on. 'As you know, we are meeting at 1600hrs tomorrow afternoon at Brands Hatch for a driving experience. There will be cocktails served afterwards, not before, and there will be a race, so I suggest we all stay sober for that element. That will take us to 1800hrs.'

'Strippers!' Yelled Big Ben again.

'Not strippers I'm afraid. There will be a coach waiting to take us to the Balmoral restaurant in Rochester.' This drew a few whistles of appreciation. The Balmoral was a steak and lobster place that was fully booked for months. I had to bribe the Maître' D heavily to get us a table at short notice. It would be worth it though. I had never eaten there but had read the reviews and knew it was frequented by local celebrities and the rich. It had appeared on several TV shows where top chefs struggled to find enough superlatives to match the location's appeal.

'Then strippers?' asked Big Ben, his voice now starting to sound hopeful.

'Yes, Big Ben. Then strippers.' I replied exasperated.

'Really?' Thank goodness. I was starting to think you hadn't arranged any.'

Around the table all the faces were looking at me. 'Of course, I didn't arrange any strippers, Ben. Strippers are the fantasy of teenage boys. When we have finished our dinner, there is the option of heading into Rochester where the mile-long High Street contains no less than twenty-seven pubs and bars. We shall toast Jagjit in a gentlemanly style.'

'So, no strippers.' Big Ben wanted to confirm.

'No, Ben.' Any ladies we meet will most likely be inclined to keep their clothes on.

'Well, that sounds shit. Anyone else want to see some tits on our night out?'

There were some rumblings from around the table, but no one said, "Yes please".

'Honestly.' Big Ben was shaking his head. 'This is because you are worried I will just shag them all and leave you lot with nothing, isn't it?' His raised his hands in mock surrender. 'I get it. I do. The likelihood of you pooftas getting any action when I am around is limited, but I'm not totally insensitive. On a chaps' night out like this one, I would make sure there were some ladies along with lower expectations that would be happy to settle for one of you. I'll make a call now, just give me a minute.' He had his phone out already and was scrolling through his contacts. 'Strippers coming right up.'

I slapped his phone away to send it skittering across the table. 'No strippers.'

He eyed me incredulously. 'Somebody's tired.' It was all in jest, of course, a bit of banter because he loved to annoy me.

I had to finish the point though, just in case he brought a bus load of scantily clad ladies along anyway. 'Ben, what is the attraction of strippers? Please explain, because so far as I understand it, they take their clothes off, hopefully in a sensual manner that a lady might as an intro to a night of sex, then they dance around a bit, gyrating and such, which one might also sometimes benefit from if the lady is so inclined right before the whole sex thing gets underway. Then, once one's motor is running at full speed and the old blood is pumping, they pick their clothes up and go home. The sex thing they have been getting you very much ready for doesn't happen. Why would we want strippers?'

'Because, you dung trumpet, we are men out doing manly things. Without some women around to marvel at our magnificence, we might as well turn in our heterosexual badges and be done with it. The strippers aren't there for us to look at.' He looked around the table making eye contact with everyone in turn. 'Although, to be fair, we probably will. However, in my experience the ladies will spend more time looking at us.'

Big Ben liked to forget that the rest of us look like normal, average men, not like an Adonis.

'I don't want strippers.' Said Hilary. 'Not just because Anthea wouldn't approve, which she very much wouldn't, but mostly because like Tempest said, I find them pointless.'

'Pointless?' Asked Big Ben. 'They are female perfection personified. They are the epitome of everything that attracts men to women.'

'Exactly.' Agreed Hilary. 'That's why I don't want to see it. Real women don't look like that, Ben. My wife is lovely but producing children has side effects. I am very content with what I have got. Most especially so recently.' He added extra quietly. 'And I don't need to be reminded how she used to look a decade or more ago.'

Arjan chimed in with, 'Hear, hear.'

'I think that settles it, mate.' Big Ben looked less than impressed. 'No strippers.' I concluded.

We went through the details of timing and transport to the venue. Hilary, Arjan and Aditya were all to collect others and would abstain from drinking until we'd arrived at the restaurant whereupon they would abandon their cars at my office, thus avoiding parking fees and we would all get taxis home when the drinking was done. There were twelve of us in total.

Jagjit, Tempest, Hilary, Basic, Big Ben, Arjan, Aditya, Rajesh, Vihann, Kit, Ross and a chap called Ian that I hadn't met yet. Ian was a friend of Kit's, an old school friend that was apparently a local fellow but short on friends. When I had first emailed the group, Kit said that Ian knew Jagjit and asked if he could come along. I wanted to say no but couldn't come up with a reason to justify it and his inclusion made it an even dozen, a nice balanced number. So, he was coming as well. How he and Jagjit knew each other would become apparent tomorrow.

I got up and went to the bar calling, 'My round.' As I went. I had printed out an itinerary for the next day which provided all the relevant times and addresses, it was a belt and braces move because everyone had already joined a WhatsApp group and had a link to a cloud-based itinerary. It was also a bit nerdy, which Big Ben helpfully pointed out, but I had willingly accepted the burden of the task of best man and I was going to be good at it because I hated when people did things half-arsed.

The Landlord dutifully poured the drinks and I left him my card while I zeroed in on Hilary. He was already talking with Big Ben.

'Good evening, Hilary. How is everything with you?' I asked, shaking his hand cautiously. 'How's the shoulder?'

A week and a half ago his right shoulder had been dislocated in a life and death battle at my house. He had done it to himself but in doing so had saved both my life and Big Ben's. We were both grateful, but it is not the sort of thing chaps talk about more than once. You thank the guy, then you move on, otherwise it becomes a big thing and is always there when you talk, hanging around in the background waiting for someone to bring it up.

'It's good actually. The doctors said the damage to my rotator cuff was minimal and I should expect to recover fully in eight to ten weeks.'

'Good. That's good.' I replied. Then I got to the point I wanted to discuss. 'You seem different. What's going on?'

'That's what I said.' Said Big Ben.

Hilary looked at him. 'No, you didn't, Ben. You said that I seem less totally gay than usual.'

That did sound more like something Big Ben would say. I brought Hilary's attention back to me. 'So, what is it then? You seem... deeply content.' It was the best description I could come up with.

Hilary shrugged a sly shrug. 'Let's just say that things have changed at home. The little incident with the witch has altered the dynamic between Anthea and I for the better. I am feeling pretty good about life right now.'

Big Ben laughed and slapped him on the shoulder. 'You mean you've been smacking that ass. Good for you, buddy.'

Hilary pursed his lips. 'I do wish you wouldn't talk about my wife like that.' Then he smiled and brightened. 'But yes, smacking that ass is pretty much what has been happening. Anthea was very remorseful about kicking me out, about treating me badly and about underestimating me. Somehow I went from loser to hero in just one act of madness.'

'Maybe that's all it takes.' I nodded my approval. 'Good for you, man. Oh, there are drinks at the bar for you guys.' The landlord was signalling for me to enter my pin number. 'I'll get them.'

We chatted for a while, I made sure I talked to everyone and asked Kit about his friend Ian. He said he wasn't sure himself how Ian knew Jagjit, only that he did, and that Ian had a job that made meeting people and making friends a little tough. I empathised, it had been tough making friends in the army. Once I had been promoted several times, there were few peers in any of the environments I would find myself in and everyone I saw on a daily basis had to call me boss or sir and had no desire to hang out with me socially. Except for Big Ben that is.

I checked my watch to see that I would need to get moving in a few minutes. Big Ben caught my eye from across the room, he was aware of the time too. We finished up our drinks, said a round of goodbyes and left the chaps with a promise to see them the next afternoon.

Cleaning Duties. Tuesday, November 22nd 2030hrs

Emptying the bins was a task that had to be completed every day and no one else wanted it at this time of year because it was dark and cold. Maybe in the summer months it was a more popular job, but for now we were assigned to it as the new boys and that suited us just fine despite the howling wind whipping around and between the buildings. The only other outdoor cleaning task was the road sweeper that went out each night to take care of discarded sweet wrappers, cigarette butts and any other detritus. That was driven by an old Ukrainian man who's name I had heard but could neither say nor spell.

As the cleaners filed out, Big Ben and I went with them, collecting our supply of bags to refill the bins as we went.

Pasha had given us ninety minutes to get the job done. It was longer than we needed but not if we were going to sneak off to look for the map, it wasn't. I had explained to Big Ben about the map when we met in the car park outside.

'So, we just have to hope it is easy to find.' Was the comment he had made upon hearing my second-hand description of where it should be located.

Now it was 2030hrs and we had dutifully pushed our wheelie bin through the Dockyard as far as the museum. There were no bins here, none outside anyway and there was a cleaning crew visible inside the museum. We could see them through the windows. They would be attending to the visitor areas though, not the back rooms where Big Ben and I were heading.

Glancing around to make sure we were not being observed, I slipped the key into the lock again, gripped the handle and gave the door a shove. The hinges squeaked once and then were silent. The door opened into a short corridor and a flight of stairs that ascended to the next floor. Like everything else in the Dockyard, the building was at least two-hundred-years old, so the staircase was wooden and would creak like mad if we attempted to ascend it.

Thankfully there should be no need to do so as the library should be beyond the door ahead of us with the archive and map room leading from it. We were at the far end of the building, well away from the cleaning crew in the tourist area, but caution dictated we move stealthily.

Big Ben closed the door to seal us inside, the noise of the wind dropping to almost nothing as he did. Neither of us would speak of it, but it was cold out – unpleasantly so, which meant the unheated room we were now in was gloriously warm compared with outside.

'This door?' Big Ben asked while rubbing his hands together.

'It should be.' I replied. He placed his hand on the handle, listened for a moment, then opened the door. There was darkness beyond.

'It looks like a library.' He said as he went into the room.

He wasn't wrong. It reminded me of the Royal Navy Archive I had visited with my father in Plymouth a few weeks ago. The bookshelves were all ornate wood and stretched to the ceiling. The information contained within the pages could all be managed on a single hard drive now, yet there was a recognisable nostalgia in the books before me, many of which would be as old as the Dockyard itself.

There were three doors leading from the library if I didn't include the one we had just come through. One would lead out of the library toward the visitor area. We didn't want that one. Big Ben was asking me which door we did want by pointing and shrugging.

I shrugged back. They were not labelled, so we would have to guess.

A shadow played across the room. There was someone outside. Big Ben and I froze. Nothing would give us away quicker than movement. It was movement that had alerted us to their presence. However, when a flashlight came on, its sharp beam drilling holes in the dark, I stepped into a shadow. They were shining it through the windows, but we were hidden from view.

Were they looking for us?

Big Ben had stepped behind a bookcase, I could see his eyes in the dim light coming into the room from outside. He glanced down and nodded, drawing my attention outside. I glanced, my movement furtive and small, not wanting to give myself away.

Outside were two ghosts.

Obviously, I need to caveat that statement though. What I could see outside were two security guards dressed as ghosts. They had on the ornate Royal Navy uniforms with the brocade running across the epaulettes and silver buckles on their shoes. That they were carrying flashlights gave the game away or would have if I had ever been convinced they were anything other than two dummies in costumes. The costumes had a frosted appearance to them. I couldn't tell what it was at this distance, but it looked like flour. Poor Cedric would have a fit if he saw his priceless artefacts being abused like that.

As they moved away toward the end of the building we had entered, Big Ben said, 'We better get moving.' As he went for the nearest door.

It opened to a storeroom filled with boxes. The next door also opened into a storeroom, but this one was vast, its shelves and spaces filled with everything but books. There were uniforms, paintings, and boxes upon boxes of all shapes and sizes, each labelled to say what the box contained. Wooden wheels taken from ships, flags and pennants, and weapons. Lots and lots of weapons from old flintlock pistols, to swords and knives and everything in between. No cannons, I noted. Perhaps cannons were kept somewhere else.

'I think this is it.' I called quietly to Big Ben. I had found a door at the end of a pair of shelves that formed a corridor in the room. There might have been a label on the door, but in the dark, I just couldn't see it.

Big Ben crossed the room. 'I think those guards are in the building.' He did not sound concerned about it. Knowing Big Ben, he was probably bored with all the sneaking about and ready for a fight. It worried me though. I was nowhere near to working out what was going on yet. Getting caught where we ought not to be would only get us fired and possibly prosecuted for attempted theft. A vision of CI Quinn's gleeful face played in my head.

'Let's hurry then.' I said as I pushed open the door. It was instantly clear we had found the chart room because there were charts everywhere. On shelves, on counter tops, pinned to the walls. Mostly they were rolled, and many were in containers – the long thin tubes designed to house and store such things.

'Tell me you know how to find it, Tempest.' Pleaded Big Ben.

Cedric had started by telling me that he didn't know where the map was and that he hadn't seen it in years but had changed his tune once he learned my plan. He knew precisely where it was and what it looked like. He had even drawn me a basic schematic of the room. I pulled the piece of paper with his drawing from my pocket now and held it to the light coming through a solitary window.

As I orientated myself to the room, a noise came from the archive we had just been in. The only way out of the room we were in was back the way we had come. The guards were blocking our exit. It must have been the wheelie bin that had tipped them off. We should have hidden it around the corner, not left it outside the door.

'I'll deal with them.' Big Ben said, swinging a few practise punches as he went for the door.

I grabbed his shoulder. 'Not yet.' I needed us to stay under the radar. For now, at least. 'Get the window open.'

He disapproved but he didn't argue. I worked out where the map I wanted should be, prayed no one had moved it since Cedric was fired and started moving through the room. It was located on a high shelf above my head on the far wall. Safe inside a red cardboard tube, it was easy to spot but not so easy to reach. I wasn't tall enough.

The sound of the guards talking was getting louder. They might spot the door leading into the chart room and walk through it at any moment. Quelling my rising panic, I looked around for something to stand on.

'Here you go, short round.' Said Big Ben as he reached up with one of his impossibly long arms to take the tube from the top shelf. 'Can we go now?' He asked with humorous faked impatience.

I slapped him in the ribs and went out the window to drop lightly to the cobbles below. We were in the lee of the building and in shadow, the dark working for us finally. I caught the map as he threw it and checked around while he lowered himself down and closed the window once more.

Then light filled the room we had just vacated as two guards spilled through it, their flashlights sending shafts of light to bounce off everything.

We hugged the wall, crouching beneath the window where we could not be seen. As the guards blundered about above us, I tapped Big Ben's leg, it was time to go. The chance that they might open the window and look out was too great.

We gained the corner, stood up and went back to our cleaning duties as if we hadn't just stolen a map to the underground lair of whatever was going on here. The tube containing the map went into one corner of the wheelie bin. I would have to work out what to do with it later. I couldn't leave here with it tonight. It was four feet long, I hadn't arrived with it and it looked like an ancient old artefact.

Any triumph I felt over finding the map and getting away was short lived though. A voice called out from behind us. 'Where have you two been?'

It was Pasha. She was flanked by two more guards and they were all coming toward us, their pace fast and determined.

Thinking fast, I could not come up with a decent lie. As they closed the distance, the two guards dressed as ghosts that had been inside the museum rooms looking for us, came back out the door we had opened. All four guards could have been brothers, their silhouettes were so alike. Each had crew cut light brown hair and a blockish frame. Their uniforms barely fitted them, especially the two old Royal Navy uniforms which were stretched tight across enormous chests and thighs.

'Well?' She demanded. She had taken up position in front of us while the four men spread out to surround us. The two dressed as ghosts were behind us now. I turned to get a better look and decided that the frosted effect on the old uniform was indeed flour. I wasn't going to be the one to tell Cedric.

Acting my way out seemed the only option. 'We got cold and went inside to warm up for a bit.'

She said something in Ukrainian, smiling while she did it. The guards laughed to prove she had said something derogatory but the threat they posed did not diminish. The laughter left her eyes as she turned them back to me.

'You have no place here. You should both quit.'

'I need the job.' Big Ben lied.

'I don't care.' She spat back. 'All you English are weak. Hiding from the cold like little children. Taking trips to the bathroom, always taking longer to get simple jobs done. I expected you to quit after last night.'

'Why?' I asked.

'Because you saw one of the ghosts. No one else has stayed once they have seen the ghosts. They all ran away screaming like babies. Like little English babies.'

She paused, waiting for us to respond. When neither of us filled the silence, she pressed on. 'You should quit now, and these gentlemen will escort you from the premises. It will be better for everyone.'

Stupidly, I decided to challenge her. 'Do you have a copy of the company equality policy? Does it endorse your opinion that English should not be employed?'

Her eyes diverted to a point beyond my face as she nodded to one of the guards. Suddenly, my arms were grabbed from behind in a steel-like grip. I was fast to react, but hadn't seen the other guard moving in. The punch to my gut took the breath out of me, just as the same thing happened to Big Ben.

'You hit like a girl.' Said Big Ben as he straightened up. 'Go on, have another go, see if you can add two punches together to make one good one.'

The guard sneered and belted in three more gut shots in quick succession.

'Yes or no?' Big Ben asked me. I understood the question. We could fight back right now. Big Ben wasn't used to letting people hit him without then turning them into a bleeding mess. Despite the size of the guys holding him, I believed he would beat them both to a pulp. I might struggle with my two, but my concern was that once we had shown them what we were capable of, we would no longer be viewed as two weak English cleaners but as something far more dangerous. Dangerous things get treated differently, which in this case, might mean they just kill us.

'No.' I replied quietly.

They were not done with the gut shots though. Twice more they hit each of us. Gut shots because they don't show up and there's no blood or split lips or missing teeth to explain.

Gritting my teeth against the pain, I locked eyes with the man that had hit me. 'I won't forget your face.' I promised.

He smiled and hit me again.

'Feel like quitting yet?' Pasha asked as the guards let us go and we slumped to the cobbles.

I put a hand to the cold cobbles as I started to get up. 'Not even slightly.'

'I need the job.' Big Ben repeated his lie.

Pasha said something in Ukrainian again. Another joke as the four guards laughed, but the show was over. They were leaving us, and the map was still tucked safe inside the wheelie bin. They hadn't even looked in it.

Pasha paused before she walked away. She had a final comment. 'This is your last shift, boys. If you are here tomorrow, it will go badly for you.'

Big Ben gave me a hand to straighten up. Bruising to my abdomen was going to bother me for a few days.

'Just tell me I get to beat the crap out of them later this week, Tempest.'

I put a hand on his shoulder. 'That's the plan, big man. That's the plan. I have just reviewed my policy of never hitting girls and discovered it is no longer politically correct.' They were guilty of far more than scaring off English workers. I was going to find out what it was and bring it all crashing down around them.

For now, though, we were just going to have to suck it up and finish our shift.

'What do we do with the map?' He asked as we pushed the wheelie bin toward the next set of bins. What he had done was identify the shortfall in my plan. I had been so absorbed in getting my hands on it, I hadn't considered how I would get it out of the Dockyard.

I could only see a couple of options. I could leave it in the bin and retrieve it in the morning. Or I could stash it somewhere else and retrieve it in the morning which did nothing to improve the first plan other than reduce the risk that it went to the tip – I had no idea what day the bins got emptied. The final option was to remove it from the protective tube and carry it out, folded flat against my body. They didn't search the staff at any point because there was nothing here that could be easily stolen.

'What about the two Daves?' Big Ben asked when I outlined my options.

'Top idea. Let's give them a call and find out.' I pulled my phone from my back pocket with a small groan – my abs were complaining already.

'Hello.' A cautious voice answered.

'Dave. This is Tempest Michaels. I need your help.'

'Oh, err. Give me a minute.' He didn't hang up and came back on the line a few seconds later. 'Sorry, I was in the rest room warming up. Dave and I have all the worst shifts now. I am starting to wonder if they will just ban us from the rest room. They are trying everything they can to get rid of us. What is it you need from me?'

'It will be easier if I show you. Are you going out on patrol again soon?'

He said that he was and gave us a place to meet him.

The underground. Wednesday, November 23rd 0037hrs

We went to my place with the map because it was closer to the Dockyard than Big Ben's. The two Daves had dutifully done as requested, smuggled the map out and placed it inside my car. Their belief that no one was paying any attention to what they were doing proved true.

'Hey dogs.' Big Ben called out as my Dachshunds recognised him and tried to climb his legs. I shooed them into the garden to empty their bladders, then made two coffees while Big Ben extracted the map from the tube and rolled it out on my dining room table.

The contents of the tube turned out to be three maps, each drawn at different times when the tunnels had been added to. They were not complete though and failed to show where the buildings above ground were in relation to what we were looking at. What I needed more than anything was a way into the underground chambers. Finding it was proving frustrating.

Big Ben sipped his coffee. 'Got anything stronger?'

'Are you planning to stay here?'

'Yeah. Too late for shagging now. I should have set something up earlier. This will just have to be one of those rare days when I don't get any. I'll make up for it at Jagjit's wedding this weekend.'

I was listening to him as I fetched tumblers and rum from the kitchen. 'Want it over coke?' I asked.

'Nah. Ice will do.'

I poured two drinks and focused back on the maps. Big Ben wasn't done with his plan for the weekend though. 'Jagjit doesn't have any sisters, does he?'

'No, four brothers. All older.'

'Many female cousins that will be attending?'

I laughed at his continuous need to meet new ladies. 'I believe so. Alice will also have a selection of friends along. I am sure some of them will be single.'

'Doesn't really matter if they are, mate, so long as they don't bring their boyfriends with them.'

'Didn't you only just get a girl pregnant? Do you not remember how scared you were a couple of weeks ago when you thought it was more than one?'

'Oh. Did I not tell you? Bianca isn't pregnant anymore. I think what she meant to say was, her period finally came a month later than expected. Do girls get that? Their period just misses a cycle?'

'I couldn't tell you mate. It is not the sort of thing I remember from my biology classes and I have never found myself in a position where I needed to ask.'

'Fair point.' He conceded. 'You know, this map might not tell us how to get in, but it looks as if there is an entrance at the water.'

'Where?' I asked, my curiosity making me stare harder than I had been.

'See here.' He pointed. 'The elevation changes. The river sits well below the level of the Dockyard but at high tide this tunnel might be low enough to be accessible. Why build it that way otherwise?'

A water entrance. What a great way to sneak in and out. It wasn't definitive, but what he had suggested made sense. 'If we assume you are correct and where they have drawn the terminus of that tunnel is the river, then we can orientate the maps.'

We spent the next minute working out how the maps overlaid. The oldest-looking map had a single tunnel and a set of stone steps drawn leading down into it. It was more pictographic than the others, clearly hand drawn, as each of them were, but there was no scale to it, which made it hard to work out if the whole tunnel was represented on the later maps or if it had been extended at some point. Neither of the other two maps showed a way in. So, we had a possible river entrance and a set of stone steps that led down to the original tunnel but no way of knowing where they started.

It was quite frustrating.

'This is a bit difficult without a scale to work from.' Big Ben observed. 'Plus, I'm not confident of the direction the tunnels are running.'

I scratched my head and yawned. 'If people are coming and going from the tunnels they must be doing so visibly. Maybe I need to stake the place out during the day and see if I can spot human traffic where it shouldn't be.'

'What about the river entrance? Do you want me to look for that?'

'Have you got access to a boat?' I asked.

'I have a canoe if it comes to it, but that seems like the long-winded version. I'll pop down to the marina tomorrow, there's bound to be a boat with a lady on board.'

'And what? You flash her your winning smile, she throws her knickers off and then lets you take the boat down the river to scout out the Dockyard?'

'Pretty much.'

Annoyingly, that tactic would probably work for him.

'I need some sleep.' I announced. 'Come on boys.' I gathered up the dogs, carried them up to bed and left Big Ben to sort himself out, he knew where the guest bedroom was.

Drifting off to sleep, I wondered what this was all about and how long it was going to take me to solve the riddle I faced.

Murder. Wednesday, November 23rd 0715hrs

The day started with an unwelcome phone call. I didn't recognise the number when it rang so gave my standard answer. 'Blue Moon Investigations. Tempest Michaels speaking.'

'Tempest, this is Alan Page. There's been a development.' He said the word *development* very carefully like it wasn't the word he wanted to use.

I hedged a bet, 'Who's dead?' I was guilty of sometimes forgetting that people didn't like to talk about death. I had grown hardened to it through my almost two decades in the Army. Iraq, Afghanistan and a few other places I had been deployed to were as unpleasant as you might imagine. I wasn't too worried about Alan though, he would have endured much the same experiences.

At the other end, Alan licked his lips before saying, 'Julia Jones.' The name hit me like a slap to the face.

My question contained only one word. 'How?'

'They found a suicide note in her office. She washed up a few miles downstream in her car.'

A suicide note. I didn't believe it for a second. They had killed her. Whether it was to get rid of her as part of their plan or as punishment for hiring Big Ben and I, there was no way of telling.

'How do you know already?' I asked when I realised it was too early for him to even be at work. I was only up because I had wanted to go for a run.

Alan had an answer for me. 'I woke up to a message from Dave Saunders. I guess they found out at some point in the night.'

'Alan, I will see you at the Dockyard. I'll be there soon after opening time.'

When the phone disconnected, I stood in my kitchen staring at the wall. I started to tell myself that they had escalated to murder but caught myself. I doubted Julia was the first person they had killed.

'Hey, man, what's up?' Big Ben asked as he wandered into the kitchen.

I was gripping the edge of the counter with my head bowed. Now I had to tell him what had happened.

He did not take the news well. The thing with Big Ben is that he genuinely believes he is performing a service for the ladies he sleeps with. He gives them the best sex of their life as far as he is concerned, providing one golden memory for them to treasure for all time. I would accuse him of being hugely egotistical, but I worry that he might be correct. He might go through them at a rate unprecedented outside of the adult film industry and not even try to learn their names, but on some level, he still connects with them.

He had slept with Julia Jones to bribe her into giving the two of us jobs. It had cost her dearly and he felt guilty about it. The guilt manifested as anger and he was ready to split heads.

When he left my house, he was fired up for finding the river entrance. We both really wanted to get back to the Dockyard tonight, but we couldn't blow off Jagjit's stag party for it. The draw of the case, the thirst for blood if you will, was beckoning. Neither one of us felt like going out socially right now, but our next chance to sneak around the Dockyard in search of the entrance to the tunnels was going to have to wait until Thursday. This morning he was going to look for the river entrance while I scoped out the Dockyard itself. Using the map, we had narrowed the entrance points down to a handful of options. Between us we needed to obtain hard evidence, like video footage maybe, of a criminal operation so we could force the police to take notice.

My plan, in fact, was to present my proof to the CEO of the Dockyard, Alex Jordan. He could call the police himself and remove any danger that they might ignore it because it was me calling.

Alone in my house, there was nothing constructive I could do this early, so I went for a run. I had been slacking on the exercise front and my guilty conscious wouldn't shut up about my fat belly. I argued that I had a distinctly bruised abdomen from the beating last night. In reply, the gym instructor in my head called me several non-PC names and made me put my running shoes on. Outside, clouds had cleared overnight leaving a thick frost on the cars and hedgerows. It sparkled where the streetlamps touched it but made the pavement a little dicey.

Rather than be defeated, I ran in the road. Early morning traffic around the village was light though there were a few cars I needed to dodge. The purpose of the run was partly to alleviate the growing stress I felt about not exercising. I don't know whether that is normal or not, but I always find that after a few days away from the gym I begin to get twitchy. This would take care of the twitch, but it also gave me time to think. There were few distractions when I went running, habitually I used the time to organise my thoughts regarding whatever was bothering me.

What was bothering me today was the Ukrainians. What were they capable of? I had accepted that I had met with organised crime. I had suspected it from the start, right back when it became apparent there was a strong Ukrainian flavour, but the death of Julia Jones nailed the thought home. So far though, all I had seen them do was guard the Dockyard and keep it clean. It had to be a front to the real operation. Whatever that was had to be criminal. It would have helped if Quinn had talked to me. Maybe I had been too hasty in leaving the police station yesterday. He had finally found his way onto my hook once I said I had evidence, by then though his aggravating nature had done a trick on me and I no longer cared for his company.

I had left the village through the vineyards. In the pre-dawn darkness there was no sound from critters running back into their holes in the ground and no traffic noises penetrated this far away from the roads. It was quiet, the only noise my laboured breathing as I slogged up the hill that would eventually cross the main artery into Maidstone known as Bluebell Hill. Before I reached it, I turned left at the edge of a field and began the route home, pushing myself despite the slippery grass under my feet. The frost coated everything, but the soil was not frozen. There were puddles I could see and navigate around and soggy patches of mud I could not.

Back at the house, I had to strip off my socks and shoes outside and carry them in. They went in the sink for me to remove mud from later. At the top of the stairs, having heard me come home, were Bull and Dozer, wagging their tails and waiting for me to fetch them.

Despite any misgivings about the case and the danger I might face, the dogs always made me smile.

Thirty minutes later, I was placing a freshly dog-licked plate into the dishwasher. The plate had once held bacon, eggs, spinach and courgette, a healthy breakfast that had met my needs if not exciting my taste buds.

My watch said the time was 0841hrs. It was time to go to the office.

Round Two with the Chief Inspector. Wednesday, November 23rd 0900hrs

The second I opened my car door to get out, the dogs bounced over my lap to plop on the tarmac and scurry to the office back door. Quite what they found so exciting about getting into work would forever be a mystery. They stood at the door, impatiently waiting for the slow-moving human to open it, looking at me, looking at the door and repeating the action until I locked my car and produced a key to open the office.

Having raced inside, their little paws skidding on the plastic tile from their furious effort, they were once again defeated by the inner door that led from the storage, toilet and admin area through to the office proper.

Had they been teenagers they probably would have sighed and tutted. Dachshunds though seem perpetually in an optimistic mood, so they did not complain, they just barrelled through the gap as I pushed the door open, Bull riding briefly on Dozer's back as they both fought to occupy the same space.

Jane was making coffee. 'I thought you would be along any moment.' She said as she held a small white cup to collect the brew being dispensed. 'Amanda has been and gone already.' Jane was dressed today in a pair of fake, black, leather, wet-look leggings. A vague memory was telling me the correct name for them was jeggings. Whatever they were called, they were skin tight on her slender legs which, to my mind was not a good look as the legs were not shapely like a woman's. Rather, they were skinny, like a skinny man's. Involuntarily, I noticed that where I would expect to see a bulge in the front of her groin area, the fake leather (is it pleather?) was completely smooth as if Jane were in fact post-op.

I opened my mouth to ask how the effect was achieved but closed it again quickly before the words made it through my teeth. I didn't want to know the answer. Jane's top half was covered by a loose-fitting jumper that hung off one shoulder to reveal the strap of her bra. Jane didn't have any boobs to fill a bra but whatever was going on inside her jumper would remain a mystery as it was another question I was unwilling to ask.

The dogs had scurried across the carpet to search for biscuit crumbs, their busy noses leading them in an ever-hopeful search for food. By the time I arrived at the coffee machine, they had either found and eaten all there was to eat or had accepted defeat and stopped searching. Bull hopped onto one of the chairs set out for clients to wait on, turned around twice and settled down to sleep.

'Thank you, Jane.' I said as I accepted the offered cup. 'Not having one yourself?' I asked as she returned to her desk.

She shook her head. 'It's strong stuff. I have had one already and find that more than one in an hour makes my pulse begin to jitter.'

I knew what she meant. But, oh, it was good.

As Jane sat back in her chair she said, 'I got a hit on the paper you found.'

It was to be the first thing I was going to ask her. Now I didn't need to. I joined her behind her desk to see what she had.

'The writing is Ukrainian. That's what you expected isn't it?' I nodded. 'The maker's mark on it is for a firm that makes all kinds of different paper-based products from tissues to writing paper. I had a good look at them, but they appear to just be a firm that makes paper.' She sounded disappointed because she knew I was hoping this might be a lead or a clue of some kind.

'What is this particular paper used for?'

'Oh, ah.' She clicked the mouse to check her information. 'The manufacture of cigarettes. Specifically, this is the paper that goes around the outside of the tobacco.'

As I thought about that the front door opened. I glanced up, unsure who it might be coming in, but very much expecting a customer. To my great surprise, the lean form of Chief Inspector Quinn let himself into my premises. He was accompanied by a younger man in a business suit. I took the younger man to be a plain-clothes police officer, but where most plain-clothes guys wear crappy, cheap, ill-fitting suits, this chap's suit looked hand-cut and of fine material.

CI Quinn's eyes met mine. His lips were pursed tight and I could instantly tell that he was here to admit that I was right about the Dockyard. His pride was stopping him from doing what he should and leading with an apology. I really wanted to make him squirm and mess him around, but I took the mature approach instead.

'Chief Inspector, so good to see you.' I crossed the room and shook his hand vigorously. 'Might I interest you in a coffee? It's the good stuff from Columbia.'

His face was fighting with competing emotions. He didn't like me, and we were always adversarial, but here I was greeting him like an old friend and offering him the best of the house. Finally, the attraction of my coffee, no doubt aided by the wonderful aroma already in the room, forced him to speak. 'Thank you, Mr Michaels. That would be acceptable.'

Acceptable. Quite the concession.

'I'll get them.' Jane said, sidestepping us to get to the machine.

I turned my attention to the chap in the good suit. 'Tempest Michaels.' I introduced myself as I offered him my hand. He seemed quite caught off guard. CI Quinn had no doubt been warning him that I would be problematic or aggressive.

'Joseph Kushnir.' He replied automatically. The name sounded distinctly European but was delivered in a local accent.

'Detective Sergeant Joseph Kushnir.' CI Quinn reminded him before turning his eyes to me. He opened his mouth to speak but I got in first, guessing what it was he wanted to see me about.

'Counterfeit and smuggling.'

'I'm sorry?' He replied.

'That's what the Ukrainians are up to at the Dockyard. They are using the Dockyard to smuggle in goods from outside the UK and are manufacturing counterfeit goods like cigarettes. No doubt there are other criminal activities such as prostitution going on elsewhere.'

'Once again, I find you surprisingly well informed, Mr Michaels.'

'Like I said yesterday, I found evidence.' It was time to see how much the Chief Inspector knew. 'Are you aware there are tunnels that lead to chambers beneath the Dockyard? They can be entered from the river unseen by people on land.'

His eyes betrayed that he did not. His younger colleague looked startled at the revelation. CI Quinn didn't answer my question though. Instead he posed one of his own. 'What is your relationship with Julia Jones?'

A brief flutter of worry zipped across my gut. Was the idiot here to see if I was involved in her death? 'I don't know her at all. We spoke on the phone once.'

'And yet she employed you at the Dockyard, did she not?'

'You know that she did.' I snapped back with a touch of impatience. I hated being asked leading questions when everyone already knew the answer. 'The Ukrainians murdered her. For what, I cannot tell so you can forget any daft ideas that I might be involved in her death.'

He nodded. 'Shall we sit?' He asked. The question was a change of tack and caught me by surprise. I was still standing when both he and his detective sergeant took their seats. Jane was just serving the coffee. 'Please, Tempest.' He added.

It was the first time he had addressed me by my first name.

I asked, 'What are you up to, Ian?' As I reversed into the seat opposite him.

CI Quinn looked up as Jane handed him a cup, thanked her and only paused for a half a second when the petite blonde said "You're welcome" in a deep manly voice. I think he wanted to make a comment on the subject but to his credit he refrained, choosing to get on with what he had to say finally. 'For eighteen months I have been spearheading a taskforce to tackle a growing organised crime problem. The Ukrainians are gaining ground and have been impossible to catch in the act as they flood the market with counterfeit tobacco products. There are alcohol and narcotics as well, and prostitution but on a lesser scale. The goods just appear on the streets. All our attempts to determine where they are coming into the country have resulted in wasted effort.'

I watched the dynamic opposite me. Quinn was relaxed in his chair, his back resting against the material behind him. He was doing all the talking. His colleague in contrast, was poised on the very front edge of his chair, almost twitching with nervous energy. He remained silent but hung on every word that came from his superior's lips. The younger man looked a bit like the Chief Inspector, but not so alike that I thought they could be related. His brown hair was buzz cut to a length of perhaps a half inch on top and almost nothing on the sides. It was a very military cut and I observed that he was muscular beneath the suit, not hugely bulging like Big Ben, but athletic and toned like me.

I pushed my way into the conversation. I wanted to move it along. 'You came here with a plan. What is it?'

'My detective sergeant will be joining you on the cleaning crew.'

His statement caused my eyebrows to rise. 'Just like that? How do you propose to get him a job on the cleaning crew?'

'His parents are both Ukrainian. Aren't they Joseph? His grandparents came to England after the second world war. Joseph speaks enough Ukrainian to make a phone call and secure a job. He did that yesterday afternoon.'

About eight seconds after I told you about the Dockyard, no doubt.

'That's right, sir.' He confirmed like a dutiful puppy.

I thought about it and shook my head. 'I have no need of a companion on this venture.' I held my hand up to silence Quinn before he could speak. 'I recognise though that I have no sway over his presence at the Dockyard. Rather than conduct two separate investigations, I will work with you. What is that you need before you can raid the place?'

'To prove its existence would be a good starting point. So far, I have no evidence that anything criminal is happening there at all. Can you prove the existence of this underground system?'

I considered what I genuinely knew. 'Not yet.' I had to conclude. I had some old maps, but they could be forged from imagination and I had noises coming through pipes in the rigging room that appeared to run into the ground. I still had no way into whatever was down there though and that was a key fact. Even if we knew for certain they were down there committing crimes, we couldn't raid the place if we didn't know how to get in. It was quite clever on their part.

I took the time to explain what I had been able to glean so far and what my next move was. Having CI Quinn on side for once was both refreshing and unsettling. I wasn't sure I could trust him. I was certain that if I solved the case, revealed the ghosts, which were fast becoming nothing more than an aside, and presented the criminals to be arrested, Quinn would claim the victory for himself and his taskforce, reducing my involvement to a by-line somewhere.

By 1000hrs, Quinn was ready to leave. 'I am leaving Detective Sergeant Kushnir with you, Mr Michaels. He will report back to me, so that you do not have to.'

It spoke volumes about CI Quinn that he had automatically assumed he was now in control of my investigation and was acting as if he was letting me off the hook of having to report to him. I managed to avoid reacting, although I made sure I did my best to crush his hand when I shook it goodbye.

'There is a key point that neither of you know yet.' I had their attention. 'I am not going to the Dockyard tonight. I have a prior engagement.' I didn't elaborate. It was none of Quinn's business.

Quinn nodded, thinking. He turned to his subordinate, 'Sergeant Kushnir, it falls to you to act alone it would seem.'

'Probably better to not involve civilians anyway, sir.' He replied. 'I shall report my findings in the morning.'

'Very good.' Quinn turned his attention to me again. 'Good day, Mr. Michaels.'

When the door closed behind him, the only sound in the office was Jane's fingers dancing across her keyboard.

I watched out the window as CI Quinn walked along the High Street, nodding his head in acknowledgement at the people going by like a noble acknowledging serfs from his horse. As he vanished from sight in the crowd, I asked, 'Do you have a car with you?' Just to make sure Joseph wasn't expecting a lift to the Dockyard.

'I do. It is parked in the public car park with a ticket displayed.'

It was more information than I needed. Detective Sergeant Kushnir came across as a boy scout. Not that this was necessarily a bad thing, he just seemed a little bit too shiny, like he only just left the academy. Perhaps he was a direct entry detective. I knew the Police did that, giving applicants with suitable qualifications or experience an entry point above the usual constable rank that other police officers started at. It had been one of the options open to me when I left the Army, but even though I could have applied to join as a Superintendent, it had not been attractive to swap one uniform for another. It occurred to me now though that I would have an entirely different relationship with CI Quinn if I had taken that route – I would have been his superior.

Cheered by that thought, I turned away from the window. It was time to get on with the day. 'I have some admin tasks to take care of. When did you last visit the Royal Dockyard?'

'Not for some years.' He admitted. 'And then it was a school trip and we mostly skived off to smoke cigarettes and drink lager that Billy Scraggs had smuggled in his school bag.'

It sounded like every school trip since the dawn of time.

'Best you get there and familiarise yourself with the land. Memorise the layout. The Ukrainians running the place are unfriendly, my colleague and I were assaulted last night in a bid to scare us off. They don't want English there, or, more accurately, they don't want anyone that is not Ukrainian and on their payroll.'

'You were assaulted? Surely you can identify your assailants and we can arrest them right now?' He had taken a step toward me in his instant excitement.

'Bigger picture, old boy. There is something far more heinous than a little roughing up going on. If you want to deliver the Chief Inspector a crime syndicate, we have to catch the big fish that runs the pond. Not his little minnows.'

I could see his cogs turning before he nodded his agreement. 'What do you think I should do?'

His question told me how new to police work he must be. I could have been condescending or even steered him onto a ridiculous path that would have embarrassed him. Big Ben would have. However, it was not my nature to take advantage of people. 'Go to the Dockyard, buy a ticket and act like a visitor. Look around. Watch the security but don't look like you are watching them. Somewhere in the Dockyard there is a way into the underground tunnels. We don't know what is down there, but I think they killed Julia Jones to protect it. Go there, fit in and observe. I'll be along shortly.'

I took him through to my office where I had the map of the dockyard on one wall. On it I pointed out the rigging room, the Admiral's office and the museum and using a handy pencil, drew a rough guide of where I thought the tunnels ran. We exchanged mobile numbers so we could communicate and rendezvous more easily later and he went back out the door he had come in more than an hour before.

Left alone in my office, I called my sister.

The Invitation. Wednesday, November 23rd 1042hrs

'Hey, sis. How you doing today?' I asked when her voice came on the line.

'Um. Okay, maybe.'

Her answer told me that she was trying to not tell me something while at the same time also telling me that there was something she didn't want to tell.

I flashed back another question, 'What is it? Is dad okay?'

'Oh, yeah. Yes, dad is fine so far as I know. So is mum.' She was hesitating, unwilling to say what she wanted to say.

'Rachel, just tell me what the issue is.' I demanded.

'Okay, dickhead.' I guess she wasn't happy with my forceful attitude. 'I think the baby is coming.'

I felt the earth tilt beneath me. What was I supposed to do now? I had not the slightest experience with babies. 'Do you need me to do anything?'

She actually laughed at me. 'No, Tempest. I've got this. It will be many hours before I even need to go to hospital. I will take mum to see dad later. You can just get on with what you are doing.'

'If you are sure.'

'This is my third, Tempest. It's really no big deal.' She sounded relaxed and confident. I wished her luck and ended the call. There was a baby coming. I had never seen a new born other than on television. When Rachael had given birth to the previous two, I had been out of the country, seeing them for the first time only once they were several months old. The concept of a new born was a little terrifying. What if they expected me to hold it?

I distracted myself by going to speak with Jane. 'Have we had many enquiries this week?' I asked. I had barely been involved in the business this week. Since mum's phone call on Sunday evening, everything else had gone on hold.

'Quite a few, but no more than the usual amount. Mostly nutters, but there were some with merit amongst them.' We got a lot of emails and phone calls from people who had felt a cold draft in their house and instantly assumed it was a recently dead relative coming to haunt them or give them a message. Also, people got confused, or rather chose to confuse themselves about the service we offered so there were weekly requests for exorcisms, magical banishments, palm reading or prediction of the future, which were almost always about relationships and will this boy cheat on me, and we got a lot of enquiries on whether we did kids parties. Even once Jane had filtered out the ridiculous, the remaining enquiries were still filled with nutters claiming their father's new girlfriend is a ghoul or their new neighbour had created a pet cemetery and was going to bring their cat back from the dead. For every one-hundred enquiries we received there would be one or two that had genuine merit.

Jane had to find them.

'Is there something I need to attend to?' I was going to remain focused on the Dockyard case, but I didn't want to lose clients through lack of communication.

'No. Amanda has been dealing with it all. She has four cases she is pursuing concurrently.'

'Jolly good.' There seemed to be nothing that I needed to do. As I was about to consider my next move, my phone pinged in my pocket.

I took it out to read the new message. It was from Natasha which should have generated a zing of anticipation, but what I felt was dread because I knew I had been ignoring her.

Hi Tempest. Is your dad any better? I just wanted to message and check on things as I have not heard from

you in a few days. If you feel like taking your mind off things, I think I know something we can do...

The message ended with a winking emoji. I was a bad person. It would be the easiest thing in the world for me to go to her and indulge in some harmless, consensual adult activity. It was what she wanted. I couldn't do it though, because I knew there was no future for us. I wondered how to respond, tried to frame a reply but deleted it. Tried again, deleted that one as well and stuffed my phone back into my pocket to deal with later.

Not for the first time, I wondered how I made relationships so complicated. Standing next to the wall, I let my head droop forward until it touched it, then knocked it twice against the plasterboard. I needed to stick to doing what I was good at and just leave women alone.

'Everything alright, boss?' Asked Jane. I had forgotten she was there while I knocked some sense into myself.

'Girls.' I replied, one word telling her all she needed to know.

'Tell me about it.' She agreed incongruously with her deep voice and Adam's apple.

There was nothing else to say, so I grabbed my bag and car keys, let Jane know I was heading back to the Dockyard and got going.

Jane stopped me before I got to the door. 'Boss, I almost forgot. You have a letter here.'

'A real one? Not a bill?'

'No, it's got gold embossed lettering. It looks fancy.' She was holding it up and it did indeed look fancy.

I took it from her and used a pencil to slit the top of the envelope open. Inside was an invitation.

Dear Blue Moon Investigations,

I request the honour of your attendance at an event in honour of my 80th birthday at Hale House on the weekend of December 10th and 11th. The invitation extends to all employees of the Blue Moon Investigations firm and their partners.

For three hundred years, every second generation has lost the heir to the family in mysterious circumstances. The creature known as the horror of Hale House has claimed the life of the elderly heir on his 80th birthday.

The last Lord Hale, my father, died peacefully in his bed aged ninety-three. So, you see, the visit may be quite eventful. In addition to providing you with full access to all areas of Hale House, which includes a full spa and gymnasium, swimming pool, room service and personal butler in each suite, I will pay your firm the sum of £25,000.00 for attending, providing you stay the entire weekend and ensure that I survive until my birthday has passed.

I look forward to receiving, by return, your confirmation that you will attend.

Yours

Lord Hale

I blew out my cheeks when I read the number he had written. The firm wasn't hurting for money, not by a long shot, but this was something else.

Seeing my face, Jane asked, 'What is it?'

I was rereading the handwritten letter for the third time but stopped to meet her eyes. I handed it to her. 'Read it for yourself.'

I stayed quiet while she did, my mind whirling, watching her face to see the changes in expression as her eyes reached different points. Her eyes damned near popped out and I knew she had just seen the number.

'Is this for real?' She asked as she handed the letter back to me.

I pursed my lips and twitched my nose, something I have been told I do when I am thinking. 'I think it is.' I answered slowly. 'I need you to do some research. Are you doing anything for Amanda?'

'Not really. A couple of bits, but nothing pressing.'

'Then drop everything and pull together everything you can find about Lord Hale and the Hale family tree, the creature he mentions and anything else you can think of. See if you can find out what his financial position is.' I didn't want to get too excited about the potential windfall if the whole thing was a bluff or a ruse.

'Will you go?' She asked as she started typing.

I didn't want to commit to anything until I knew more, so I said, 'Maybe.' Waved goodbye and went out the door.

It had brightened outside, the clouds lifting to reveal cold blue sky that promised more frost tonight. Traffic was light through Rochester and Chatham to the Dockyard, although as I passed the Pentagon shopping centre, it picked up and there was some bumper to bumper action where early Christmas shoppers were beginning to converge.

Alex Jordan. Wednesday, November 23rd 1101hrs

The Dockyard itself was busy. Eight coachloads of children from different schools had descended on it. Educational trips no doubt a constant source of income throughout the year. With the dogs on their leads, I bought a ticket for the third day in a row but noted that the two ladies that had served me previously were no longer there. It could just be that they had the day off, but the lady with the heavy Eastern European accent now fumbling to work the till had never worked this job before if I was any judge. I had to wait while she conferred with a colleague in Ukrainian. Finally, she found the right button to press and my ticket was dispensed.

The Ukrainians were taking over every position as the old Navy boys had predicted. Were they next? I went to find them.

Sergeant Joseph Kushnir was here somewhere. I was in no hurry to find him though, if I didn't spot him in the next hour, I would call him. As I made my way to the dry docks where I would find Alan and the others, I called Big Ben.

'Hey, dung trumpet, what're you up to?' He asked as the call connected.

I replied with, 'Good morning, Ben.' He had a new insult or name to call me every time we spoke. I had to wonder if he had a book he used to generate them. 'I am at the Dockyard. Did you find a boat?'

'I hired one.' He replied. 'There was no one around to borrow one from so I have a tiny little dingy. It's fast though, or at least it feels it. I should be alongside the Dockyard in another half an hour.'

I said, 'Then I hope the entrance is easy to find.' and pressed the red button to disconnect the call.

I had arrived at the dry docks and already been spotted by Boy George. I was easy to pick out with my dogs pulling along in front of me and I stood three feet higher than eighty percent of the schoolchild visitors around me.

I threw him a casual wave. He was sending a group of kids below deck on the destroyer, leaving him free.

'Wotcha, Tempest.' He called as he crossed the concrete. 'Bad business with Julia Jones, I don't mind saying.'

I started to agree, wondering if they even suspected she had been murdered when I noticed that he wasn't looking at me, but beyond me over my left shoulder.

'Look out. Here comes the boss.' He said. As I turned to see who he meant, I noticed that Alan and Fred were also approaching from wherever they had been performing their jobs.

Boy George had been referring to Alex Jordan though. He was approaching from behind me, wearing an elegant suit and a long winter coat of a wool-blend. It looked like it might cost an average person's annual wage.

'Mr. Michaels.' He extended his hand as he greeted me. 'How is your father?'

'No different.' I answered. 'Thank you for asking though. I am sure he will recover and be able to identify his assailant soon enough.'

'Well, let's hope so.' If the death of his colleague, Julia Jones, was having any impact on his day, there was no sign of it. 'What brings you here today?'

His interest was suspicious. How had he known I was here? Was it chance? 'Why do you ask, Alex?' I decided to push my luck. 'What are you hiding?'

The question was inflammatory, designed to make him react. I expected an angry response, perhaps that it was a perfectly reasonable question to ask while avoiding giving an answer to my other question about what he might be hiding. Instead, I saw a flutter of panic in his eyes. Then he grabbed my arm, so he could whisper in my ear. 'I'm in trouble.'

He moved back to put a normal distance between us again. I checked behind me to see where Alan, George and the others were. They hadn't heard what Alex had said and were waiting patiently for me to speak with them. 'I'll be back shortly.' I said as I moved away, taking Alex's elbow to guide him.

Quietly I said, 'I'm listening.' He seemed nervous, skittish. His eyes were darting about. 'If we are being watched it will be best to act and move normally, smile, gesticulate and speak at a volume that is only slightly lower than normal. There is plenty of ambient noise to drown out what we are saying.' He swallowed, looking nervous and looked about again. I stopped walking. 'Here will do. Face me and you can check one field of vision while I check the other.' I was trying to calm him so he would talk and act naturally. He was drawing attention to himself with the scared rabbit act.

Finally, he pulled himself together and spoke again. 'I think Julia was murdered.' He blurted. 'I think she was murdered, and I think I might be next.'

'Why?' I asked. 'Why was Julia murdered and why would you be next? Better yet, who is it that you think killed Julia? Just what is going on here?' I had made several mistakes I realised as I stopped speaking. I should have stuck to one question at a time. Too late to take them back though.

'It's the Ukrainians.' He hissed. 'They invested some money two years ago when I wanted to expand some of our attractions. Everything costs so much and then there is upkeep and maintenance and cleaning and extra staff to show the tourists around. I think they even sabotaged some of the new attractions so I would need to borrow more money from them. Then, as old staff retired, or we needed to hire someone for a new position, it was always a Ukrainian that got the job. Before I even knew it, the security guards were all Ukrainian. When I took the money, they insisted I hired that ox Danylo Vakhno. He terrifies me.'

'Why didn't you tell me any of this on Monday?'

'I think my office is bugged. And my house and car and phone. They have made it quite clear I am to keep the place running and not ask questions.'

A light bulb came on in my head. That was what he had been trying to signal to me on Monday. His office was bugged. That was why he kept touching his ear. 'Why haven't you gone to the police?'

'And tell them what? I have no evidence of anything. I know they are up to something, but I have no idea what it is.'

'Mr Michaels.' The loud voice calling my name came from behind Alex. He spun around shocked like he had just been stabbed with an electrode.

'Who's that?' He asked, panicked.

'A colleague.' Detective Sergeant Kushnir could remain anonymous for now. He was certainly trying to do just that with his coat collar turned up and dark sunglasses to hide his eyes. He looked like a spy from a bad nineteen eighties movie. I hadn't wanted anyone to see him with me. Secrets are best kept by those that don't know them. I waved for him to stay where he was. Thankfully he understood the gesture. 'So, why are you telling me now?'

His eyes flared with surprise. 'Because they killed Julia. I don't know why. Maybe it was just because she wouldn't step down and they didn't need her. I heard she hired a couple of chaps that were not Ukrainian, so it could be just because of that.'

I grimaced.

'You have to help me. All I need is some hard evidence that I can use. Something tangible I can take to the police.' He had locked my eyes with his, his expression desperate. Then they widened again. 'Oh, God. It's him.' He squeaked.

As the colour drained from Alex's face, I turned to see what had scared him. Looking menacing just by standing still, Danylo Vakhno was staring directly at us. His blocky frame and head even more impressive in person than in the photograph I had seen. He was standing in the lee of the Admiral's office building at least one hundred feet away.

'I have to go.' Alex had already started moving away. 'Evidence, Mr Michaels. I need evidence.' Then he was out of range for me to say anything without shouting. I had wanted to ask him about the tunnels. If I were the CEO of a place, I would expect to know everything there was about it. Accepting that it was now too late to quiz him, I looked back at Danylo Vakhno. He stared at me for a few seconds more, then he turned and went out of sight behind the building.

It felt a lot colder on the Dockside suddenly. I shivered. He was a person I really didn't want to have to fight. Ever.

Joseph caught my eye, checking it was now okay for him to approach. I waved him over.

I knew he was going to ask, so I started talking before he could. 'That was Alex Jordan, the CEO of the firm that runs the Dockyard. He is concerned that the Ukrainian presence here is up to no good and would like for us to find some incriminating evidence.'

'He doesn't know what they are up to?'

'He claims that he doesn't. Always difficult to tell when people are lying, and they rarely tell the whole truth no matter what the circumstances.' I changed tack. 'Have you had a good look around?'

He nodded. 'I wasn't able to hear anything in the rigging room, there are too many people in there making noise, but I have memorised the layout and I am ready to infiltrate the underground base.'

Infiltrate an underground base? He sounded like James Bond.

'I need to talk with the gentlemen waiting over there.' I gestured toward Alan and the chaps.

As I started toward them, Joseph grabbed my arm, 'We shouldn't involve civilians in our mission.'

Our mission?

I looked at his hand on my arm meaningfully. He removed it. 'Those gentlemen are colleagues of my father. I have questions for them. Specifically, whether they know anything about tunnels under this place.'

'Are you sure we should be involving them? How do you know you can trust them?'

I started to retort that he was being ridiculous. Before I could speak though, I remembered some of the recent subterfuge I had encountered during other cases. Instead of arguing I shrugged. 'I don't know. I choose to though. Like I said, they are friends of my father and that is good enough for me.'

I didn't wait to hear what he thought of that. Turning, I walked toward Alan. The dogs had been sitting still long enough in their opinion, instantly pulling at their leads to get to the next destination.

'Who's your friend?' Alan asked, always the spokesperson for the group, he was looking beyond me to Joseph as he sidled nervously along, keeping to the shadows and contours of the buildings to stay invisible. He looked like a moron.

'This is Detective Sergeant Joseph Kushnir.' I introduced him as he caught up with me.

'Don't use my real name.' He squeaked.

'Bit late now lad.' Alan pointed out.

It had become quickly obvious that poor Joseph was in over his head. What training and experience he had I couldn't tell. I assumed it was minimal though. I was going to have to use him only for communicating with CI Quinn. He could relay instructions and information if there came a point when I learned anything useful.

I addressed the four old Navy boys. 'What do you know about tunnels under the Dockyard?'

'Tunnels?' Fred repeated.

The four men looked at each other, each as equally mystified as the others. They had no idea.

'There are tunnels beneath the Dockyard. The first was dug more than three-hundred years ago. They link with the river somewhere and can be accessed in at least two other points, I believe.' They were staring at me with rapt fascination, wanting to disbelieve, but seeing that it instantly explained some things. 'The Ukrainians are up to something here. Something criminal, I just don't know what, but the point is, the whispers you can here in the rigging room are the voices of people below ground. The noise is travelling up what I guess are ventilation pipes.'

'Where are the entrances?' Asked Stuart.

'That is the thing I don't know. I have a map but all it shows is the layout. It was drawn with some artistic license so there is no scale one might use to locate the way in. The entrances must be within the buildings though.'

The chaps looked at the building behind me, probably searching their memories for anything that might fit what I had described.

'You guys know of anything that fits the bill?' Alan asked his friends. They all shook their heads. 'No, me neither. Sorry, kid. We're not much help on this one.'

It was what I had expected. 'Not to worry, chaps.'

'I will find the way in.' Announced Joseph. He was standing so close to my shoulder I had to turn to look at him. He still had his collar turned right up and his dark glasses on. 'Give me a few hours. I will find the entrance. The Chief Inspector deployed me to bust this gang, so that's what I am going to do.'

Joseph was over-excited and playing out some kind of secret agent fantasy. I wasn't sure what to make of it, or what to do with him. He was fast becoming an unnecessary distraction though.

'Joseph, these are dangerous people. They probably killed Julia Jones and have run off most of the English staff here. If they catch you, they will not let you go. We need to tackle this in a coordinated fashion, not rush in and get caught.'

'I am surprisingly well trained, Mr Michaels.' He tried to make it sound like he had Chuck Norris level fighting skills, but he was just coming off as youthful and stupid.

'Nevertheless, we will be more successful if you and I operate together. I have someone looking for the river entrance already. We can monitor and observe on land. The way into the underground system is here, we just need to find it. There will be signs if we look for them.'

'Won't that take too long?' He was positively vibrating with nervous energy. I had to question whether I had ever been that gung-ho.

'It will be slower than storming the buildings and demanding to know what their evil plan is, yes. If the stairs down to the tunnels are inside the buildings that are not accessible by the Dockyard visitors, we would have to break in or sneak in just to take a look around. That is something I might be able to do tomorrow night on my cleaning shift. There are a lot of buildings to cover though.'

'What are you proposing then? We stand around and watch, while under our feet criminals commit crimes and get away with it?' There was impatience in his voice. He wanted to be the hero, to save the day and get the medal.

'For now, yes. Think about it. If your Chief Inspector had sufficient evidence that there were criminal enterprises occurring beneath the Dockyard, he would descend on this place with a taskforce of officers, storm the buildings, find the way in and arrest everyone. He hasn't though because we don't actually know anything.'

Deflated, his shoulders slumped as he accepted that I was right.

Joseph appeared to have calmed down but I still felt mired in difficulties. I had the unexpected but very welcome support of the police for the first time ever, but until I could deliver them something tangible to prove the Ukrainians were using the space beneath the Dockyard as a criminal headquarters, Quinn would not move. I was certain they were down there, but until I could find a way in to take some pictures or video I was stumped. Even getting into the buildings I believed might house the stairs down to the underground chambers was fraught with difficulty. Each building was filled with people and guarded. At night I might be able to move unrestricted, but the buildings were locked. I was content to break in but could not be sure that if caught I would be turned over to the police. It was an organised gang of criminals – there seemed a distinct chance they would just kill me and make my body disappear.

I got no further with my thoughts as my phone rang. Caller ID told me my mother was on the line.

'Mother.' I answered.

'Tempest!' Her voice was filled with panic. My adrenalin spiked instantly, and my head filled with imagined misadventures she might have encountered. 'It's your sister. The baby is coming!'

'Oh.' I replied, my pulse returning to normal. 'Okay. Are you off to the hospital with her?'

'Tempest this is not the time for being calm.' She snapped. 'How fast can you get here?'

My brow furrowed. 'Get where? Are you at home?'

'Yes!' Her voice was beginning to concern me. My mother was given to dramatic notions, she often made more of a situation than was necessary, but she was upset and worried, her agitation obvious.

'Do you need me? Why not call an ambulance?'

A torrent of swearwords split the background noise on the phone. My sister was having a contraction. I didn't know what that was like to experience, and had never seen it up close, however, the TV and film people liked to portray it as an uncomfortable event. I doubted they were all hamming it up.

'We need you.' Mum insisted and then she was gone, the line dead in my ear.

'Problem?' Alan asked.

'The baby is coming.' I answered absentmindedly. I was thinking about what I was going to do. I checked my watch again. It was 1130hrs. I had more than four hours before I needed to get to Brands Hatch for the start of Jagjit's stag party. I wasn't going to miss it, but I wondered how much time would get eaten up taking my sister to the hospital. Did I need to stay with her? Or was it okay to just drop her at the door and wish her luck?

I had a nasty feeling my best-laid plans were about to get torched.

Alan said, 'Congratulations.' moving in close to shake my hand, a universal reaction to the announcement of a birth. Alan had misunderstood me though, or rather, I hadn't expressed myself clearly.

'Sorry, no. It's not my baby. It's my sister that's in labour.'

Alan pumped my hand anyway. 'That means our pal Michael Michaels is just about to get another grandchild. That's something to celebrate.'

I couldn't argue.

'Are you leaving?' Joseph asked.

'I guess so. I can't imagine what I am needed for but my other engagement will prevent my return today.'

'Well, don't worry. I will handle things here. Leave it to me to find the way into their lair.' He saw my reaction and raised his hands in supplication. 'Don't worry, I won't do anything daft, I won't break in anywhere and if I do work out where the entrance is, I will observe only.' He got an A for enthusiasm, it was misguided though and likely to get him into trouble.

'I think it would be far safer if you start your shifts here tomorrow when there will be three of us.'

'Nonsense, Mr. Michaels. The Chief Inspector's instructions were clear. Besides, I am Ukrainian, they will welcome me with open arms.'

'Ah, the confidence of youth.' Alan said. There was no negative inflection in his tone, but Joseph took offence anyway.

He fixed Alan with a hard stare. 'Yes, it always wins against the tired acceptance of old age.'

Alan merely shrugged in acknowledgement, too experienced, wise and astute to be drawn into an argument.

'I'm leaving.' I said, breaking the stalemate as Stuart, Fred and Boy George moved in to flank their pal. 'I'll be back as soon as I can.'

I put my hand on Joseph's shoulder to steer him away and moved the pair of us back toward the exit and car park.

'Why do you tolerate them?' He asked meaning the old Navy guys.

I didn't bother to look across at him. 'Because they have been there and done it and have the t-shirt and they know more than they will ever let on. Never let their age fool you into thinking they are less capable.' He nodded his head in acknowledgement of what I had said but didn't offer a verbal agreement. We were almost at the exit. 'I advise against trying to get into the tunnel system, Joe. Check and observe what is happening around you. Tonight, do the cleaning duties they give you and monitor the movements of the guards. Otherwise, try to fit in.'

I guess he was tired of me trying to dissuade him from saving the day because he said, 'I don't take orders from you, Mr Michaels. I'm the police officer here, not you. Perhaps you should take instruction from me in this investigation.' He had stopped walking and turned to face me.

'Good luck then. I urge you to stay in touch and consider everyone working here to be a potential threat. I will drop everything and come running if you feel you are compromised and need help.' My words were intended to show him we were on the same side. I waved a quick salute as I reached the exit building and lost sight of him.

Baby. Wednesday, November 23rd 1143hrs

With Bull on my lap to look over the steering wheel and Dozer riding shotgun, I headed out of the car park. It was midday and mid-week, so traffic was still light, but it was still sticky as I went through the bit of Chatham next to the Pentagon shopping centre.

I was driving to my parent's place in Rochester. It was not a task I had intended to include today. I needed to focus on the case and found myself a bit irritated by this latest distraction. Sensing my ire rising, I quelled it, finding my centre as many different senseis had taught me over the years. With one hand I ruffled the fur on Bull's neck.

The information from Alex Jordan was disturbing but not surprising. I had idly wondered how he could fit into what I was seeing at the Dockyard. As CEO, he must know what was going on around him. Now the picture was complete. He was trapped by his own need to find investors. He had taken the wrong offer and now it hung over his head like a deadly storm cloud. I needed to rescue him as well.

It took twelve minutes to make the journey to my parent's house. Twelve minutes. Was that a long time if one was in labour or was it little more than the time between contractions at the early stages.

I had not the faintest idea.

Pulling up to the curb though, I got a sense that things might be moving along a little faster than my sister had indicated. She was framed in the doorway with my mother holding her hand and frantically waving for me to hurry up.

Confused and concerned, I opened the car door forgetting the dogs who both bounded over my lap and up the driveway to scoot into the house.

'Quickly, Tempest.' Called my mother before I could get moving. 'Your sister needs to get to the hospital. Take her car.'

I had a stack of questions fighting for first place in order of priority such as why is there not an ambulance here? What am I expected to do once we get to the hospital? Have you told her husband yet? What am I supposed to do with my dogs? What are you doing that is so important you cannot drive her to the hospital yourself. I dismissed them all though. I was already here, my sister's face was a mask of discomfort and I was clearly taking her to the hospital no matter what, so I elected to just get on with it.

I offered her my hand to get her down the step from the door, but immediately regretted doing so when her grip broke every bone in my hand. I swear she could have turned a steel bar into foil with that grip. Mum thrust Rachael's car keys at me and ushered me back to the road where her car was parked.

What felt like thirty seconds after arriving, I was leaving again. Rachael was in the passenger seat but braced against the ceiling and dashboard as if we were about to flip over.

I tried a tentative, 'Everything okay?' As I pulled away.

It was the wrong question to ask apparently as it elicited a torrent of expletives that ought not to come from a mummy's mouth.

'So, just get to the hospital then?'

More expletives, mostly about men and what they could do with their todgers. I drove cautiously at first, not wanting to throw the lady next to me around too much.

She grabbed my arm, her steel grip around my left bicep cutting off the blood flow to my hand instantly. 'Hurry up, Tempest.' She hissed between breaths drawn in through her teeth.

I proceeded a good deal faster after that.

I swept the car through the tunnel under the river just as the latest contraction subsided. Calm returned as I scanned the roads for cameras and police cars as I was doing twenty more than the speed limit and wanted neither a ticket nor the delay getting pulled over would cause.

'Okay. I'm okay.' Rachael panted next to me. 'Sorry about this, Tempest.' She patted my forearm. 'Things have advanced far more quickly than with Martha or Fallon. I got caught out by it.'

Now that we were having a conversation I asked, 'Why is it that mother couldn't drive you or call an ambulance?'

Rachael laughed. 'Have you been in a car with mum recently? She is dangerous behind the wheel. Besides, she had a meeting with some church ladies this afternoon and didn't want to miss that. She will catch up with us at the hospital.'

That mum would believe her meeting took precedence was entirely in keeping with her world view. I would be able to go back for my dogs and car once I had settled Rachael at the hospital labour ward. I kept quiet about the very important engagement I had this afternoon for two reasons. Firstly, I recognised that it was insignificant when compared with what my sister would be doing, and secondly, I was concerned that she might try to force feed me my testicles if I mentioned it.

'Is Chris on his way?' I asked.

'Yes. I called him an hour ago. He was in a meeting but was off to collect the kids from school. I told him not to hurry.'

'Why?'

Rachael laughed at the mystified tone in my voice. 'Because it is our third, Tempest. It's really not that big a deal anymore.'

'Will you tell the child that?'

I was being flippant; my sense of humour was not well received though and was timed to coincide with the start of the next contraction. As she started to suck air in through her teeth again and utter a long string of words her children ought to not even know, I swung the car into the hospital car park. Thankfully, there was a barrier dispensing tickets, so I didn't have to scramble for change to buy a ticket.

'Which way to the labour ward?' I asked needlessly as we approached the reception desk. Anyone with eyes could see my head turning purple from her grip on the back of my neck and the space hopper looking bump jutting out through her top.

Of course, my sense of urgency was not reflected by any of the staff in the hospital. They saw this every day, possibly even every hour, but their anaesthetised reaction to my predicament did nothing to calm my nerves.

Next to me, still crushing my neck as she held on to me while I guided her down the corridor toward salvation, Rachael muttered more obscenities under her breath. She was sweating like a pig and turning red with the effort.

I tried to focus my concerns and thoughts on her and how she was feeling. Truth be told though, she was my twin sister and that familiarity gave me confidence that she was going to be fine. I was more worried about my bruised hand, bicep and neck.

Finally, and with a final torrent of cursing from Rachael, I handed her off to a pair of women that introduced themselves as midwives. I guess they were used to four letter words as neither seemed to even notice.

I leaned against the counter that formed the reception desk for the antenatal ward, relieved that I had made it. A clip board with several sheets of paper landed next to me.

The lady behind the counter advised, 'You'll need to fill these out presently.'

Before I could respond or look at them, the larger of the two midwives that had taken Rachael away came back to get me. 'Hurry up, or you'll miss baby.'

'But I'm not...'

'No time for any of that.' She snapped, probably used to dealing with bewildered fathers-to-be. 'Mum needs company right now.'

I was in the labour room before I knew what was happening. I opened my mouth to protest, but once again Rachael grabbed my hand and crushed it.

'Oooooooooooh.' She wailed. Actually, she didn't say *ooh* at all but let's say that she did. 'Oooooooh, Tempest.'

She was lying on a torture table that had been designed for birthing. It was tilted at an angle so the person laying on it had their back and head raised, then under the bum the device split in two to make the legs go in different directions.

'Look.' Said the midwife that had fetched me. 'You can see baby's head.'

Without thinking, I looked. The sight causing me to utter an expletive of my own. I had never expected nor wanted to see the parts of my sister that I was now seeing. Not only that, but the sight was putting me off seeing the same parts on other women at any point in my future.

Drawn in through the sheer horror of it, I saw my sister sucking at the gas and air mask like it was the only thing keeping her alive and the midwife between her legs literally grab hold of the infant while it was still inside her and pull it out with a twist.

Baby, all covered in goo and muck, was plopped onto my sister's chest whereupon she pulled down her top to show me another part of her I had never expected to see. With a little encouragement, my new niece started feeding.

'A daughter.' Said midwife number two from by my ear. 'I can tell this is your first.' She meant me not Rachael. 'She has your eyes though, the same piercing blue.'

'I'm, ah. I'm not the father.' I managed weakly.

'Oh.' She replied, sounding surprised or confused. 'Um.'

'He's my brother.' Rachael filled in the blank helpfully. 'We both have our father's eyes and now my children have them.'

Rachael looked tired. The baby was snuggled on her chest, warm and safe and in the best place in the world. I was a spare part with no purpose, a designation that had been true since the beginning of proceedings.

'I just need to clean her up a bit love.' Said the smaller of the two midwives. She was holding out her hands ready to take the baby but waiting for Rachael to acknowledge that she was going to take the baby away.

When Rachael removed the arm she was using to cradle it, the midwife scooped the tiny human and expertly carried it to a table across the room. The baby started mewling. The midwife was cooing at it while patting the muck off with a white towel that didn't stay white for very long.

A nappy went around the little girl's bum, then I watched, fascinated as she was lifted into the air again. 'Would you like to hold her?' The midwife asked.

'Goodness, no!' I recoiled. All three women laughed at me. I had no idea why they were laughing. The tiny human terrified me. What if I dropped it, or it moved when I was holding it? I would commit to picking her up when she was old enough to go to school and could be relied upon to bounce.

'Back to me please?' Rachael said. She soon had her new daughter nestled on her chest feeding again.

'Sis, do you need me for anything?' I asked.

'No, Tempest. Can you let Mum know, please?'

'Sure.' The midwives were busy doing midwife things. I knew the placenta still had to come out, I had no intention of hanging around to witness that. My phone had silently buzzed in my pocket several times in the last hour, whatever messages I had received remained unread but might be important, so I kissed my sister on her head and left the room.

I had missed calls from Big Ben and Jane. I called Big Ben first.

'What have you got for me, brother?' I asked as he came on the line.

'I got chased off as soon I approached the Dockyard. There must be something there to see. Two boats about fifty times the size of mine told me to go away in quite certain terms. They even bumped me at one point. I nearly capsized, but I couldn't do much about it, so I had to back off.'

'You're okay?'

'Of course. I would have happily boarded their boats and knocked them around a bit, there was no way to easily achieve that though. I can report that they were Ukrainian, or at least they have the same accent as everyone else at the Dockyard.'

'You couldn't get close enough to see an entrance though?'

'No, I saw it. I was just too busy manoeuvring the boat to get a good look though. I had planned to take pictures. It is around the corner from the dry docks where the river twists toward Gillingham. I would guess that you can only get boats in and out of it at high tide because I could see the bottom lip of it and the water was still going out. There's no steps or anything going down to it though, so the only way in is by water.'

I pursed my lips. This was great news. We had one entrance located and if the Ukrainians were protecting it, then my assumptions about goods coming in or out of there were likely to be right. How to get to it though? They had boats there now so would have boats there the whole time.

'Where are you now?' I asked him.

He said, 'Just getting back home. I need some lunch and I need to get changed before Hilary picks me up to go to Brands Hatch. How are you getting there?'

I thought about that for a second. 'I'm not sure actually. I'm at Medway hospital. My sister just had a baby in the last hour.

'Will you be late?' He asked, straight to the point.

'I don't know yet. I don't intend to be.' I was still wondering about it though. 'I'll keep you posted.'

We disconnected, and I made a second phone call. This one to Jane.

Her voice came on the line almost immediately. I imagined her sitting at her desk, a pencil tucked behind one ear as she researched whatever enquiries had come in today, the phone rang on the desk next to her and she would snatch it up with her right hand, her eyes never leaving the screen in front of her. 'Hi, Boss.' Her deep masculine voice said. 'What can I do for you?'

'I'm just returning a missed call, Jane. Did you call about the Hale case?'

'I didn't but I do already have a stack of data for you to sift. From my initial scan, it all looks genuine. There are accounts of mysterious deaths, all on eightieth birthdays and always the incumbent Lord Hale. One could write that off as coincidence, but the accounts all refer to the appearance of a creature. Also, the family has money. I cannot see their bank accounts, of course, but the Hale estate recently bought stocks in Berkshire Hathaway, Warren Buffet's firm.'

I whistled. The shares started at three-hundred grand a piece. 'So, what did you call for?'

'What do you know about demonology, inverted pentangles and missing girls?' She asked.

I had an immediate answer. 'Not a lot. I would recognise the inverted pentangle as a demon worship symbol but that's about it. What was that about missing girls? More specifically, what age do you mean when you say girls?'

'Sorry, I should have been more clear. I meant young women. We don't have a case by the way, it was more of a general question because of some feed trends I am reading.'

'Go on.' I encouraged.

'Some of the paraweb news sites, the conspiracy nuts and suchlike have reported the appearance of inverted pentangles which has led to a discussion about demon worship. I have been tracking it for over a week, purely for interest, then yesterday there was a report of two missing women that had been linked to the practice.'

'Local girls?' I asked.

'Both from Kent, but it doesn't say whether they have been seduced and run away to join them or have been snatched from their homes for something unpleasant. How's the Dockyard thing going?' She asked, switching topic.

I had been walking while I was chatting on the phone, my route taking me through the rabbit warren of Medway hospital to the Special Care Unit my dad was in. At the doors outside, I stopped to rub my hands with the alcohol gel stuff they expect everyone to use. Inside, one of the ladies on the reception desk had spotted me and buzzed the electronic doors open. I needed to finish up my call. 'It's proving to be bigger than I had thought. The ghost thing was nothing more than a distraction, a ruse to scare off staff they didn't want. I hope to have it sewn up in a few days.' That part was certainly true, but I deliberately didn't tell her about the organised crime gang I was antagonising, there was no need to make people worry. 'I have to go, I'm at the hospital to see my father.'

I promised to stop in at the office the next day and left her to get on with things as I pushed through the now unlocked door and went inside.

'Hello, Tempest.' Said the lady on reception, making me feel bad that she had memorised my name, but I hadn't even looked at hers. 'You got the message then.'

I raised my eyebrows. 'What message?'

Her quizzical look matched mine for a second before she said, 'Your dad is awake.'

I paused while the news processed through the outer limits of my brain, reached the decision-making bit of my head which sent a message to my feet. I ran to the room he was in without looking back or even thanking the nameless lady on reception.

In his room, dad was sitting up in bed while a doctor made notes in a manila folder.

'Hey, kid.' He said as I entered the room. Then he looked to the door behind me, 'Where's Mum?' He asked, wondering why she wasn't following. He didn't know I was here with Rachael.

Since he was very clearly feeling back to normal and was still being dealt with by a doctor, I pulled out my phone and dialled the number for mum's phone.

It rang for a while before she answered. 'Hello, Tempest. I'm still at my meeting. Has the baby arrived.'

'Yes, it has….'

I had stopped speaking because I could hear that she was no longer listening to me. She was speaking to other people at her end, no doubt the group of women she was with and she was now telling them about her latest grandchild.

'Well, come on, Tempest. Do I need blue wool or pink?'

I sighed. 'Dad's awake.' I blurted. It was the only way I could change the course of the conversation.

'Oh. Oh, jolly good. Now how about that wool?'

The news that her husband had woken up from a head injury which had kept him unconscious for several days was accepted, acknowledged and parked in favour of having something juicy to tell the ladies she was with. 'Pink, mother.' I supplied.

Again, I could hear the background babble of voices as the news was delivered. 'What is her name, Tempest?'

'I have no idea, mother. I…'

'Well, go and find out, Tempest.' My mother demanded, cutting me off yet again.

'Mother I would imagine the task of naming the child will be conducted only once Rachael's husband arrives. Now, if you please, my father is awake, and I am going to see him. Should we expect you here any time soon? Or is your meeting still the priority?' I was being a little harsh. My mother had always been able to compartmentalise her life. Dad was awake therefore she probably felt no further concern for his well-being and was content to focus on other things.

'Tell him I will be along shortly. Honestly, men are so needy. And tell your sister to text me the name of the baby.' With that she was gone.

The doctor was finishing up whatever checks he had been performing. While I had been on the phone losing a conversation to my mother, the doctor had been shining a light into my dad's eyes and moving his head around. He seemed satisfied, so was leaving. With a final instruction that my father should keep up his fluids and rest, he left.

'Hey, Dad.' I finally replied. 'How are you feeling?'

'Would you believe I am tired?' He asked, a wry smile on his face. 'Four days sleep and I wake up tired. Your mum will probably have a stack of jobs lined up for me because I haven't done anything for four days.'

'You might be right.' We both knew he was. 'I have been investigating at the Dockyard.' My announcement grabbed his attention. 'Did you know there were underground tunnels and rooms beneath the cobblestones?'

His surprised face told me he didn't. It was a well-kept secret that somehow the Ukrainians had found out about. 'Big Ben and I have taken jobs there as cleaners on the night shift.' He listened as I filled him in on the events of the last couple of days and what I had learned so far. As a tour guide on the ships during daylight hours, he was mostly shielded from events in other departments but had noticed the Ukrainians were slowly pushing everyone else out. He had heard about the ghosts and that several of the staff had quit after being scared by them. However, he had only been poking around in the rigging room because, like me, he had an inquisitive nature.

'Did you see your attacker?' I asked.

'I caught a reflection only, but it was a woman. A big one. With muscle to spare like one of the ladies you see doing shotput at the Olympic Games.'

Pasha.

'I believe I know who it was. Would you be able to positively identify her?' This was important because I was only really trying to catch the person that had hurt my dad. Now that I was embroiled in the case it would be hard to step away, but we were a little short staffed to be taking on an entire gang of criminals. If dad could point the finger of blame at one person, it might give the police the start point they needed to crack the gang's activities apart. Then I realised that I was being too hopeful. Yes, it might give the police a starting point, but it would take them too long to achieve anything and even if they did arrest Pasha, she would be out the next day, if not the same day. In the meantime, the gang would continue to operate, and the Dockyard would be a dangerous place to be. Most especially for my father as he would have identified one of the Ukrainians as a criminal and therefore identified himself to them as a target.

He shook his head no anyway. 'I only caught a brief glance. I don't think I saw her face and I doubt I would recognise her. If I picked her from a line up based on her muscles, I couldn't allow a jury to convict her. I just wouldn't be sure I had the right person.'

I was going to have to do this myself.

Then I remembered the baby. 'Oh, err. Rachael had her baby.' I said, turning around to deliver the news halfway out the door.

Dad looked at me. 'I seem to have missed a lot. When?'

I looked at my watch. 'Twenty-eight minutes ago.'

'Right. Is that why you are here without Mum?'

'Yes, it is. She had a little girl but hadn't named it before I left.'

'I wonder if they will let me visit her.' Dad was looking around for his call button to summon a nurse.

I saw the folly in his intentions. 'Perhaps it will be best to wait until she can visit you. Chris is on his way with the kids and mum will no doubt be along later as well.' He looked unconvinced. He was bored with being in bed and wanted to do things. I understood how he felt, but I also knew how deceptive head wounds could be. 'Also, you only just came around. If you get woozy or are still suffering any ill-effects, you won't know about them until it is too late.'

He made a disappointed face but accepted the wisdom of my words. 'Are you off again? Back to the Dockyard to tackle the case?'

'Not right now, no. It's Jagjit's stag do today.'

'Oh, is that today. Hold on, what day is it?'

'Wednesday, November 23rd.'

'Wednesday.' He repeated. 'Isn't that an odd day for a stag do?'

'Some might say, but it is today for several reasons starting with because it is an Indian family, so the wedding starts on Friday. If we had it Thursday night instead, which is kind of the same thing, we would run the risk of hangovers. This way any ill-effects from overindulgence will be gone before the big event and it was the only day I could book the events I wanted. It was all very short notice.'

He nodded his head. 'Fair enough.'

I checked my watch again. 'I need to get going actually. My dogs are at your house, so I have a round trip to perform before I can get to the venue.'

'Okay, kid. Have fun. I should be out of here tomorrow. Maybe then I can help you at the Dockyard, be your inside man perhaps?'

My instant reaction was that I didn't want to involve him in what I considered to be a dangerous situation. I didn't say that though. I hadn't explained to him about the Ukrainians, not in any detail anyway, so I gave him a thumbs up. If they did let him out and mum didn't put a ban on him leaving the house, then I would tackle it.

Even though I could feel the time ticking away, I went back to the maternity ward to catch up with Rachael and the new baby. Enough time had passed that they had moved her out of the delivery room to a much nicer room where there was a proper bed for her and a TV and a crib thing for the tiny infant.

I knocked on the door, waited and went in when I heard Rachael say, 'Come in.'

She was dressed in a hospital issue gown, robe and slippers and was laying on the bed. An empty tea cup was cooling on the night stand next to the bed while in her hands a plate showed the remaining crumbs of a recently devoured sandwich. The TV was on, some daytime soap I didn't recognise, but Rachael was looking at the baby instead.

'Have you named her?' I asked.

She shook her head. 'I will wait until Chris arrives, but we have discussed it. I like Summer as a name. possibly Summer-Storm. Dad would like that.'

She jolted my memory. 'Dad's awake.' She looked up in surprise. 'Sorry, I should have led with that. I didn't know myself until I arrived at the ward. He is talking and sitting up and says he feels fine. He wants to come to the Dockyard with me to solve the case there.'

'That sounds about right. The two of you are the same. Nothing is allowed to slow you down for long.' I almost argued, she was right though, that was how I approached life.

I checked my watch yet again. Rachael saw the motion. 'Do you need to be somewhere?' She asked.

'Kind of. It's Jagjit's stag do today. He gets married this weekend and I am best man.'

Her eyes widened then she started shooing motions. 'Go, Tempest, get gone. I don't need you here. I will join the baby shortly and have a nap. Go have fun.'

'Okay.' I said with some relief. I crossed the room to kiss her cheek then left the room and started hauling ass. I had less than seventy minutes before I was due at the venue and about seventy-five minutes of stuff to do first. I was supposed to be getting picked up so that I could leave my car at home, but couldn't see any way of achieving that without making more people late.

By the time I got to the car park I was jogging.

Man stuff. Wednesday, November 23rd 1600hrs

Getting across to my parent's house to collect the dogs was easy enough, but by the time I tried to get from there to my house the schools had kicked out and the roads were clogged with mums in cars.

Sitting in my car, I had watched the minutes tick away unable to do anything about it. When I finally got home, the walk I had wanted to give the dogs before dropping them off next door became an abridged run around the garden to make sure they were empty of waste fluids. They got a treat from the jar and a hug before I dropped them off at Mrs Comerforth's for the third time that week. Then I had to run back into my house to grab a fast shower and a change of clothing.

We would be driving adapted race cars for the next two hours so I used the thirty-minute drive to Brands Hatch race track as a warm up in my nippy, red Porsche. The fact that I made it in thirty minutes, testament to how fast I had driven as it should have taken closer to forty-five.

At 1600hrs, I had been there less than a minute and was just coming into the bar where Jagjit, Big Ben and the others were gathered.

The eleven chaps were already in their race suits, a one-piece leather outfit designed to make the wearer feel like a race car driver. A young chap asked me my size on the way in before scurrying away to fetch another one for me. Another gentleman, this one older and vaguely familiar, was addressing the chaps who were all seated in a single row in front of a lay out of the track. He was explaining how the afternoon would proceed and about racing lines and how to get the best out of the event.

Then, just as I was about to take my seat, I saw him. Two in from the far left, sitting next to Kit was his friend Ian. The one that knew Jagjit but Kit couldn't remember how.

Well, I knew how. He had arrested him. And me. And Big Ben. And several other people I knew. It was Chief Inspector Ian Quinn.

Now the comments about not being able to make friends in his job made sense. Kit looked to be early forties, which made the two men about the same age. Kit claimed they went to school together, although I hadn't enquired whether he meant University or a younger period in their lives.

This threw a curve ball into the day and I had to wonder how Jagjit felt about it. I would find out soon enough. For now, the chap standing in front and talking was in full-flow and had indicated for me to take a seat. All heads turned as his attention lifted from those seated, so I gave a quick wave of hello as I took a chair and tried really hard not to scowl at CI Quinn.

Just then, the young man that had scurried away to find my race suit returned.

As it turned out, Jagjit hadn't even recognised Ian Quinn. They had been introduced only briefly and the subject of where he knew Jagjit from had not arisen.

'He arrested you.' Big Ben pointed out when I asked. 'Or rather, he had you arrested.'

Jagjit's jaw had dropped. 'Let's all play nice now that we are here, shall we?' My tone was aimed at Big Ben and demanded compliance. It was a well-established fact that I was the sensible one in the group. The one that would do the right thing and could be relied upon to be diplomatic. In the same way, Big Ben was labelled as the one most likely to take offence and push someone's head through a wall.

Big Ben muttered something that rhymed rather well with mucking runt but promised to be agreeable for the duration of the stag party. I crossed the room to speak with CI Quinn.

'Ian, this is something of a surprise. When I emailed thebigchief@bossnet.com I had no idea the Ian I addressed it to would turn out to be you.'

'I see. Am I to assume I am not welcome?' He asked, his tone guarded.

Kit, who was standing next to him looked quite taken aback. 'What's going on chaps?' He asked. 'Is there something I should know?' He looked poised to step between us.

I smiled as congenially as I could. 'Not at all. Ian and I know each other through work and have never had the chance to socialise before.'

'Yes.' CI Quinn joined in, 'Yes, we met through police business as Tempest here is a detective.'

'Oh, I know.' Said Kit. 'Getting quite famous too. Jagjit is always telling us about your adventures.' Kit was addressing me now so didn't see the briefest sign of displeasure sweep across Ian's face. To his credit Ian quelled it no sooner than it arose.

He caught himself at that point, clapped his hands together loudly then raised them in the air. 'What say you, chaps? A wager on the winner today?' Our relationship had always been adversarial, but for now at least, we were going to tolerate each other and act as if we were nothing more than two chaps out to celebrate another man's loss of singledom.

I pulled out my wallet. 'I say fifty pounds per man, winner gets the first round.' I held aloft a crisp fifty pounds note, someone produced a clean pint glass and the notes started going into in. Everyone had come cash-heavy, ready for a night on the town. Having been first to support Ian, I moved away to let others get to the pint glass he was holding.

Then I saw my mistake. Basic was behind me. Jagjit's brothers were in banking and real estate, Big Ben had a huge inheritance, I was a successful business owner and Basic parked shopping trolleys at a local supermarket for a living. As my cheeks warmed, I quickly crafted a lie I thought he would believe: That his mother had given me some money for him to spend.

I went over to deliver my well-intended falsehood to find him pulling his wallet from his back pocket. It was a mangy-looking canvas thing with a Velcro strap that was stuck up with all manner of fluff. Before I could open my mouth, he lifted a crisp fifty pounds note of his own and walked by me to deposit it.

'Hi, Tempest.' He said in passing. Then, 'I never had a fifty before. They look funny and they don't really fit in my wallet.'

He was right in that they were too large for many wallets. The Royal Mint's odd habit of making notes increase in size along with value made the fifty almost ungainly in size. I worried he had just spent half his week's wages.

'Have you been saving for today?' I asked, trying to work up to the lie about his mum giving me money.

'No. I have lots of money now, Tempest.'

Jagjit was within earshot. 'Haven't you heard?' He asked as he turned to face us. 'Basic is an entrepreneur.'

I waited for the punchline, not wanting to say anything that might be offensive. When no one spoke, I gave up waiting and requested, 'Do tell.'

'I sell guitars.' Said Basic.

I couldn't help the quizzical eyebrow from lifting. I had never once heard Basic talk about guitars or suggest at any point that he was even slightly musical. 'Do you make them?' I asked.

In return, Basic looked at me like I was being particularly thick. 'No, Tempest. The guitars don't exist.'

Now I was really confused.

Jagjit laughed but came to the rescue. 'Our good friend, Basic, discovered that he can sell air-guitars online.'

'You have to be joking.' I didn't know what other response I could come up with.

'Nope.' Basic was grinning like the Cheshire Cat.

'Shall I tell the story?' Jagjit asked Basic. When Basic nodded, he turned his attention back to me. The chap that had been giving instruction on the racing event when I walked in, was now calling us all to proceed to the track. As we walked, Jagjit started talking. 'James,' He used Basic's real name for once, 'filmed himself messing around playing air-guitar to an ACDC track a few weeks ago, just one of those random things you do when you are bored. He uploaded it to YouTube and as these things sometimes go, it started spreading. Then he came up with the idea of advertising signed copies of his air-guitar for sale via a well-known social media platform and linked that to the video feed.'

'What's going on?' Asked Hilary because we were dawdling behind everyone else. 'You are going to be last on the track.'

'Never mind that. Listen to this.' I said.

Jagjit backtracked slightly to catch Hilary up on the story so far, then pressed on. 'So, anyway. It was just a bit of a joke. Wasn't it, Basic?'

'S'right.' He agreed.

'But then they were actually selling. They are ninety-nine cents with a seventy percent profit margin and purchases are global.'

'How many?' I asked. 'How many sales?'

'Basic?' Jagjit prompted.

'Dunno.' He replied.

'Let's just say it's a lot and the sales graph is going up still.'

I shook my head in awe. Maybe it took someone with Basic's intelligence to come up with such an idea. I doubted it would even occur to me. 'What's next? Film yourself on a skateboard and sell the wicked airtime?'

I had been joking but Basic was clearly giving the idea some serious thought.

'Oi, Jizz weasels. Get in your cars. It's time to race.' Big Ben was always a delight. 'Or in your cases, it's time to lose like the snot-soaked, Justin Bieber t-shirt wearing, limp-wristed losers you are.'

His goading got us moving. The cars were lined up like you would find in a Grand Prix race and each car had a co-driver that was there to guide us through how best to handle the car we would be racing. As I got to mine, deferring to Basic, Hilary and of course Jagjit so that mine was last on the grid, the cars at the front were already peeling away.

The two-hour slot we had bought got us fifteen minutes of orientation, thirty minutes of instruction, thirty minutes of racing and thirty minutes of free drinks as we watched the action as filmed by a number of remote and manned cameras around the track. It wasn't a cheap afternoon which would have been enough motivation for the chaps to want to make the most out of it, but the wager had ensured we were all chomping at the bit to get the race underway. Six-hundred pounds wouldn't change anyone's life, but it would look fat in anyone's wallet.

By 1700hrs, we had finished our practise laps, stretched our legs and taken on water. Now we were back in our cars and waiting to go. The cars had been arranged on the grid according to lap times recorded during our practise laps, just like they would on a Grand Prix. I was tenth somehow, which I had decided was due to my car being faulty. I drove a Porsche every day. Surely, I should be better at this than anyone. My disappointment was only slightly mollified by Big Ben sitting dead last. I put this down to the cars all being equal and him weighing fifty pounds more than anyone else. He also had to drive with his head on slightly sideways. His daft height and the full racing helmet for safety meant even scooching down in his seat didn't really work.

The bank of lights ahead of us turned from red to green resulting in the engine noise cranking up to the accompanying sound of wheels spinning and the twelve race cars blasted away from the grid.

Stag Night. Wednesday, November 23rd 2051hrs

My stomach was filled to capacity with dinner, but the steak the size of a box folder had absorbed some of the beer I had drunk just when I was starting to feel its effects. The food had been glorious, rich and decadent. It was a meal to remember and capped the afternoon off perfectly.

The after-action review of the race was still going, there didn't seem to be room for another topic of conversation. All twelve of us had dispensed with any form of transportation, along with any sense of sobriety, the moment we arrived in Rochester. My car was parked in its usual spot behind my office with the other cars piled in around it. There was a rather tenuous plan to fetch the cars early tomorrow morning so they would not cause a problem when Jane and Amanda arrived just before 0900hrs. Looking at the drinks now flowing through the group, I wasn't sure anyone would make it back in time.

It was a minor concern though, I had already sent them both a text to say I would reimburse any parking fee they needed to pay elsewhere, and Amanda had said she was working late and would not be in first thing.

I shot my cuff to check my watch: 2051hrs. I needed the gents. Thirty seconds later, with Mr. Wriggly performing his less interesting function, I started worrying about the case. It was far from ideal that I had taken today off. Would they even let Big Ben and me back in for our cleaning shift tomorrow? Our absence today could not be helped, and we had both called in sick but the Dockyard business was not one that struck me as being concerned about employee's rights given their willingness to hand out a beating for turning up.

We would go back anyway and see what happened. If more extraordinary measures were called for, like breaking in because next time they denied us access completely, then so be it. I wasn't worried about getting caught trespassing and arrested, the police would release us without charge once I could get a message to CI Quinn, however, I wasn't sure they would bother handing us over if caught. They were capable, possibly even inclined toward murder. It was a concern. I wasn't stopping though.

On my way back to the bar I used my phone to call Joseph. The music in the bar was loud, but not so oppressive that conversation was impossible, but further into the bar, in the utility area I found myself in now, it was quite quiet. I ducked into an alcove when he came on the line.

'Dobryj den.' He answered, speaking Ukrainian to maintain his cover.

'Joseph, it's Tempest. Are you able to talk?'

He whispered quietly, 'One moment.' Then spoke at normal volume in Ukrainian again, most likely pretending the caller was his girlfriend or his mum or something. He could have been saying anything, the words were gibberish to my ears. 'Yes, I can talk.' He said after a few seconds.

'I'm just checking in. How's it going?'

'No problems. I was immediately accepted and welcomed. I am quite the hit with the almost-all female cleaning crew in fact, although I will say there is an air of disappointment that someone called Big Ben is not here tonight. Is that your colleague?'

I sighed. It was always all about Big Ben where the ladies were concerned. 'Yes, that's him.'

'Well, there are several ladies here of varying ages that have plans for him, if you know what I mean.'

'Well, tell them he will be back tomorrow if you can do that without blowing your cover. What have they got you doing?'

'I am emptying bins. According to Pasha, the lady in charge, the two useless, weak English goluboi's, that's Ukrainian for homosexuals, didn't turn up today so someone else needed to do it. They paired me with an older man, but it was clearly a bit much for him, so I found him a warm place to rest and have got on with it by myself. I am poking around as I go.'

Good. This was good. After his promise to find his way into the tunnels earlier today I had worried that my overly adventurous and confident new acquaintance might do something rash like ask where the bad guys were and then try to arrest them all. He was playing it cautious and sensible though.

Tomorrow, with three of us there, we could make a concerted effort to find the landside tunnel entrance. Even though we had identified the river entrance, it appeared to be guarded. Big Ben and I could borrow some scuba gear and maybe get in undetected underwater to avoid being chased off by the boats. Not impossible, but also not simple either.

'Roger. Stay safe. Let's touch base in the morning and agree on a plan of action, yes?'

'What time do you start work?' He asked.

'I'll be in my office for 0900hrs. Does that suit you?'

'Perfect. I'll see you then.' We disconnected. My concerns were somewhat placated. Pasha was making fun of us but had not verbally committed to others that we were not returning so she was expecting to see us again even if she was hoping we had quit.

Back at the bar, Aditya had a drink for me. 'Here you go, Tempest.' He handed me a fresh pint. 'I'm not sure how many more of these I can drink. I took tomorrow to recover from today, well done for arranging the stag party for today to give us recovery time by the way.' We clinked glasses in salute to my great planning. 'Then it's the wedding all weekend.'

'Well, that should give you time to forgive Vihann for cutting you up on the last corner to win the race then.'

He frowned. 'Maybe.'

The race had been competitive from the start, everyone tearing away from the line to make the first corner. We had ten laps to complete, however it was clear by the end of the first that there were only three cars in with a chance of winning. Aditya, Vihann and Hilary. The five Singh brothers had fought each other though, their efforts aimed more at beating their siblings than at winning the race as if old brotherly disputes over whose turn on the Scalextric it was were now being settled. My tactic to hang just a bit off the lead and let them tussle it out before swooping in to win at the end proved folly, but I had been happy with fifth place. There were more people behind me than ahead, unlike Big Ben who had started last and finished last and would be smarting about it for years to come.

The only disappointment was that Ian Quinn had beaten me. He came up the inside of me on the penultimate lap, cutting off my driving line as we approached a vital corner. I had been forced to go wide to avoid a collision which gave away my position. He then doggedly prevented me from passing, his effort seemingly focused on keeping me behind him instead of trying to catch the car in front. It was the sly grin he had given me as he cut me up that was stuck in my craw though.

I had put it down to the excitement of the race, but I couldn't shake the feeling that he had gone into the event with the sole aim of making sure he finished ahead of me.

I was standing at the bar, chatting with Jagjit about his planned honeymoon when I spotted a face I knew, then I noticed that conversation in the bar had dropped significantly. The face I saw was Brunilda's, the sexy as anything brunette I had met briefly at Big Ben's penthouse suite on Monday. She was in the bar and leading a procession of other gorgeous women. All had on cocktail dresses that contained very little material, high heels and little else. They were all clearly cold from being outside, but the door was open and there was still more coming in. I could already count twenty.

Big Ben, never easy to lose sight of, towering over everyone else as he did, was greeting them all and handing a credit card to the barman.

He leaned across so we would hear him, 'I told the girls there was a bachelor party and I needed them all to look sexy and mingle.'

They had managed the first part of the task easily enough. Big Ben started handing out drinks to the ladies and kissing cheeks. A couple of them got a playful smack on their rumps which was warmly received by each of them. He was a master at work.

As a space opened up at the bar next to us, Big Ben stepped into it, accompanied by a dozen or more beautiful women all sipping sparkling wine from tall fluted glasses.

'I felt there was a need to liven things up and you were insistent that there be no strippers, so I compromised. I can't guarantee that they will all keep their clothes on though, a couple of them do like to dance and just happen to work in gentlemen's clubs.'

'So, by default, you managed to invite strippers anyway.' I laughed.

'Only sort of. Anyway, Jagjit, as it's your stag do, last night as a single man and all that, why don't you pick one? My treat.'

Jagjit's jaw dropped as the gaggle of gorgeous women all smiled at him. An athletic blonde woman in her early twenties with green eyes like emeralds, smouldered at Jagjit in a way that would have made Mr. Wriggly burst out through the front of my trousers had it been aimed at me. I swear she made her nipples harden on command as they were suddenly visible through the sheer fabric of her dress.

'Only joking.' Big Ben said. Jagjit exhaled in relief. I understood his plight, such temptations are easy to resist when there is no way you can make it happen anyway, but far less so when put on a plate in front of you. He didn't want to go into marriage having just cheated on his intended any more than I would. Big Ben wasn't done though, 'You can have three.' He said with a laugh.

I couldn't tell if he was serious or not, or even begin to work out how the ladies before us were his to command. Jagjit said, 'I'd better pass, thanks all the same.' Just in case the offer was genuine.

As the girls filed away, some of them looking genuinely disappointed, Jagjit grabbed my arm, 'Dude I need a stiff drink like right friggin now. I'm freaking out, man.'

I waved for the bartender's attention, 'What's up, buddy.' I asked while I waited for the man to finish serving his customer.

'Am I crazy?'

'I need some context, mate.'

'I'm getting married this weekend to a girl I met a month ago. Did you see all those amazing women just then? I'm not just getting married, I'm giving up any chance to ever be with them or anyone like them or anyone ever again for that matter.'

The bartender arrived, took my order of single malt doubles, Irish not Scotch and I waited for them to be served before answering. Damn Big Ben and his stupidly attractive harem of women. Jagjit had been rock solid until sixty seconds ago.

I handed Jagjit his drink as I paid with my card then grabbed mine from the bar intending to sniff the heady scents and savour it while trying to come up with something wise to say about the conflict between head and heart. With my glass in my hand I turned back to face Jagjit.

He slammed his empty glass down on the bar and signalled the barman for another.

So much for savouring it.

'Jagjit, you need to calm down. The only thing that has changed since you were talking so animatedly about your lovely Alice an hour ago is that a bevy of unapproachable, untouchable, unrealistically perfect women got wafted under your nose.' I sipped my drink. He was served a second glass which I had to intercept on its way to his face. He was about to down a second large hit of very alcoholic whisky. 'Tell me when you last had any form of relationship or even interaction with a woman that looked like any one of them.'

'Err, I haven't.' He admitted, feeling that he was making a valid point.

'Exactly.' I replied. 'Normal men like you and I don't get to have relationships with women that look like that and I, for one, am glad about it.'

Jagjit considered that for a moment before shaking his head. 'Nope. No, you're going to have to explain this to me. Why is it that I don't want to have sex with the perfect women?'

'Precisely because they are perfect, mate. I'm going to hit you with some wisdom. Are you ready?'

'Um, I think so?' He asked, confused now.

'Really attractive women are terrible in bed.'

'Who cares?' He implored.

'Exactly, mate. Guys don't care, so the perfect women never get to be good in bed because the men they end up with only demand that they turn up. They don't have to try. They get used to men following them around dribbling and offering them things because men are just so utterly crap. You think any of those girls has had to buy a drink this year?'

He had no answer. 'What number is Alice on the hot scale? If those girls are a ten, what score is Alice?'

Jagjit looked a little stunned although it might be the whisky hitting his system and making him woozy, not the power of my wisdom making him look dumb. 'I'm going to say a nine?'

'At least.' I agreed. 'Your lady is one hot number. If you don't go through with the wedding, if you decide that you have been hasty, then it has to be for a better reason than because there are other women on the planet and they have tits too.'

'Fair point.' He conceded. He took a sip of his drink. 'This is good stuff.'

I nodded my agreement.

We were silent for a while. Across the bar, Big Ben's entourage of perfect women were getting a lot of attention from the other men and women in the place. There were several girlfriends with unhappy faces trying to get their boyfriend's attention back.

'Thanks, Tempest. You're a good best man.'

I clapped him on the back. 'Don't sweat it. You're entitled to one wobble. Do you need to rethink the wedding?' I was testing him. No matter what had been spent or who he would hurt, if he really was rushing in and needed time, then he had to take it. He would do more harm marrying her and learning his mistake only later.

'No. No, I'm good. Alice is wonderful.'

'You've been saying that for weeks.'

Jagjit had a distant look to his face and was swirling his whisky in his glass when Ian Quinn approached us.

'Chaps, I wanted to thank you for a thoroughly entertaining evening. Kit assured me I would be accepted, although I was dubious given how we met, I must say that I have learned I sometimes form opinions that prove to be false.' I inclined my head in a gesture that said, "I know". 'I have to go, I'm afraid. I am on duty in the morning at five o'clock.'

We all shook hands and watched as he weaved his way through the bar saying goodnight to all the other stag night attendees. As he went out the door a whoop went up and I thought for a moment the two events were linked until I saw Basic standing on a table playing air-guitar as Big Ben's ladies cheered him on.

Seeing the attention Basic was getting, one of the bartenders put the volume up. In seconds, the girls were dancing around him like he was a genuine Rockstar. Phones were coming out around the bar, random people filming the scruffy, air-guitar playing, crazy-haired doofus. Egged on by the crowd around him, Basic redoubled his effort and he must have known what the track was when he got started because it was nearing the end and had become a magnificent guitar solo.

On the last chord, and with an almighty sweep of his arm to strike the last note, he jumped into the air to land on his knees among the baying crowd at his feet. There was an almighty cheer and applause, which Jagjit and I had to join in with and girls were kissing him, not just one or two, but damned near all the hot women were pawing him, touching him and kissing his face.

Finished with his act and with the crowd now settling back down, he actually mimed taking off his air-guitar and placing it on a stand before coming to the bar with an empty glass. I guess playing the air-guitar is thirsty work.

I bought him a drink and shook his hand as I marvelled at the hidden depths one sometimes cannot even perceive in the people that are closest to us.

'Dat was fun.' He said, a smile splitting his face.

Dat is going to sell even more air-guitars.

The thought played through my head and I had to consider that maybe Basic was an absolute genius sheathed in the body of a Neanderthal and not the lumbering dopey ox we all took him to be.

'Hey, where did you go?' Asked a delightfully petite Japanese girl. Not one of Big Ben's thankfully, her interest in Basic looked real. 'That was really fun, can I buy you a drink?' She asked him.

'Sure fing.' He replied.

I backed away a pace to give her room at the bar next to him. Basic was taller than me, though his height was a mystery as he never stood up straight. The young lady, in contrast was at least a foot shorter than him and she had on heels.

'What's happening?' Jagjit whispered in my ear. I was just as mystified as he was. The lady had her purse in one hand and her other hand was on Basic's arm as it rested on the bar. She was being tactile and playful.

'I need to learn to play the air-guitar.' It was the only answer I had for the magic trick unfolding in front of me.

As the dutiful best man, I stayed until the very end and made sure I escorted Jagjit to his door, which is to say I paid for the taxi we were both in and had the driver wait in the road outside his parent's house until he was safely inside. It was his last night living there, although in truth he had moved out a week ago to move in with Alice and moved back in to his parent's place two days ago so he wouldn't see the bride before the wedding. I hadn't asked but it was probably something Alice had requested.

It was 0043hrs when I wobbled ever so slightly over the threshold and into my house. The two wonderful dogs I live with came to greet me at the door, stretching and yawning themselves. My arrival would have woken them from a deep sleep on the sofa. They were pleased to see me and just as pleased to exit the house via the back door so they could water the garden and bark at imaginary creatures.

I found enough energy to make overnight oats for the morning, fill a glass with water to take to bed and clean the scuzz of the day from my teeth before I flopped weary and happy into bed.

I drifted into a contented sleep, but I wouldn't have if I had known what was happening at the Dockyard.

Rude Awakening. Thursday, November 24th 0800hrs

I was woken by the muffled sound of my phone ringing. I had forgotten to switch it to silent, but when I saw the time, I ruefully acknowledged that it was time to get up anyway.

I had a faint buzzing at the back of my skull when I sat up, the barest trace of a hangover which might have been far worse had I not stayed off the alcohol until we reached the pub after dinner and then bought myself a bottle of water every third drink. Most of the chaps had taken today off and were at the wedding tomorrow so had attacked the bar with abandon. I would be suffering had I attempted the same.

The phone was inside a sock. How it got there would be one of those mysteries one never solves. The missed call was from Alan Page and I had three missed calls from Joseph plus two text messages.

I called Alan first. 'Good morning, Alan.' I said as he answered the phone.

'Mr. Michaels there has been another development.'

I sat up sharply. 'Another death?'

'No. Not that I am aware of. I always get here for about half past seven in the morning. Me and a few of the other boys use the time before we start at nine for a bit of practice. Anyway, we usually see the two Daves and recently we have been making a deliberate habit of meeting up. They are coming off shift as they finish at eight and we are all just arriving.' I waited patiently for him to arrive at the point. 'They weren't here this morning. Neither one of them and I checked the log; they both started their shift last night.'

A sense of dread was settling in my gut. My gut that was still bruised as a reminder of the violence the Ukrainians were willing to perpetrate.

'Have you tried calling them?'

'Of course. Neither one is answering their phones. I can't leave now that I am here, but I was hoping you could go to their houses and check if they are there. Maybe they got fired or something.'

I had Alan give me the phone number and address for Dave McKinnon as I already knew where Dave Saunders lived and told him I would make it my first task.

Then I called Joseph. While I was in the bar last night, he had been acting the role of Ukrainian cleaner to poke about and see what he could learn from the other cleaners. I wasn't sure there was anything to learn from them, but he would be able to glean what information they did have far more easily than Big Ben and me.

He didn't answer his phone though, it went to voicemail instead. Rather than leave a message, I checked the text he sent.

My heart plummeted as I read it.

I think I have found the entrance to the underground. There are stone steps leading down into the dark. I cannot raise you, so I am proceeding. I will send you video footage of what I find.

I clicked on the second text message. Sure enough, it was video footage. The forty-two second clip started playing, displaying the shaky hand-held image one always gets. It was dark, but I could make out what appeared to be a damp and curving wall.

An underground tunnel.

The camera advanced a couple of feet, the picture then showing the view around a corner. A large room came into focus. Soft overhead lights provided illumination, the cables to power them draped loosely across the floor. What I could instantly see was perhaps two dozen people operating machines and boxes upon boxes of branded cigarettes. The quality of the picture was too indistinct to make out the faces of any of the people. It was evidence though.

'Tell me how you got in.' I pleaded, my voice a quiet hiss as if any noise I made might be heard by the people in the video.

The clip ended.

Dammit.

I tried calling him again. I had told him not to do anything alone. Still no answer.

Three men missing. The Daves might be at home asleep having finished early or something but it felt like a hopeful stretch. My money was on the Ukrainians having done something with them.

Swearing under my breath, I sent CI Quinn the message containing the video clip and called him. After weeks of trying to get to him through the main switchboard at Maidstone police station or having to go there in person, I now had his mobile number. I got it more than two weeks ago when I was setting up the stag party but hadn't realised who the Ian in question was.

'Chief Inspector Quinn.' He answered.

'Ian it's Tempest. I just sent you a video clip. Young Joseph has... is not answering his phone. Have you heard from him?' I picked my words carefully, not wanting to say that he had gone missing because I didn't not know that to be the case.

'I have not heard from him.' He said slowly. 'Are you saying he is missing?'

'He reported that he had found the entrance to the underground system I told you about. Against my advice he went in by himself, the clip is from him and shows the underground facility at the Dockyard and the illegal manufacture of counterfeit cigarettes. I haven't heard from him since. Whether he has switched his phone off and is still sneaking about or has been discovered, I cannot say.'

'So where is the entrance that he found?'

'He didn't say. Check the video.' I was unhappy about admitting how little I knew, even though Joseph wasn't my charge or my responsibility, I still felt I had a duty to keep him safe.

'Wait please.' I waited while he watched the clip. 'The footage could be taken anywhere.' He concluded.

He was right but would have to be a moron to believe it was anywhere other than below the Dockyard.

'He didn't… Hold on, where are you?' CI Quinn asked.

'At home. I just got up. Also, I should tell you that my father woke up yesterday. He remembers only vague details about the person that attacked him, I think I know who it is, the same person oversaw a beating for me on Tuesday, but a positive ID will not be possible.'

'Nor helpful.' He agreed. 'I need the whole gang, not some lesser minion. If you still don't know the way into whatever might be beneath the Dockyard, then there is little I can do at this time.'

'Your man might be missing Quinn. At what point do you organise a rescue? When his body turns up? Or shall we move before that?' I was pushing him to do more than he was willing to.

'Mr Michaels.' We were back on last name terms it seemed. 'Thus far the only reason my man is even there is due to hearsay on your part. I have taken a leap of faith because I will reluctantly admit that you have a knack for being right. I have no evidence though. Nothing I can reliably use.' He added when he heard me begin to protest. 'What you have sent me is not proof that there is a base of criminal operations beneath the Dockyard. It is not sufficient to justify deploying more resources. Even if I wanted to raid the place, I would never be able to get the Superintendent to endorse it.' It was the first time I had ever heard him refer to someone superior as if it pained him to not be ruler of the universe. 'No, I'm sorry, Mr Michaels. My hands are tied for now.'

'Until I risk my life to break in to the criminal's base of ops and deliver you a risk-free excuse to do your job?' I snapped in response. 'What will your excuse be when they fish Joseph's body from the river later?' I pressed the red button to disconnect the call, once again at loggerheads with the Chief Inspector. Our truce had not lasted long.

I frowned as I organised my thoughts. The bottom line was that I needed to act soon. Really soon. The two Daves were missing, as was detective sergeant Kushnir and no one was going to help them unless I did. There was a chance they didn't need rescuing, but I wasn't prepared to take that chance.

I got off the bed and started moving. I needed a shower, but it could wait. I made do with some deodorant and aftershave, even though I didn't shave, and a quick brush of my teeth.

I yelled, 'Come on, dogs.' Along the corridor to rouse them. As usual they ignored me, content and warm in the duvet. With some exaggerated stomping to get to the bedroom, I scooped them, one under each arm and took them downstairs to start their day as well. Of course, their day consisted mostly of sleeping anyway so I could never understand why they resisted their few chances for activity so much.

I called Jane. I figured she would be on her way to the office by now. It was 0831hrs and as it turned out she had already arrived.

'Everything alright?' I asked when she answered in a tone that suggested it was not.

'Yup. It's just really freezing this morning.' I looked out my window. There was a slight frost. Civilians tended to exaggerate about the cold. I kept quiet about it, but in my head, I acknowledged that they had no idea what cold was. Jane fell firmly into that subset, although she has so little body fat and was so slight that perhaps she felt it more keenly than most.

'Jane, I need you to check a few things this morning. I might not make it to the office at all today, but I also might be able to wrap up the Dockyard case and get back to paid cases.'

'Okay, Boss. What do you need?' I relayed my requests to her, laying out what I knew and what I suspected and what I specifically wanted her to look for. 'You're not in tomorrow either are you? It's your friend's wedding, right?'

'That's right.' I had almost forgotten. What I believed I needed to do today had no guaranteed end time on it, which might make tomorrow a little problematic. I had no intention of being late for the wedding but equally I wasn't going to leave men in harm's way either. First, I had to establish that they were in harm's way, of course.

We ended the call and as Jane got to work on the latest problem, I went out the door. Sliding into my car, I thought about something that had been niggling away at me since Monday. Something I had seen that didn't add up. I still wasn't sure what it meant, but if I looked at it from a certain perspective, a lot of what was confusing me about the Dockyard suddenly made sense.

My plan to quickly check on the two Daves proved to be less swift than I had hoped. Traffic through the Medway towns is awful between 0700hrs and 1000hrs every day. School run mums and people going to work clog the main arteries, so my short trip back to Dave Saunder's place in Gillingham took almost an hour and was bumper to bumper almost the whole way.

He still wasn't answering the phone and he didn't respond to my thumping on the door either. A neighbour came out of her house two doors down.

When she saw me, she said, 'His car's not here.' As she checked up and down the road.

'What does he drive please?' I asked. If I could find it still parked at the Dockyard it would provide a clear indication that he had arrived at work last night and never left.

'A tatty old, grey Honda Civic with one blue wing.' She had her keys in her hand and was getting into her car whether I had more questions or not. I thanked her and turned back to my car as she peeled away from the kerb.

The natural route out of Gillingham took me back to the Dockyard. I was following his neighbour most of the way, her eyes flicking to her rear-view mirror constantly once she saw me behind her. Her paranoia that I was some nutter finally relieved when I took the Dockyard turning.

As I went through the gate to the carpark, Jane called. It was a short conversation in which I mostly listened, and she relayed information to me that confirmed what I had thought likely to be true. It was 1002hrs when I pulled on my handbrake and got out of my car. There were coaches in the carpark already and a stream of recently arrived schoolchildren making their way across to the entrance. Otherwise the carpark was mostly empty, and it was easy to spot the car Dave's neighbour had described.

It was parked on the far right-hand side of the carpark against a hedge with a number of other cars. The concentration of cars in one area made it look like this was where the staff had elected, or perhaps were instructed to park. Whatever the case, his car was still here so he had not left last night.

It was evidence enough to convince me that he, and by association, the other Dave, had met with an unfortunate situation. What that meant exactly, I had no idea, but it wasn't good. If they were being held here, they were not necessarily dead but the longer I took to find them, the greater the likelihood they would meet with an unfortunate end.

I was ill-prepared, but I was going in anyway.

I locked my car, pulled out my phone and called Big Ben.

'Hey, buddy. What's happening?'

'The Daves are missing.' I included both even though I hadn't confirmed anything regarding Dave McKinnon. If he was home safely sleeping in his bed it made no difference to my need to find Dave Saunders, or Joseph for that matter.

'What's our play?' It was a simple question that meant everything in one go. He was in no matter what, by my side until we won even though he had no idea what we were getting into.

'Are you sure you want to do this?' I asked. I knew what he would say, because it was what I would say too. I had to provide an exit option though.

He said, 'There are some Ukrainians I owe a slap. I would hate to miss my chance.'

Okay then. I had the vaguest sense of a plan.

'Is that it?' He asked when I finished outlining it to him. 'That's your plan.'

'Yup.'

'It's a little thin mate.'

He wasn't wrong. There was a piece of the case that didn't add up. It had been bugging me since Monday although I had only realised what it was this morning. Now that Jane had confirmed it, I wanted to test a theory.

I would be right or wrong.

'What if you are wrong?' He asked.

It was a valid concern. 'Then I am in trouble.'

'Oh. Well, you've thought about it then. For the record, I don't think this is a good idea.'

'Neither do I. If you come up with an alternative plan, please let me hear it.'

'How soon are you going in?'

That was the question. If I waited for other playing pieces to reach their position on the board, I risked whatever fate might be in store for the two Daves and Joseph to reach its appointed time. Time was not my friend. Besides, my plan had a distinct chance of failing two minutes after I started so I would be looking for a new plan anyway.

I shrugged. 'Right now, mate.'

He was silent at the other end for a while. When he spoke, he said, 'I'll get my gear on. I'll see you later.'

As I walked to the Dockyard visitors' entrance, I sent one final message and wished I had put better shoes on. My brown leather dress shoes matched my outfit, completing the smart but casual office look I generally went with. As I paid a Ukrainian lady the daily entrance fee and pushed through the barrier under the watchful gaze of a Ukrainian security guard, I considered that the outfit might very well prove to be inappropriate.

My first task was to see Alex Jordan. He wanted evidence and I was going to give it to him.

Alex Jordan's Office. Thursday, November 24th 1128hrs

I had to go through the lengthy process of going to the Admiral's building to have them call through to his office with a request that he see me. I then had to wait because he was busy in a meeting of some kind so that by the time I got called forward to go upstairs to see him, I had lost almost an hour and knew that I could have spent the time doing something more constructive.

As I jogged up the stairs, it was concern for the missing men that motivated me. Alex Jordan could make the call that would get the police here. His authority to raid his own facility would remove the hesitation CI Quinn currently felt.

That was what I was about to propose anyway.

Andriy Janiv met me at the door to Alex Jordan's office. He was wearing a different suit to that which he had been wearing the last time I had seen him. Like Danylo Vakhno's, it had to be hand-cut in order to fit his enormous frame. What it told me was that there was no shortage of money going around the Ukrainians if a personal assistant could afford multiple hand-made suits.

'Mr. Michaels, so good to see you again. Mr Jordan is expecting you, please go straight through.' He led me through the outer office where his desk was located and held the door open to let me into Alex's private office.

'Thank you.' I said as I passed him.

'Mr. Michaels.' Once again, Alex Jordan crossed the room to greet me and shake my hand. Behind me Andriy closed the door, shutting himself outside. With my hand still in his, Alex leaned in close to whisper, 'Do you have something for me?'

'Indeed, I do.' I was keeping my volume low, but I wasn't whispering. In many ways, I was here to call the Ukrainians out. They had played their hand, clearly believing they were unbeatable or invulnerable and could get away with making people vanish if they chose to. 'You asked for evidence.' I said, fishing out my phone.

'Shhh!' He insisted, panic in his eyes as he looked around the room. Rather than argue or tell him it was time to man-up, I opened the message with the clip and played it.

His eyes widened as he understood what he was seeing, perhaps recognising some of the people in the short film.

'There is a complex of rooms beneath the Dockyard, dug several centuries ago and accessed via hidden tunnels. Your Ukrainian friends are using them as a secret base for illegal activities. In the room seen in the clip they are manufacturing counterfeit cigarettes which they will sell without paying tax and make a fortune from. Doubtless there are other nefarious enterprises we cannot see.'

He put his hand to his chest as if to steady his heart. 'Goodness. What do I do?'

'You call the police.' I replied, the answer obvious to me. 'I don't know where the entrances to the tunnel system are but with a squad of armed officers here, I doubt it will take long to find them.' He stared at me, caught between a nervous desire to do exactly what I had just suggested and a terrified fear he might get killed by the Ukrainians before he could rid himself of them.

He had gone to sit at his desk, indecision like a mask on his face. I put my hands on the desk and leaned across to get in his face. 'You do this now or you will never be rid of them. Grow a set, will you? It has to be you that places the call. The police will listen to the man that runs the place calling a raid on his own facility.'

He nodded. 'Yes. It is time to act.' He locked eyes with me, opened his mouth and yelled, 'We're busted. Come on in.'

Dirty Truth. November 24th 1142hrs

The office door opened to allow Andriy Janiv and Danylo Vakhno to enter. Their faces were impassive, no emotion showing of any kind. They were followed by a pair of the oversized uniformed guards so that I had Alex Jordan in front of me and four men blocking my escape, each of them roughly fifty percent heavier than me. Any thoughts of barrelling through them to escape were benched.

I turned back to face Alex.

He was smiling an exaggerated smile. Putting his arms out on each side in a gesture that said, "Oops". What he said was, 'Sorry to disappoint you, Mr. Michaels. I'm the bad guy.'

I opened my mouth to speak, the words never aired though as a wicked blow struck my left kidney, shocking me like a bolt of electricity. My legs buckled, and I suffered a brief bout of fuzziness that passed quickly only because my head was now close to the floor.

Strong arms hauled me back up, the two security guards now flanking me and holding me in place.

'Well done, Mr. Michaels.' Alex Jordan had taken up a relaxed position sitting on the front edge of his desk, one foot on the carpet, his hands resting lightly in his lap. 'I underestimated you. At first that is. When you first visited, I saw an amateur with good intentions but too little brain to achieve what no law enforcement agency has been able to. I kept an eye on you though, it was the cautious thing to do and I am a cautious man, Mr Michaels. I will admit I was impressed when you found your way onto the night cleaning crew, but I did expect that Pasha's tactics would convince you to withdraw.'

My mind was whirling. I needed to fight my way through five men. If I could get out into the open, with the public around me they wouldn't dare touch me. I was still being held by the two security guys, but their grip had loosened. Waiting wasn't a clever option.

So, I didn't.

I jinked forward, a simple tactic designed to make them move their centre of gravity forward. As they dived after me, I countered my direction and as I went backward, I made sure the back of my head connected with the face of the man to my left. His grip on my arm came loose exactly as I had known it would. In anticipation, I had already started to twist so that I could use the whipping effect of my arm coming free to strike upwards at the guard to my right.

They were big, and they were strong, but they were not fighters. Big Ben would have taken them apart. As I broke free of both guards, the second losing his grip as my open palm contacted his jaw to snap his head back, I turned my back on Alex Jordan. Gritting my teeth, I went for Andriy and Danylo.

A nanosecond. That was all the time I had to plan. Grab the arm of whichever one of them moved first, use their weight against them. They would both want to use their greater mass to force me backwards, which I could use to my advantage. If I could pull them off balance all I needed was one accurate strike to land a crippling blow. No matter how big you are, the throat, the testicles, the way the joints of the body work were always just as vulnerable, but bigger men didn't see the danger coming.

As I lined up on Danylo, the first to move between he and Andriy, the blow from behind caught me by surprise. It was hard and decisive, and wisely it landed in exactly the same spot as the first blow to my left kidney.

This time I threw up.

I had dismissed the smallest man in the room. Why was it that I couldn't listen to my own advice? While the big men weren't fighters and relied upon their size and strength to see them through, Alex Jordan needed the skills because he was that much smaller.

Looking up from the floor, I saw in him the lightness and balance of a martial arts master.

'That was fun.' He said as he settled back onto the front of his desk again. 'Get up.'

For a second, I considered replying with a tirade of swearwords. Then I realised he wasn't talking to me. The two guards I had felled were getting back up and looking not only ashamed but afraid. Alex Jordan really was the big cheese of the operation.

'Mr. Michaels you interrupted me. Please refrain from doing that again.'

With a grimace devoted to the pain in my lower back, I pushed myself upright. I didn't respond though.

'When I played the role of the victim yesterday morning, it was nothing more than a safety net to drive you to me if you did find something.' He laughed. 'It was quite brilliant actually. You were so ready to defend me. A real man of the people, always looking for someone to protect or save. You were surprisingly easy to read. I must say though that I had no notion that you might discover the operation beneath our feet. I would like to shake your hand for that.' He said as he extended his hand toward me.

I looked down at it. 'You have got to be kidding.'

'Not at all, Mr. Michaels. You have played a good game. It is not my fault that you lost. I am just better than you, but I acknowledge your skills. We should part as gentlemen.' He offered his hand again, insistent almost.

'I'm going to have to pass.'

He blew out a breath of disappointment. 'Very well. He can go out tonight with the others.'

Danylo Vanhkno spoke for the first time. 'Do I put him with the others?

Alex Jordan was getting up to return to his seat behind his desk. 'No. He is a bit too capable. Give him a beating and make sure he is well restrained.' He didn't even face his number two when he spoke. Everyone was dismissed.

My arms were grabbed again. This time the two nameless guards made sure they had me. I wouldn't shake them free again. Automatically,

I turned my feet toward the door. However, we were not going that way. Andriy walked to what I had assumed was Alex Jordan's private bathroom and opened the door.

As the guards shoved me toward it, I saw Andriy begin to descend.

It was an entrance point into the underground tunnel system.

Captive. Thursday, November 24th 1201hrs

The stairs led down and down and down, the bare stone walls giving off a familiar damp smell I associated with churches and cellars. The stairs were also stone, made to last forever in an age when other materials might be less easy to obtain. The stairwell itself was rectangular, the flights leading down around a central stone column, ten steps, then a corner, six steps then another corner, another ten steps on the longer side.

I counted in my head. Allowing a six-inch drop per step every circuit took me down sixteen feet. The Admiral's office was on the second floor, so deduct ten feet for that. By the time we reached the bottom of the dimly lit stairs I had descended roughly one-hundred feet, which by my reckoning put us below the level of the river at high tide.

Cross matching that information with what I remembered about the height of the river on Tuesday when I went to Upnor… gave me nothing useful. The tide on the day had been most of the way in I thought. There was six feet of beach between the waves and the obvious high tide mark, but not only did I not know whether the tide had been coming in or out, I also didn't know how fast it moved on that piece of beach. It was a very gentle slope, so it would move slowly. Slowly wasn't a useable measure though.

I decided to ask. 'Hey, guys, what time is high tide today?'

In answer Danylo thumped the back of my head. 'Shuddup.'

We had reached the bottom of the stairs and a large wooden door. There were faint sounds coming from the other side of it like ghostly echoes. It wasn't locked though, Andriy in the lead opened it by grasping an ancient iron handle and putting his shoulder against it. It opened inward.

As I went through it, the two guards still gripping me tightly, I spared a glance at the door to see if it had a lock. At this moment all information was vital. I was doing my best to keep my head clear but there was no denying that I was in peril. I was alone, I still had my phone, but I doubted that would last long and it wouldn't work this far underground anyway, plus I was surrounded by enemies that would probably kill me if I gave them any trouble. Alex hadn't made my fate clear, he said I would be taken out with the others tonight, but if they planned to kill me later somewhere else, they could just as easily kill me now and take me out dead.

I had wagered my life that this was not to be the case. If I was to be taken somewhere else to be executed, it meant I had several hours in which to escape. The clock on the wall behind Alex's head had given the time as 1201hrs when I was led from the room. It would be dark in less than five hours.

Behind the door was a tunnel, dark and poorly lit, but with overhead fluorescent lighting strung lazily from hooks in the ancient ceiling just as I had seen in the clip Joseph sent. It curved gently to the right eight feet ahead of me so that I could not see where it went. The tunnel was rounded at the top and only just a little more than six feet in height. Ahead of me Andriy had to tilt his head to one side to avoid scraping it.

I didn't bother to resist as they led me along it. Doing so would just waste energy. All my focus was on memorising everything I saw and plotting a map in my head. We had wound around the stairs four times so had ended up pointing in the same direction we had started. The river therefore was behind me and we were now turning east toward it with the curve of the tunnel.

Glancing back, I could no longer see the door. Danylo was so wide that I could see little other than his chest and blockish head. He was kind enough to give me another shove, no doubt to discourage me from looking at him and face forward.

Then we reached a room. It was small, about ten feet in each direction with a table and lockers taking up one wall. That was all I was allowed to see as a bag was roughly shoved over my head from behind to an accompanying gut punch from the front.

What was with the constant gut punches?

As I doubled over, still held by the guards each side, my jacket was ripped off and my hands were drawn back, and I felt a plastic restraint on the skin of my wrists. It was ratchetted tight. Though I couldn't see it, the zip sound it made as it closed convinced me it was the same type of plastic cuff I had used on prisoners of war in Iraq. They were designed to stay on. Then hands were in my pockets and my phone was gone.

Alex had told them to give me a beating and secure me. I was secure now, so I was really trying to take my mind to a place where I could endure what I was sure was to come next. They were speaking in Ukrainian as I made sure my mouth was closed but my jaw was loose. My head was down but no blow came.

Instead, I was grabbed by the arms again and led away again. I tried counting steps, tried keeping myself orientated by noting any turns in my head so I might be able to find my way out again if I could escape once they left me alone. It didn't work though. For all I knew they were walking around in circles to ensure I was disorientated. We passed through what sounded like a large room, the noise of our feet was different as if the walls were further away for the noise to bounce off. Then another room which I heard coming for some time because there were machine noises coming from it. In my head, I imagined the room Joseph had shown me with the cigarettes being made.

It seemed like we covered a lot of distance, but it was less than two minutes of walking so less than half a mile in total when we stopped, and my arms were released. More Ukrainian speech, which could have been instructions to kill me or a discussion about Manchester United's hopes in the league this season. A door opened in front of me, I heard the handle turn and felt the air move as the door swung inward. Then I was shoved hard from behind and tripped to land on the cold stone. With my hands fastened behind me, I did my best to keep my face up. I avoided a blow to my jaw or skull and took most of the impact on my right arm and shoulder. I had protected myself, but it proved to be a senseless act though as the beating was now overdue it seemed.

In retrospect, I have to be glad that they didn't use weapons on me. Being whacked with a steel pipe would have ended my plans instantly.

Thirty or more blows landed on my back and ribs, my arms, buttocks and my head, which without my hands I could not protect.

Then laughter and they were gone.

I was alone in a poorly lit room, deep inside the underground lair of an organised criminal gang. I was bound and blinded and beaten.

I rolled onto my back and laughed.

I had them.

Not Trapped. Thursday, November 24th Roughly 1220hrs

Plastic cuffs are considered by many to be an acceptable alternative to steel handcuffs. They are not. Once on my back, I rolled onto my shoulder blades, pulled my hands under my bum to get them to my front and then stood up.

The next bit was going to hurt, and I had to do it on top of all the bruising I already had. With my hands behind my back, the natural position was for my palms to be facing outwards. I had ensured they were not in anticipation they would use the plastic cuffs favoured by everyone other than the police. Doing so allowed me to create a small gap between my wrists so the cuffs were tight, but not as tight as they should have been. I lifted my hands away from my body then drew them back in sharply. As my wrists hit my stomach wall, my elbows flared either side and the cuffs shifted slightly. They also dug into the skin on the back of my hands quite cruelly, but they didn't break. I was trying to shock the little ratchet inside over the lip of the lug keeping it in place. I tried again, this time harder. The same effect. It took four attempts which I considered to be a poor show on my part, but they were loose enough for me to slip out of. The hood came off and I could take in my surroundings.

I guess this is where the story started, with me escaping from the room with a pipe wrench in my hand. Had the Ukrainians received any training on prisoner handling at any point they would have removed my footwear. I might be wearing leather office shoes, but they were a lot better than nothing. I wanted my combat boots on, and my Kevlar and my black ripstop clothing. However, if I had arrived dressed in my fighting gear it would have given the game away. I needed Alex to have no idea that I was onto him.

I had found the pipe wrench, slipped out of the room and almost immediately been spotted by three Ukrainians. As I ran along the tunnel with the mob chasing me and gaining, I had been looking for the river entrance. I had found it and the plan was almost complete. But now, in the moment of truth, I felt more worried than I had at any point thus far. Now that I had my back to the door to the river entrance, my surge of confidence at finding it left me.

What if I was wrong?

'It was a good try, Mr. Michaels.' A familiar voice echoed in the confined space. 'Unfortunately, that door only opens from the other side.' It was Andriy Janiv, still in his immaculate suit and very clearly the boss of the twenty thugs around him.

I glanced at the door. He was right. There was no handle this side.

Andriy beckoned for me to come back to them. 'Come along, Mr. Michaels. Enough silliness now.'

The moment of truth was here. How clever was I? How reliable were the people I had placed my trust in?

I reached out behind me to knock loudly on the solid wood door three times. Even in the dim light of the tunnels, I could see the curious expression on Andriy's face and I got to watch the expression change to one of disbelief and then horror as everyone in the corridor heard the mechanism turn and the door behind me open.

'How's it going, Army?' Asked Alan.

Without turning, I answered, 'Honestly? I've been beaten, blindfolded and locked up and the worst part of this is still that I had to get the Navy to rescue me.'

Behind me, he chuckled. 'Don't sweat it, Army.' Then he growled. 'Let's get 'em, boys.'

Tunnel Fire Fight. Thursday, November 24th No Idea What Time it is. Don't Really Care.

Alan, Richard, Boy George and almost two dozen other pensionable aged men stormed into the tunnel. It had been a risky play. I hadn't counted on the beating, a few punches maybe, but I had run close to being incapacitated. It wouldn't have taken much more for them to have broken one of my bones.

The gamble had been that Alex Jordan was not the innocent that he claimed to be. There were two clues that had smuggled into my head and stayed hidden, waiting for the rest of my brain to catch up before revealing themselves at a time when I would understand what they meant.

The first was the Ukrainian/English dictionary. I had thought nothing of it at first. With so many Ukrainian staff, it was a natural choice to learn a few words; a good managerial tactic. Only this morning did I realise that it was the wrong way around. If he was English, he would have wanted an English/Ukrainian dictionary. By itself it was too tenuous. Then there was the firing of Cedric Tilsley. Cedric claimed that Alex dismissed him when he reported the missing uniforms. The uniforms were those being worn by the ghosts which suggested to me that Alex knew what the uniforms were being used for. Also, firing Cedric felt out of character for the man I had met, a man that played the role of caring boss too well to have made such a move so easily. In isolation I would have dismissed my thoughts, but then there was the clock on the wall opposite Alex's desk.

Once again, I hadn't picked up on it at first but somewhere in the dark recesses of my head the maker's mark on the clock had stuck. Kleynod was a Ukrainian clock manufacturer. I didn't know that, of course. My general knowledge far too limited to name the Ukrainian manufacturer of anything. However, the clock was a modern item and out of keeping with the centuries old feel and look of the room. It had been enough to ask Jane to look it up and dig a little deeper into Alex's genealogy. It had taken her minutes to find out that Alex Jordan was indeed English. He had been born and raised here, but his grandfather had travelled to England from the Ukraine at the end of the second world war. What had started out as a tenuous link had become a working principle.

Alex Jordan was the man in charge after all.

I really didn't know how he would react when I took him the evidence, yet I thought only one or two scenarios were likely.

The first was that he would do exactly as he had and try to make me disappear. The second was that he would thank me and take the evidence, bluffing his way out by saying he would take it from there onward. It had occurred to me that a third option existed where he just had me killed on the spot, but I had elected to ignore that as it was unhelpful.

Choosing to force Alex's hand was my best way into the tunnels beneath the Dockyard. A belief that held true and was vital to the next part of the plan. The plan I outlined to Big Ben required that he find Alan at the Dockyard, round up all his colleagues and friends and meet me at the river entrance to the tunnel system.

Alan Page and his friends were retired from the Special Boat Service, a Royal Navy version of the SAS. That was the tattoo they had shown me, silently telling me everything I needed to know. My father had one as well, though he and I had never talked about his time in the Navy or about my time in the Army. It was a well acknowledged fact that one didn't talk about your service if you were special forces. This was mostly because it made those that did stand out as liars. If someone said they were special forces, then they weren't.

If I were locked in a battle of banter with the Navy boys, I would have called them a watered down, weak, slightly-drunk version of the SAS, but in truth they were every bit as elite and well-trained as any other special forces unit on the planet. I knew what it took to earn the badge, so when I needed help and getting it required a water-borne infiltration, I didn't hesitate to include them. Sure, they were old. What did old mean though? They still worked a full day. They were still mobile and able, though people would call them sprightly rather than athletic now. I would get a full report from them later. Right now it was fighting time. I went with them as they charged into the tunnel, wet suits shedding water and each of them armed and ready to do violence.

In the confined space of the tunnel the first shots fired were impossibly loud. After that, my hearing was impaired, and it didn't seem as loud even though it was. The Ukrainians had gone from looking startled to acting scared. Many had already turned and were fleeing the ageing army advancing on them. Others were armed and had drawn their weapons to return fire. None of them had anything bigger or more accurate than a hand gun though.

'Shoot to wound!' I yelled as loud as I could. It occurred to me that we could just kill everyone we saw and deny we were ever actually there. Alan's crew might be up for that as well, but I couldn't be sure there were not innocent persons down here that had been coerced into the work they were doing.

The first volley of shots had been aimed at the ceiling as Alan and his motley crew charged into the tunnel. Shooting a warning rather than trying to kill anyone. With fire being returned, the tactic changed. The distance between opposing sides had been no more than fifty feet when the door opened. Now it was less which meant that whoever shot first was going to win.

I was unarmed but hadn't let that deter me from charging toward my Ukrainian opponents, so I had a front row view to the first four of them being cut down. The pensioners were all firing single shot not automatic fire, each target receiving only one or two hits, which took them down right enough, but probably wouldn't kill them unless it hit something vital.

Devoid of sympathy for the wounded, I snagged a handgun, and made sure we did not advance beyond anyone that was still armed lest they shoot us in the back. In the three seconds since the first shot was fired, the tunnel ahead of us had emptied. There were no Ukrainians still in sight other than half a dozen that had been shot and were now groaning on the damp stone floor.

I swung around to face Alan's team. 'Anyone wounded?' I asked. Several bullets had come in our direction, in the tight space it would have been hard to miss us all.

A voice said, 'Yeah. Over here.' The owner of the voice wasn't wounded though. At his feet was Boy George, his weapon discarded next to him and blood coming between his fingers as he pressed them to his leg.

'Oh, for heaven's sake, Georgie. Are you some kind of bullet magnet?' Alan sounded genuinely annoyed. 'You're making us look bad in front of the Army boys. Get up, will you?'

'Not this time, Al.' Boy George replied leaning back against the wall.

'Let me see.' The request had come from a new voice, but one I was very familiar with.

'Dad, what are you doing here?' I asked, my head bowed in defeat.

He didn't answer straight away. He was examining the wound, but as I crossed the few feet to him, he looked up, a big grin on his daft face. 'The doctor let me out. He told me to take it easy but didn't specifically say I couldn't get involved in underground gun battles while rescuing my son from a gang of organised Ukrainian criminals.

'Right.' I drawled. 'Does Mum know where you are?'

'Of course. I told her I was going to the supermarket for rum. That's where she thinks I am.'

I thought about that for a second. 'How long ago did you go out for rum?'

'About three hours.' He giggled. Actually giggled. He was going to catch hell when he got home. I wasn't going anywhere near their house for the next few weeks because Mum would most definitely find a way to blame me.

'Can we do the family reunion thing later?' Big Ben asked as he crouched down next to me. 'I can't stand up straight in these stupid tunnels made for puny humans.'

'What are you then?' Asked Alan.

'Man plus.' His instant reply. 'Also, I think it likely they have gone for reinforcements or better weapons, so we need to scarper before they come back.'

'Righto.' Said Alan taking charge again. 'Bob, Charlie, Whizzer, get Boy George here back to the river and out. He'll need to get that scratch properly attended to.' He turned to me. 'What do we do with the enemy wounded?'

'We leave them here. I don't think they are getting better weapons and I don't think they are coming back.' I stopped talking to create a moment of silence. 'See? Nothing to hear. This was always part of the plan. The police are on the surface...'

'Are they?' Big Ben interrupted me, his voice full of surprise.

'They should be. I gave Quinn an easy way to be the hero and make the big bust. I told him I was going in and would be driving them out. All he had to do was bring officers in wearing plain clothes and have uniformed back up waiting around the corner. Since none of us know where the stairs come out, I couldn't direct him to a specific point, so he is up there now looking for a flood of people exiting a building and blinking in the sunlight because their eyes are accustomed to the dark.'

'That's a bit thin, son.' Dad observed.

'This whole plan has been a bit thin. It's working though, and we are nearly there.' I scanned around the tunnel. Two ex-army guys and a good handful of well-trained but ultimately almost geriatric former Royal Navy against an unknown force. I really wanted to send my father away, but I knew he would never leave unless I was going with him and I wasn't convinced the Ukrainians would be caught unless we forced them into the open now and let the police do what was necessary. On top of that, I still believed that the two Daves and Joseph were also captive down here somewhere. Remembering them made the decision easy.

'I'm off to clear some vermin out of this sewer. Anyone who wants to come along is welcome.' Then I set off, a handgun in my right hand and Italian leather shoes on my feet. My feet were long since soaked through from splashing in puddles on the damp floor. The shoes would be going in the bin and were the least of my concerns.

My greatest concern was that I was wrong about the Ukrainians getting reinforcements and weapons.

Henchman are Hard to Beat. Thursday, November 24th (still no idea what time it is)

I filled the rest of them in on the likelihood of hostages as we advanced. I wanted to find the two Daves and Joseph as a greater priority than anything else, certainly it was more important than catching anyone. I had all the evidence I would ever need for the police to raid the place, plus it was my investigations that had placed the three missing men in danger. Sneaking along the tunnel, fanned out as best we could so any shots fired in our direction wouldn't get us all, we were trying to balance caution with a sense of urgency. There was no desire to give them time to regroup but also no wish to run headfirst into an ambush. It took less than a minute to get back to the room I had been held in and pass it. Ahead the tunnel formed a tee junction.

'Which way.' Asked Alan.

I shook my head. 'I was blindfolded.'

'Best we split up then.' He turned and issued a fast order, splitting the group. 'We'll take right. You go left?' He asked me.

I simply nodded and wished him luck. Half a dozen of his men, including my dad came with me.

The tunnel to the left quickly curved away to the right and as it did, we began to hear noises. Voices echoing along the corridor and then the faint sound of machinery in the distance. I picked up the pace, the others keeping up with me easily enough despite Big Ben having to move in a permanent crouch.

There was a shout ahead of us. A word in Ukrainian that was followed by a volley of bullets. The shooter wasn't hanging around though. We saw three men duck into view and quickly vanish again before anyone could get a shot off. They were running away, which was good news, I wanted to drive them to the surface, but there was bad news as well. Everyone else had already left and these three had been left behind to torch the evidence. The stink of petrol hung heavy in the air as we skidded to a halt in the room they had just fled.

It was the room they made the cigarettes in. There were boxes of cigarettes stacked next to several machines and boxes of paper and tobacco and other raw materials. Some of the boxes were exact duplicates of the one I had found on the beach. How it had arrived on the shore of Upnor would forever remain a mystery, but my best guess was that it fell off whatever they used to bring it in.

'We saw loads of these in the tunnel we came in through.' Said Big Ben by my ear. 'They have a pair of small ribs that tow what looks like a pod in and out. It was all rigged up next to the pontoon where we came in.

I wanted to hear more about it, but the smell of tobacco one might expect was overwhelmed by the smell of the accelerant. Before anyone could say anything else, I heard the petrol catch ahead of us and out of sight. Around the next bend in the tunnel, they had lit the petrol, the light from it scaring the dimness away. I screamed for everyone to get back. If they made it out of the room, they would have to fight against the fire drawing oxygen from the tunnel to feed itself, but they would escape the heat and flame and be out of danger.

I had travelled too far into the room though. To go back was further than to go forward and my brain was trying to remember how fast a flame travels in petrol. As time slowed down, an old science teacher drawled out numbers for equations. Fifty metres per second sounded right. It was a terrible last thought to have.

The force of Big Ben slamming into my back drove my breath from me as he lifted me and ran toward the line of flame now whipping down the centre of the tunnel floor toward us. It became a wall of intense heat for a heartbeat as he dived over it, bearing me to the floor where the cold, wet stone had mercifully already forgotten the passing flame.

Then Big Ben was hitting me. Slapping out a fire on my shirt. Smoke was rising from both of us as the light overhead twitched once, twice and went out.

'Bugger.' Said Big Ben.

Fortunately perhaps, the cigarette room was an inferno. Standing once more, I could just about see the faces of those on the other side. My dad was with them but all I could do was wave that we were alright. The fire created too much noise and it was beginning to deliver some serious heat. I didn't know all that much about thermodynamics, but I worried the tunnels were about to be a very inhospitable place.

Big Ben thumped my arm to get moving even as we were being forced to back away from the oppressive heat. We turned and ran.

Straight into Pasha, Andriy and Danylo. They were emptying cash into bags from a large locker.

Both Big Ben and I had lost our weapons escaping the flames. Now unarmed, the three hugely muscular opponents presented a difficult obstacle.

Pasha glanced over her shoulder to see who was there and was turning her eyes back to the money when she did a double take. I guess they hadn't told her it was me causing all the fuss.

Andriy and Danylo caught her reaction and turned to face us as well. Three against two. I was half beaten to pulp and they were each bigger and probably stronger than my unstoppable friend. I was really hoping they would see the danger in the fire behind us and run away.

They didn't though. Smoke was beginning to fill the top of the tunnel. I saw Andriy notice it, looking above his head to examine then dismiss it. His attention came back to Big Ben and me.

It was Pasha that spoke first. 'Do you remember when I told you I had a huge boyfriend that would beat you up? Well here he is.' She said indicating Danylo to her left.

Danylo looked confused. 'I am not your boyfriend.' He argued.

'Yes, you are, Dany.' Then her brow wrinkled. 'Hold on, what do you mean you are not my boyfriend?'

'Why would you think I am your boyfriend?' He asked, mystified.

Pasha's attention was no longer on us as she turned to face the larger man. 'You had better be thinking hard about the sleeping arrangements, Dany.' She hissed. 'You have been tapping this ass for months and you think it is just a bit of fun? Or are you getting it somewhere else as well?'

Andriy sputtered with a laugh he was trying to hold in. 'Busted.' He managed between sniggers.

Pasha raised one eyebrow, then, barely taking her eyes off Danylo, she rotated on one foot and kicked out hard with her right heel. It caught Andriy in his groin forcing an involuntary intake of breath from both Big Ben and me. He folded inward slightly, fought it, tried to recover, then accepted his fate and sank to his knees whereupon she kicked him in the head with the same heel.

Danylo now looked like a dog caught halfway through taking a poop on the carpet. He wanted to run away or make himself invisible, but he couldn't move.

'What did he mean?' She demanded. 'Why did he say busted and then laugh?' She had fixed him with a hard stare, her hands clenching and unclenching by her sides.

'I don't know, um… darling?' He tried unsuccessfully.

'It's that skinny blonde bitch that does the books for the protection rackets, isn't it?' Pasha was working herself into a frenzy, there was spittle on her lips and she looked angry. Like bite a man's cock off angry.

Danlyo, the huge man that he was, took a pace back, looked at us, considered his options and ran away. Suddenly, the blocked escape route was open, and we hadn't needed to do anything. Only Pasha blocked our path. But whatever else was going on in her head, Pasha was planning to leave with the money in the bags at her feet and we had to get by her to get out.

'I'll get this one.' Big Ben said as he advanced toward her. 'You have a rest, this won't take long.' He took two loping paces toward her and swung a hard punch that I have witnessed to great effect on several occasions. It was the sort of punch that a lumberjack would use to fell trees.

Pasha caught it in her right hand, looked Big Ben hard in the face and twisted while simultaneously closing her hand to crush his knuckles.

If I was surprised, then Big Ben was shocked to his core. He was a fighting machine that never lost, and he felt he owed Pasha a lesson for his treatment on Tuesday night. He wasn't going to be the teacher today though.

She kicked out with a vicious boot to his inner left knee and followed it with a clubbing blow to his right cheekbone from her left hand. He was hampered by the height of the ceiling still, the only man down here that just didn't fit. He backed away and circled, trying to find an opening, then charged her, but he was outwitted again as she moved to meet him before he could position himself.

Her arms whipped out to deflect his, a high elbow caught his jaw and she converted his stumble from the latest strike so that she was able to grab his left arm and fold it into a lock. He was about to be pinned.

I hit her with the pipe wrench. Somehow, I had forgotten I had it in my pocket.

Pasha let go of Big Ben's arm, 'That's what you get for hitting my dad.' I sneered in her face. She blinked twice and fell over backward.

'You couldn't have done that earlier?' Big Ben asked.

'I was too busy filming you getting slapped about by a girl.'

'Ha ha, dickhead.'

'Yes. Shall we go?'

'What about them?' Big Ben pointed to Andriy and Pasha.

I considered my options. 'I need to get Pasha to the surface. She's the one that hurt my dad. I don't want to run the risk that the police don't catch her and she escapes justice.' I thought back to Deadface the Klown. I definitely didn't want her to slip away. 'We need to link up with the police and make sure the Navy boys get out before the police catch them. I also want to find the two Daves and Joseph. Let's get to the surface. We can come back down with armed reinforcements to mop all this up.'

I started to pick Pasha up. She was out cold but picking deadweight unconscious people up and carrying them was a skill the army taught. Even so, I doubted I had ever picked up anyone her size.

Seeing me struggle, Big Ben took over, hoisted her easily onto his shoulder in a fireman's lift and we got moving. Andriy was trying to get to his feet. 'I grabbed him around the collar and hauled him to his feet. 'You're taking us to the surface.' I insisted.

Knowing he was beaten, he nodded and still cupping his nuts and walking bent over, he escorted us to a door I might never have otherwise found. Behind the door was a second set of stone stairs, another rectangle just like the set I had already seen. It was the other way in from the surface.

Andriy was moving too slow, whether it was because he couldn't go any faster or because he believed he could lose us and double back I didn't know or care. Big Ben and I left him behind on the stairs, right now I wanted to see daylight and reassure myself that the Ukrainians were being rounded up because I was only mostly certain that the police were out there rounding up the Ukrainians. I didn't actually know.

Nearing the final flight of stairs though, the door opened above us sending a shaft of daylight down. Voices filled the air and the squawk of a radio told me we were safe.

The police.

It wasn't the first time I had been glad to see them, but this time it was positively euphoria I felt as I called out to them and heard CI Quinn's voice in reply.

Mopping Up. Thursday, November 24th 1504hrs

I could see the time by looking at the giant clocktower that loomed over the Dockyard. Five minutes had gone by since Big Ben and I had stumbled out of the dark and into the cold air coming off the river. Big Ben had on his combat gear, which had unnerved the armed police for a moment until we were able to identify ourselves. The Chief Inspector had come back to the surface with us, wanting a full report, but had followed us up the stairs when we should have considered how we looked and insist he lead us out. All around had been armed police in uniform and plainclothes officers wearing bright vests to identify what they were. All weapons had been trained on us for a split second until CI Quinn exited behind us with a hastily bellowed order to not shoot.

On the ground ahead of us had been more than thirty men and women in cuffs, one or two of whom I recognised. They were surrounded by a swarm of officers that were processing them. Now in with them and struggling against the two uniformed police officers holding her was Pasha. She had come around as we handed her off to them, once again proving to be a handful until Quinn shouted and three more officers nearby joined in.

Now, I was sitting on a low wall next to a hastily erected on-site command post for the police that consisted of a large van with sides that opened out. It was purpose built for controlling major incidents which was what this now constituted.

The stairs we had exited from emerged into the Dockyard from an unassuming looking square of stone that had no identifying marks on it. There was a single door with a lock that not only would I not have looked at, but had I known it was the entrance, I would not have been able to get in through it anyway.

When I asked, CI Quinn was good enough to share that they had arrested sixty-seven persons, many of whom were known criminals and all of whom were Ukrainian. He was one of the officers that had come to the scene in plainclothes. His team had entered the Dockyard posing as tourists as I had suggested then fanned out. When panicked-looking people started streaming from the small building that covered the entrance to the stairs, he had been close enough to see it for himself, describing it as like watching a magic trick where one sees an impossible quantity of something come out of a receptacle too small to hold it. Then they had seen weapons and had been able to react.

A lot of the officers were below ground now going through the tunnels. They would be down there for days if not weeks, cataloguing everything the fire had not consumed. I had worried that it would spread but in the last few minutes there had been more officers going in and more people in cuffs coming out. I had heard someone report over the radio that fire had burned up the paper but had quickly run out of anything else that was flammable.

I needed to find my father and Alan and the rest of the heroes I had been down there with. Not knowing what had happened to them was keeping me agitated though CI Quinn was insistent that no one other than police officers, fire fighters, or if necessary, paramedics was going below ground. I had only just got my father back after days of watching him lying unconscious in hospital. Now his condition was unknown again and I wasn't happy about it.

From my position on the low wall, I could see the Admiral's building where I expected them to all emerge. There were police there too and the staff inside were still filing out as the entire facility was evacuated under police control.

Just then, CI Quinn exited the mobile command centre, looked around, spotted me and crossed the short distance to where I was sitting. He looked annoyed. 'My men are getting reports from the Ukrainians that they were set upon by what they described as a geriatric special forces team.' He said. 'You wouldn't happen to know anything about that would you?'

'Maybe.' I tried to make my reply sound innocent.

'Yes. Well, they have vanished like ghosts back into the dark. That's a direct quote. Some of my officers saw them and gave chase but were fired upon. No injuries sustained though which makes me think the shots were to deter them from following, not to do them any harm. Doesn't your father work here?'

'He does.' I answered, giving nothing away.

Exasperation etched on his face, he placed his head in his palms and groaned. 'Mr. Michaels you have an uncanny knack for making my life both easy and impossible. Whoever they are they were nearly shot, you know. All in black and running around in the dark with guns. It would seem they found Detective Sergeant Kushnir though *and* two security guards and were escorting them to safety. That's what DS Kushnir is saying anyway. How do you do it? How do you bring down a firefight in my jurisdiction and walk away scot free?'

I said nothing.

'Would you like to tell me who they are? I expect the mayor will want to hang medals around their necks.'

Better make it a big one, I thought, so my dad could hide from mum behind it.

'I need to see the security guards.' Next to me Big Ben was already getting up. I wanted to check how bad they were for myself.

'Really?' CI Quinn said. 'You need to see them. You cause nothing but mayhem and now you expect me to let you wander off to see the men your private army saved?'

'Yes.' I replied.

He sighed, looking around rather than at me. Then he pursed his lips as he made a decision. 'I'll come with you. I'm about to be replaced by an incident commander anyway. This is too big for a Chief Inspector now. Way too big.' He turned back toward the command centre calling, 'Wait there.' Over his shoulder.

He came back out less than ten seconds later with two bright yellow high-visibility vests in his hand. Each had POLICE written across the back in bold letters.

'Put these on. It might stop people from thinking they should shoot you.' I think he was talking to Big Ben rather than me. He still looked like one of the armed police but without the insignia so actually he looked more like a terrorist.

'Actually, I need the gents.' Big Ben said as we set off. 'I'll catch up with you.'

CI Quinn and I walked in silence across the cobblestones to the Admiral's building where staff were still leaving. A thought occurred to me. 'Ian have your men found Alex Jordan yet?'

'Alex Jordan?' He repeated. He frowned for a second. 'Oh, you mean the Dockyard's CEO. I don't think so. Why?'

CI Quinn had been rounding up Ukrainians and anyone that looked like they might be involved in the crimes they were committing. He didn't know about Alex Jordan. No one did.

'Because he is the guy at the top of the pyramid. He's the big boss of the Ukrainian gang you are currently arresting, and he is probably being evacuated from the building in front of us by your men. Escorted to safety by the very persons that should be arresting him.' I had already started running. Not towards the building though. I was heading for the exit where the first of the civilian staff evacuated from the Admiral's building were filing out. A long thin snake of them were walking in a straight line out the large oak front doors I had not seen open until today. They passed through a cordon of officers that were recording who they were and where they could be reached and probably checking them against a list of employees to make sure they were releasing innocents not criminals.

Alex Jordan had to be among them and would be gone if we didn't catch him.

No one paid us much attention as we raced up the line of confused-looking staff in their office wear. They had been happily oblivious to the fight playing out beneath their feet and getting on with whatever their job involved when the police had descended on them like a swarm of locusts. The police would not have told them anything other than they needed to evacuate the Dockyard. So, they were going home early, which was nice, but now would be questioning whether they were coming back tomorrow and if they still had a job.

The line of people had already reached the exit building where the gift shop and ticket booths were located. As we ran toward it, I couldn't see anyone that looked like Alex Jordan. It could mean that he was still inside, waiting to file out through the police cordon or he might have gone down the stairs and into the tunnels to find his escape when he saw the police coming. Or he could have left already. All these things were possible.

However, when we entered the gift shop, I saw him.

He was in the car park and hurrying away.

'There.' I yelled to Quinn as I pointed through the now unmanned ticket booths.

Our jog turned into a sprint, my body protesting after the recent beatings it had taken. My abs a solid ball of insistent pain that demanded I stop doing things with them and take a month off.

We barrelled through the doors and out into the car park with enough force and noise to alert him. He glanced over his shoulder, saw me or perhaps saw the yellow vests and started running himself. He had a large bag over one shoulder, filled with money no doubt as Pasha and the others had been trying to do. It was slowing him down.

'Police, halt!' CI Quinn bellowed in a tone he clearly believed would generate the reaction he wanted. To my surprise it did.

Alex stopped running, dropped the heavy bag to the gravel and turned to face us. We were fifty yards from him and running, but as we drew closer, I grabbed Quinn's arm and slowed his pace.

'What are you doing, man?' Quinn asked, bewildered that I was holding him back. I had faced enough fighters, both in the ring and in life, to know that my earlier casual assessment of his skills was on the money. He was loosening up for a fight right now, twisting his ankles and his neck, bending over to place his forehead against his ankles without bending his knees. He was limber and supple.

We were not in earshot yet, but I whispered anyway. 'He can fight. This will not be easy. Best to bring in backup than risk him overpowering us and escaping.'

Quinn looked the man up and down. Alex Jordan is short and has a lean frame. Visually there is nothing to suggest that he could be dangerous which must have worked in his favour many times in his life. A police issue baton appeared in Quinn's hand as he said, 'I think I'll be okay with just one man. I can call for back up when he is in cuffs.'

Before I could stop him, he moved to take Alex into custody. Mentally I wished him luck, physically I moved to create a vee angle so that Alex had to divert his attention constantly between the two of us. If I could time my attack to coincide with Quinn's, then maybe this would be easy.

It wasn't.

As Quinn stepped in, Alex darted toward me, feigning a move that would cause Quinn to follow him, then reversed his direction and struck him hard on the side of his face. It was the sort of move I used and one I liked to believe I wouldn't fall for.

Reeling back and off balance, Quinn could do nothing as Alex grabbed his baton to wrench it from his grip. I was feeling sluggish and I hurt more or less everywhere. The adrenaline that had coursed through my bloodstream too many times today already had left me feeling spent. Adding it all up, I knew I had no option but to end the fight quickly. If Alex had the chance to arm himself with a weapon like a baton, we would not beat him.

But I had bet on him trying to get it as soon as I saw him go for Quinn and counted on his focus slipping briefly. It gave me the opening I needed.

Putting everything into my move, I took two steps, leaped onto the bonnet of a car and dived at the smaller man. I wanted to wrap him up in a hug that would encompass his limbs and take away his ability to strike effectively. While he wrestled with me, Quinn would be able to regain his feet and get a cuff on him.

As always, it didn't work like that. The car I climbed on was fresh from the valet and had a good coat of wax on it. I might as well have stepped on a cartoon banana peel while honking a comedy horn.

I crashed to the gravel at Alex's feet, hitting head first and tasting blood. Presented with an easy target, Alex drove down with his left knee to smash into my throat. Thankfully he missed as I scrambled for purchase but his knee landed on my chest instead, driving the air from my lungs and he was already raising the baton to strike my face.

Quinn grabbed the raised arm which stopped the downswing but was soon shaken loose when Alex drove a long, thin leg into his abdomen, doubling him over and forcing him to let go.

Whatever fight training Alex had was comprehensive but hadn't extended to fighting dirty in the schoolyard. Still on my back on the ground, I threw a handful of gravel and loose dust into his face, blinding him for the half second I needed to line up an elbow on his inner knee. As he collapsed inward, I lifted my head and shoulders, swept my left arm behind his head and drew him down so I could bite his nose.

Yelping in shock and pain, he couldn't get away without ripping his nose off. Panicked, he was punching and clawing at me, but I wasn't going to let go.

Then the satisfying metal rasping sound of a handcuff ratchet sliding home told me Quinn had him. He pulled Alex away from me, indentations in either side of his nose where my incisors had been. He used the cuff against his wrist to force Alex to the ground as he did so.

From the ground, I heard the other cuff clicking into place. Then Ian Quinn's face came into view, blocking out the cold grey sky. He was grinning. His top lip was split and there was a bruise already where the first blow had struck home next to his left eye, but he was grinning.

I took his offered hand and let him pull me to my feet. I slumped back against the bonnet of a car, placing all my weight on it and immediately slid off and onto the ground again. It was the same damned car I had fallen off. Quinn just eyed me like I was being strange.

I selected a different car, this time feeling the bonnet for friction before resting myself against it.

While Alex Jordan was yelling about the choice things he was going to do with our kidneys and testicles, the Chief Inspector called for uniforms to assist and gave them our location.

Only when half a dozen uniformed officers came running toward us from the Dockyard entrance did he take his weary eye off Alex Jordan.

After they hauled the smaller man to his feet and after Quinn had directed them to take the bag away as evidence, he offered me his hand. 'Well done, Mr. Michaels. It was a pleasure working with you. I need to return to the command centre where there will undoubtedly be many tasks for me to perform. I look forward to working with you again in the future.'

I shook his hand, surprised at his change in attitude. Our hands parted, and he turned to go but stopped as if remembering something. 'When I make my report later, I will state that the special forces team the Ukrainians have reported were an unknown element and not connected to you in any way. That's correct isn't it, Mr. Michaels?'

He was sort of smiling as he gave me the opportunity to lie through my face about my involvement in the firefight earlier. I smiled back, as I began to walk away. 'No, Ian. I arranged the whole thing.'

Going Home. Thursday, November 24th 1522hrs

I got to my car where I planned to wait for Big Ben. I still had on the hi-vis police vest but beneath it was a shirt that had burn holes in it and was damp from rolling on the floor in the tunnels. My feet were soaked and I was getting cold now that the adrenalin was once again leaving my system.

'Mr Michaels?' I turned to see Joseph Kushnir jogging across the carpark toward me. 'Mr. Michaels.'

Despite the cold I felt, I closed my car door before I had the chance to get in and went back to meet him. I offered my hand to shake. 'Joseph, good to see you in one piece.'

'No time for that.' He panted, drawing in a huge breath so he could get his message out. 'I have to tell you that Alex Jordan is the gang boss.'

'Yes, I know.'

'Oh. Really?' Poor Joseph was not only surprised by the news but also quite clearly disappointed. 'How?'

'I pieced it together.' I said while shrugging. 'How do you know?'

'Because he was there when they took me. I spotted the guards coming out of a tiny brick building that couldn't possibly have housed them all late last night. I picked the lock and went in after everyone else had gone home and found them making cigarettes down there. Oh, did you get the film I sent you?' His brain was jumping from one thought to the next.

'I did. I used it to fool Alex Jordan into playing his hand and to get CI Quinn to come here with reinforcements.'

'Oh. Good. Good.'

I could see he was going to launch into a long-winded account of what had happened to him, but I was getting cold and I was most definitely feeling battered. I wanted to get clean and warm and sit on the sofa with a dog on each leg while I drank a cup of tea.

'Are you hurt?' I asked. 'Did they hurt you?'

'Not really.' He replied. 'They duffed me up a bit until I stopped resisting, then put me in a room with two blokes called Dave. We tried to break out but there was an armed guard outside.'

'Are the Daves okay?'

'Same as me. They were worried though, convinced they planned to kill us. I did my best to assure them they would never be bold enough to kill a copper, but they didn't believe me.'

Neither did I. Joseph's naivety was a wonder to behold. I said, 'You will have a cool story to tell now at least.' I wasn't wrong in that assessment either. He had broken into a criminal gang's underground lair, confronted the big boss and escaped with the assistance of a special forces raid. Okay, some of that was embellishing the truth, but he could make it work.

'I really have to go.' I pointed out. I wanted to talk to my father and to Alan Page, neither of whom I could contact as my phone was gone. I needed to get home, but then, as Joseph shook my hand and started back toward the Dockyard entrance building, I saw Big Ben coming out of it.

He waved that he had seen me and was on his way over. I waited for him.

'You look like crap, mate.' He said as he drew near. 'Your ear looks like it's coming off.'

I felt my ears, the right one was crusted with blood. I must have cut it when I fell off the car and hit the gravel. It didn't feel torn though. I sagged against the front of my car.

Big Ben gave me a concerned look. 'Are you okay?'

I laughed. Looking down at my ruined shoes, the holes in the knees of my trousers where I could see my skinned and bleeding knees, the burn holes in my shirt which didn't stop at my shirt – the skin beneath would require some soothing salve, my ragged ear, the cuts to my knuckles and all the bruising I had suffered from fighting in the last few days, I had to laugh at myself. At my life.

'What is it?' He asked.

'In all these wounds you can see, the thing that hurts me most is the bruise to the back of my neck where my sister grabbed me while delivering her baby.'

He joined in laughing.

Later that evening, with a snuggly dog on each thigh and a cooling cup of tea in my hand I fell asleep. I woke only briefly when the sound of the dogs finishing my tea reached my ears.

I had called my dad at his house but as expected had got my mother. She answered the phone with a demand, 'Do you know where your father has been?'

'Where did he tell you he had been?' I asked in return, idly swishing the water and bubbles around my bath as it filled. I wanted to deny all knowledge, but that would mean lying directly to my mother. Instead I was going to dance around the truth and see if I could avoid dropping him in it.

'He says he joined a clandestine force in order to storm an underground lair and free hostages held by a criminal gang.'

'Then I guess that is where he was. I was one of the hostages.'

'Okay, don't tell me.' She snapped. 'I shall expect to see you for Sunday lunch. Two o'clock, don't be late.'

'Okay, Mother.' I was answering on autopilot, wondering how dad and I had got away so easily from her wrath. Maybe she was just glad to have him home and in one piece. Maybe she was plotting revenge. I would find out soon enough.

'Will you be bringing a date?' She asked.

I though of Natasha and groaned internally. I was going to have to deal with that soon. What I said was, 'Not unless you count Bull and Dozer.' She muttered something about never getting grandchildren and was gone.

Coomer Castle. Friday, November 25th 1000hrs

The blend of Sihk and Christian wedding traditions resulted in a ceremony at the palatial Coomer Castle just outside Rochester, on a day when the sun decided to shine, and the world felt like a perfect place to be.

I had arrived at the venue at 1000hrs to make sure that everything was being set up according to the happy couple's desires. They had a few very specific requests, but I needn't have worried as it was all being taken care of. The plush interior was matched by the perfectly landscaped acres of garden and long, winding driveway that would wow the guests as they arrived.

I kept Bull and Dozer on their leads both inside and outside the great house though no one insisted upon it. There was all too much chance one of them would poop somewhere if I let them off. I had taken the option of staying overnight in the castle when it had first been offered three weeks ago upon booking the event because it meant I could keep the dogs close by instead of leaving them at home with Mrs Comerforth yet again. After my repeated absences this week I was glad I had. They would sleep happily enough during the ceremony and come out to mingle and charm people during the reception. If I am honest, it also occurred to me that they would attract the attention of the young women at the wedding. They always brought the ladies running wherever they went, a feature I was thankful for, but rarely managed to convert into anything worthwhile.

I poked around in the main hall the reception was to be held in and asked some pertinent questions about timings though I soon came to accept that I was just getting in the way. As I wandered off, thinking that I still had an hour before I would need to drive back to Finchampstead to collect the groom, I remembered Natasha.

We hadn't started dating when I booked the room at the castle but I had raised the subject of the wedding on our third date. At the time we had been in a restaurant and had kissed as we contemplated the romantic opportunity it presented. Her eyes had twinkled thinking about dressing up and then getting undressed and I had played along, continually asking myself why I wasn't more excited about the prospect.

With the wedding looming and my body feeling like it had been run over by a truck, I had staggered home yesterday afternoon and fallen into a hot bath. None of my injuries were life threatening nor would any of them still be hurting me a week from now, but right then I could barely find the bits that didn't hurt. That was just another excuse though. I had given thought to calling Natasha to tell her about my week and my current state because I could use it to postpone seeing her and dissuade her from attending the wedding with me. I saw how weak and stupid it sounded though.

I had to break up with her. I felt awful at the prospect. I had always hated break ups. Not that I had ever broken off many relationships with girls. I was always the one that got dumped, not the other way around. This time though I needed to grow a set and be the man instead of stringing the poor girl along any further.

Making the decision to call her though didn't solve the problem as I had lost my phone in the tunnels. Andriy had confiscated it when the bag went over my head. It might still be down there but if found by the police it would be labelled as evidence and placed into a little evidence bag, catalogued and placed on a shelf in a box somewhere and never be seen again. I could suppose there existed a slim chance I might be able to get it back, but I did not consider it worth pursuing. Either way, I had no phone to call Natasha with right now.

As it turned out, I didn't need to. I had been cooling down after the heat of the bath, sitting quietly on my bed and thinking about what I should eat as my stomach was now rumbling when the dogs started barking. Someone was at the door.

With a towel wrapped firmly around my waist and steam rising from my skin, I opened the door a crack to find Natasha smiling at me.

'I heard you needed some TLC.' She said. Big Ben would be to blame no doubt. I could hardly complain though, he would have called her believing that she would come to my house, take off her clothes and make me forget the bits that hurt.

She wasn't wrong about the desire for TLC either. Mr. Wriggly certainly wanted some. It was cold out, so I invited her in, resolving to do what was right and end our relationship before she could kiss me or confuse me and get my towel off. The very thought was already making Mr. Wriggly stir.

As she passed me, and I closed the door she started speaking, 'Tempest I wondered how you would react to seeing me and hoped that I had it wrong, but I can see that my instincts were right. I'll make this easy for both of us. It's time to break up.'

I didn't say anything. I was terrible at dealing with negative emotions from women. It was a major flaw in my personality that had never done me any favours, but here I was, getting exactly what I wanted, and I had to keep my mouth shut because my natural reaction was to argue with her.

'I saw it in your eyes the moment you opened the door.' Her voice cracked just a little as she shook her head and shut her eyes. When she reopened them, she said, 'I want to thank you for not sleeping with me. I guess you were never in to me.' I opened my mouth to protest, but she silenced me by pressing on. 'It's okay, Tempest, no explanation is needed. Sometimes things just don't work out. Sometimes there is no spark even when we want there to be.'

She took a step toward me, entering my personal space where I could smell her perfume and feel the warmth of her body radiating outward. Mr. Wriggly was getting agitated three feet below my mouth which was still trying to find something intelligent and appropriate to say.

She took my hand, looked me in the eyes and kissed my cheek. 'You're one of the good guys, Tempest. Don't forget that.'

Then she was gone. Out of the door and out of my life and all I felt was relief. Relief combined with a sense of confusion because I had just allowed a gorgeous woman to slip through my fingers in favour of... what?

The question was still bouncing around inside my pitifully empty skull nearly eighteen hours later as I walked the dogs through the picturesque gardens of the castle. It was done though, and this was kind of our second break up. There would be no third attempt.

At 1100hrs I was changed into my usual smart casual clothing, a combination of shirt, jeans and shoes with a jumper on to keep the cold at bay. The temperature outside demanded a coat but the bucket seats on my Porsche were too snug to allow the extra layer. I pulled out of the car park begging the heated seats to get on with warming me up as I set off to collect Jagjit. As best man it was my responsibility to get him to the venue. What I really wanted to do was sink enough gin to dull the aches I felt. This was Jagjit's big day though so I was refusing to shirk my responsibilities or even mention my soreness and fatigue to the groom. Thankfully there were very few bruises to my face. My stomach was a mosaic of interesting colours where it had been punched repeatedly, the same effect appeared on my back, though I struggled to see it even in the mirror and in a few places on my arms, legs and shoulder. I had some scratch marks on the right-hand side of my face where I had fallen off the car but the cut to my ear was superficial and no longer visible. Other than a split lip I would be presentable enough for photographs if I got one of the ladies to apply some foundation to even out the marks I did have. I could relax and recover over the weekend; Jagjit didn't need to know how broken I felt.

It was going to be a great day.

The Wedding of Jagjit Singh and Alice Windecote. Friday, November 25th 1630hrs

After five hours of dashing about performing my best man duties, the wedding itself was done. It would be hard to find sufficient superlatives to adequately describe it, so let's just say it was perfect.

Alice had been radiant, her loveliness only surpassed by the width of Jagjit's smile as he took her hand. Parents had cried, friends had cheered and many, many, many photographs had been taken.

We were now in the brief lull between ceremony and reception where guests got to chat properly for the first time, catching up with old relatives as they got a drink together at the bar. I had slumped into a chair in a corner of the room at a table by myself. I just needed a few minutes to rest before I got started again. Jagjit and Alice had a toastmaster for the evening reception which was due to start at 1800hrs. The gap between ceremony and reception planned deliberately to give time for the additional one hundred or so guests to arrive. Thankfully my role was about done, and my next task was to fetch my dogs. They would want to stretch their legs, empty their bladders and have some dinner.

'Hey, slack pants. How're you feeling?' Asked Big Ben. He had seen me sitting by myself and was delivering what looked very suspiciously like a large gin and tonic. My first of the day. He didn't wait for me to answer though. He asked, 'Have you seen Basic's guest?'

'No.' I looked about the room, curious now about who he had with him. 'Who is it?'

Big Ben didn't answer though, he waited for me to spot our friend where he was lounging against the bar. The view to him was blocked by other people getting drinks. As they moved away, I saw who Big Ben had been referring to.

It was the cute, but diminutive Japanese lady from the bar in Rochester. The one that had liked his air-guitar play.

'Are they dating?' I asked, then heard the surprise in my voice.

'Apparently so. Hilary and Anthea were chatting with them earlier. Her name is Maisy. She's an engineer in the aerospace industry and has a thing for large, dopey men it would seem.

'Well done, Basic.' I watched with awe and a little bit of jealousy as he stood with his arm around her, they were chatting about something and looked like a couple already. He had what I wanted.

Big Ben had another question. 'Did you enjoy seeing Natasha yesterday?'

He placed my drink down which freed his hand up to make suggestive gestures.

A little tired and a little melancholy, I looked up at my big friend, 'We broke up, mate.'

'Really? Is that before or after you shagged her?'

'Before.' I picked up my glass of gin saying, 'Thanks.' As I took a gulp. 'I guess you noticed that she is not here.'

'I did. I could call you weak, but you already know that you are so instead I will point out the person that just walked in.'

Confused, I followed Big Ben's outstretched finger to see Amanda entering the hall. She was looking around, trying to spot someone she recognised. As I watched, she spotted Hilary, smiled and waved and made her way to him at the bar. He was stood with his wife, Anthea. I watched as he introduced her to Amanda. The scene played out without dialogue as their voices were lost in the general din of conversation and background music.

Amanda looked beautiful. She always did.

'You're panting.' Big Ben pointed out, derision in his timbre.

He was right. My heart was beating faster, and my mouth was hanging open.

I had it bad.

Big Ben, who was sitting next to me, leaned in closer so I would hear every one of the next words he said. 'She broke up with her boyfriend.'

It felt like a jolt of electricity passing through my body.

'Wh, how... How do you even know that?' Amanda was a private person. She didn't tell me anything about herself. How was it that Big Ben kept track of her relationships?

'I know people that know her.' He replied.

Patience. Patience would have tipped him off. And she would have done so, so that he could tell me.

I slowly got to my feet. They felt leaden. I was going to have to talk to Amanda. It was something I did every day without thinking about it because we worked together, now though I was beginning to sweat at the prospect.

'Go get her.' Big Ben cheered from behind me as I started to cross the room.

She saw me coming and waved with a happy smile. At the gesture my heart stopped for a second before restarting.

All I had to do was talk to a girl. That was what I told myself as the distance between us continued to diminish. Why was it that I felt wrestling a shark was an easier option? I checked to make sure she wasn't looking, turned away slightly and gave myself a few face slaps. I was actually standing in the middle of the reception hall slapping my face in a bid to jolt myself into a better frame of mind.

I gave myself one last instruction to get a grip, smoothed down my jacket and went to her.

With a broad smile I said, 'Good evening, Amanda. It's so good to see you. I didn't know you were coming.'

'I wasn't. Big Ben called, said he didn't have a date and promised he wouldn't hit on me.' As she spoke, she dodged my hand shake, looped an arm around my neck and lightly kissed my face.

Another lightning bolt surged through me. She was full of energy and life and was clearly very happy. 'How about you buy me a drink, boss?' She asked, her voice a playful laugh as she grabbed my hand and pulled me to the bar. Hilary and Anthea exchanged glances as we both waved them a brief goodbye.

At the bar, I said, 'How about you never call me boss again?'

'You pay my wages.' She pointed out.

I inclined my head to acknowledge her correctness, 'Nevertheless, it makes me uncomfortable.'

Amanda took a pace away from me. She had a serious expression now. One that suggested she was about to say something vital or important.

'What'll it be folks?' Asked a barman peering under the glasses hanging from the bar.

Neither of us spoke for a moment until Amanda broke the silence, 'Why is that, Tempest? Why is it that me calling you boss makes you uncomfortable?'

My throat went dry and I found myself swimming inside my own head as I formed the words in my brain and tried to connect them with my mouth. I could see her in front of me, waiting for me to speak.

Like a rubber band snapping inside my head, I found the gumption I needed and opened my mouth. 'Because I can't date my employees.'

The planet has always conspired against me, so my statement came at the exact moment the DJ stopped the music to make an announcement.

Everyone heard me.

We were standing in a crowd of people at the bar, all of them silent now to see how she would respond. Most of them didn't know me, they were guests and relatives of either the bride or the groom but they could all tell what they were witnessing and almost everyone from my immediate circle of friends was there too, frozen in time, waiting for Amanda to speak.

She didn't speak though. Her eyes had been locked with mine for the last five seconds. She broke the moment by looking down to the floor. Then as if she had arrived at a decision, she looked up again, stepped forward and kissed me.

Postscript: Call from Hilary. Tuesday, 29th November 1809hrs

I hadn't looked at my phone for hours because I had been lying in ambush and then dealing with the man I caught. The case I was on had been easy to solve, however, catching the perpetrator proved to be trickier because I couldn't predict where he would strike next. He had been targeting children's playparks and scaring the life out of kids while they played. That was all he was doing, there was nothing more devious going on, but I had met some of the kids he had terrorised and they were traumatised by the costumed idiot jumping out on them.

Anyway, it had been necessary for me to operate in silent mode until he fell into the trap I had arranged with the help of my clients and their children. It was cold out and we had been just about to give up when he was spotted approaching.

Now he was in custody, but the process of catching him, calling the police to our location and giving statements had eaten up another chunk of time. It was after the dogs' dinner time and I was getting hungry myself, but I paused in my car to check my phone.

I had a stack of missed calls from Jagjit, all within the last hour. Wondering what he wanted so desperately, I pressed the button to call him, but a fresh call connected as I did. The caller was Hilary, a surprise as I couldn't remember the last time he had called me, if ever. Usually we sent text messages.

I answered, 'Good evening, buddy. What's up?'

'Hi, Tempest.' Hilary spoke rapidly as if the message was important. 'Jagjit called me. He's been trying to get hold of you all for hours.' Hilary explained.

'I've been on a bust, dealing with the police and stuff. I was just about to call him. Did he say why he was calling?' I asked.

'Yes! He has a case for you in France. Or rather he has a client with a case. There's a yeti on the loose!'

The End

(Except it isn't, of course. Not only are there lots more adventures in this series, there is free stuff and many other series besides. Scroll down a little to see more.)

More Books by Steve Higgs

There are secrets buried in the Earth's past. Anastasia might be one of them.

The world knows nothing of the supernaturals among them …

… but that's all about to change.

When Anastasia Aaronson stumbles across two hellish creatures, her body reacts by channelling magic to defend itself and unleashes power the Earth has forgotten.

But as she flexes her new-found magical muscle, it draws the attention of a demon who has a very particular use for her. Now she must learn to control the power she can wield as a world of magical beings take an interest.

She may be damaged, but caught in a struggle she knew nothing about, she will rise, and the demons may learn they are not the real monsters.

The demons know she is special, but if they knew the truth, they would run.

Lord Hale's Monster

Every second generation of the Hale line dies at the hands of an unnameable monster on his 80th birthday. The current Lord Hale turns 80 this Saturday.

To protect himself, Lord Hale has invited paranormal investigation experts Tempest Michaels and Amanda Harper plus their friends and a whole host of other guests from different fields of supernatural exploration for a birthday dinner at his mansion.

As they sit down for dinner, the lights start to dim and a moaning noise disturbs the polite conversation. Has Lord Hale placed his faith in the right people, or just led them to share his doom?

Finding themselves trapped, Tempest and Amanda, with friends Big Ben and Patience must join forces with a wizard, some scientists, and occult experts, ghost chasers, witches, and other assorted idiots as they fight to make it through the night in one piece.

Could this be their final adventure? Will Tempest finally be proven wrong about the paranormal?

Early Shift

Don't Challenge the Werewolf

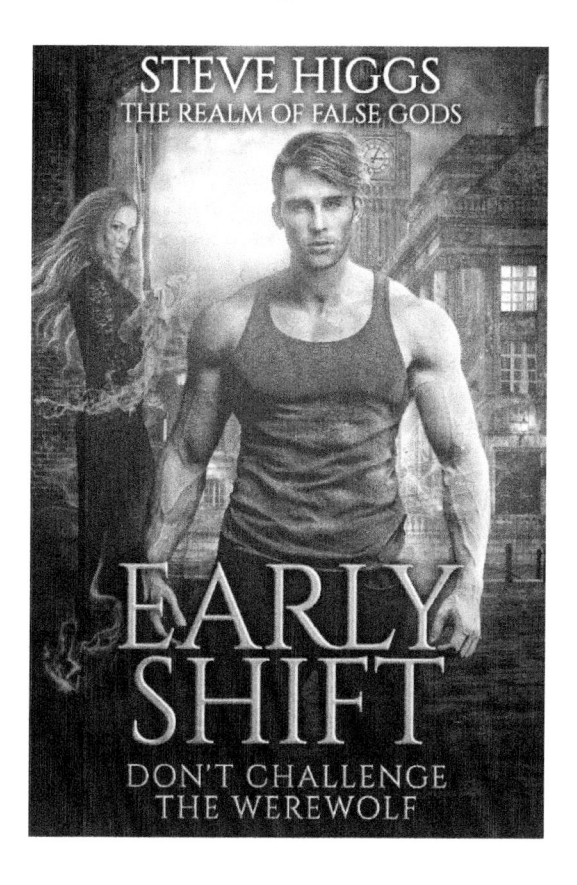

Don't pick a fight with him. You won't lose. You'll die

Zachary has a secret he tries to keep under wraps …

… if only people would let him.

When he drifts into a remote farming community looking for work, the trouble starts before he orders breakfast. Normally he would just avoid the trouble and move on, but there's a girl. Not a woman. A little girl, and the men that want to dominate the village threaten her livelihood.

And that just won't do.

There's something very rotten in this community but digging into it brings him face to face with something more powerful even than him. Something ancient and unstoppable.

He has no choice other than to fight, but who will walk away?

As the false gods find their way into the realm of mortals, how many mortals will rise to defend the Earth?

Be ready for war.

More Books by Steve Higgs

Blue Moon Investigations

Paranormal Nonsense

The Phantom of Barker Mill

Amanda Harper Paranormal Detective

The Klowns of Kent

Dead Pirates of Cawsand

In the Doodoo With Voodoo

The Witches of East Malling

Crop Circles, Cows and Crazy Aliens

Whispers in the Rigging

Bloodlust Blonde – a short story

Paws of the Yeti

Under a Blue Moon – A Paranormal Detective Origin Story

Night Work

Lord Hale's Monster

The Herne Bay Howlers

Undead Incorporated

The Ghoul of Christmas Past

Patricia Fisher Cruise Mysteries

The Missing Sapphire of Zangrabar

The Kidnapped Bride

The Director's Cut

The Couple in Cabin 2124

Doctor Death

Murder on the Dancefloor

Mission for the Maharaja

A Sleuth and her Dachshund in Athens

The Maltese Parrot

No Place Like Home

Patricia Fisher Mystery Adventures

What Sam Knew

Solstice Goat

Recipe for Murder

A Banshee and a Bookshop

Diamonds, Dinner Jackets, and Death

Frozen Vengeance

Mug Shot

The Godmother

Murder is an Artform

Wonderful Weddings and Deadly Divorces

Albert Smith Culinary Capers

Pork Pie Pandemonium

Bakewell Tart Bludgeoning

Stilton Slaughter

Bedfordshire Clanger Calamity

Death of a Yorkshire Pudding

Cumberland Sausage Shocker

Arbroath Smokie Slaying

Real of False Gods

Untethered magic

Unleashed Magic

Early Shift

Damaged but Powerful

Demon Bound

Familiar Territory

The Armour of God

Free Books and More

Get sneak peaks, exclusive giveaways, behind the scenes content, and more. Plus, you'll be notified of Fan Pricing events when they occur and get exclusive offers from other authors because all UF writers are automatically friends.

Not only that, but you'll receive an exclusive FREE story staring Otto and Zachary and two free stories from the author's Blue Moon Investigations series.

Yes, please! Sign me up for lots of FREE stuff and bargains!

Want to follow me and keep up with what I am doing?

Facebook

Printed in Great Britain
by Amazon